MOTHER LOAD

KG MacGregor

Bella
BOOKS
2010

Bella Books, Inc.
P.O. Box 10543
Tallahassee, FL 32302

First Edition Bella Books 2010

Editor: Katherine V. Forrest
Cover Design by: Linda Callaghan

ISBN-13: 978-1-59493-204-5

Other Bella Books by KG MacGregor

Aftershock
House on Sandstone
Just This Once
Malicious Pursuit
Mulligan
Out of Love
Photographs of Claudia
Sea Legs
Secrets So Deep
Small Packages
Sumter Point
Without Warning
Worth Every Step

About the Author

A former teacher and market research consultant, KG MacGregor holds a PhD in journalism and mass communication. Infatuation with *Xena: Warrior Princess* fanfiction prompted her to try her own hand at storytelling in 2002. In 2005, she signed with Bella Books, which published the Goldie Award finalist *Just This Once*. Her sixth Bella novel, *Out of Love*, won the 2007 Lambda Literary Award for Women's Romance, and the 2008 Goldie Award in Lesbian Romance. In 2009, she picked up Goldies for *Without Warning* and *Secrets So Deep*, and a year later won for *Worth Every Step*, a romance based on her own climb to the top of Mount Kilimanjaro.

KG proudly serves on the board of directors for Stonewall Library, Museum & Archives in Ft. Lauderdale. When she isn't writing, she's either on a hiking trail, a golf course, or if she's really lucky, a cruise ship.

For my mother
1934 - 2010

Chapter 1

Nothing said family to Lily like a Sunday afternoon barbecue at the Big House, her in-laws' stately home in Beverly Hills. Even after five years of weekends like this, she never took for granted how lucky she was to be part of the Kaklis clan.

Someone else was lucky too, she thought as she dangled her feet in the shallow end of the sparkling kidney-shaped pool. Five-year-old Andy, her late sister's child, swam nearby with his cousin Jonah. This time last year Andy had been in foster care in San Francisco. Now he was her adopted son and Anna's too. She almost felt guilty for her small wave of euphoria, since Anna was more stressed these days than Lily had ever seen her.

A plastic ball landed at her feet, sending a spray of water into her face.

"Trow it to me, Mama!" Andy shouted, waving his arms excitedly.

She couldn't help but smile at his struggles with "th" and

certain other sounds, the hallmark of a missing front tooth.

Jonah jockeyed for position in front. "No, to me, Aunt Lily!"

She tossed the ball between them and laughed as they crashed together in a wave. Though Andy was older than his cousin by a year, he was undersized and not as mature as most children his age, which made Jonah the perfect best friend. After only a month in kindergarten, Andy was already getting good reports from his teacher, who felt certain he would catch up to his peers soon. He certainly had come a long way from the shy little boy hiding in the corner the first time she saw him in the foster home.

On the deck at the far end of the pool Anna, Hal and George were clustered around an umbrella table mapping their next move for pulling Premier Motors back into the black. Her stress showed in her body language, the way her tall frame slouched in the armchair and her hand anxiously twisted her long black hair.

Sales at the four dealerships were down nearly thirty percent from the year before, and a return to profitability would require the drastic personnel cuts they had hoped to avoid. Anna was confident she and Lily would weather the downturn financially— her plunging portfolio notwithstanding—since she kept her personal investments separate from those of her business. She was less certain she could hold onto the three dealerships—two in Palm Springs and another in Beverly Hills—she had boldly acquired only two years earlier.

As serious as the dealership situation was, it wasn't at the top of Lily's worry list. She doubted it was at the top of Anna's either.

She turned her face instinctively to avoid the splashing war that suddenly erupted between the two boys, soaking her one-piece black swimsuit. "Hey, you two!"

"You're getting your mom wet," Jonah sputtered in an effort to slow Andy's onslaught.

"She doesn't care," he lisped.

"Don't bet on it, buster!" Lily shouted, playfully kicking a stream of water their way. Actually the spray felt refreshing in the late September heat, but if she didn't put up at least a mild protest they would douse her from head to toe.

Anna's sister Kim appeared beside her in a two-piece coral swimsuit and kicked off her shoes. A long strand of auburn hair had fallen free of the clasp that held the rest off her neck. "Is it safe to sit here?"

"If you don't mind being in a war zone."

"They better not screw with me," she grumbled under her breath. "I'm ready to put them all up on Craigslist. Children free to good home. No references necessary."

Lily chuckled at the empty threat. Kim was the best mother she knew, and fiercely protective of her son and daughter. "Did you get her to sleep?" The "her" in question was baby Alice, who had taken her first steps a week earlier and scarcely stopped since.

"Finally," Kim answered, blowing out an exasperated breath. "I was tempted to join her in a nap but Mom beat me to it. I got so jealous of seeing both of them sleeping that I wanted to poke them and scream."

If anyone deserved a nap it was Anna's stepmother Martine. She had worked all morning to prepare their Sunday feast, and then cleaned up the kitchen by herself over Lily's protests. "I don't mind watching the boys if you want to go back inside and crash."

"Nah, I'm okay. By the way, I found out it was Jonah who taught Andy the F-word, not the other way around."

"How do you know? I'm sure Andy heard the whole vocabulary when he was in foster care."

"Jonah's preschool sent out an apology. Apparently one of the kids in his class overheard his parents using it and he taught it to everyone else. Now I have to live in mortal fear of Jonah telling his whole class that he caught us having sex on the kitchen table."

"I'd be more worried about the time on the patio if I were you," Lily deadpanned, delighting in the rare look of shock on Anna's sister's face. "He told us all about it, in vivid detail. Didn't you notice when he started getting his own juice?"

"And here I thought he was just trying to show some

independence." Kim arched her eyebrows with suspicion as she looked at her son, who played on oblivious. "Sounds like Hal and I need to be more careful."

"I'll say. Or consider home schooling so he doesn't blab your family secrets."

"Boarding school is more like it. Think they'd take a four-year-old?" The two women took turns tossing a diving ring into the center of the pool so the boys could race to retrieve it. "Can I ask a personal question about my sister?"

Lily almost laughed at the perfunctory request. Since when did Kim ask permission to get into Anna's personal business? The two of them had been practically soul mates since their early teens when George and Martine, both widowed, married. She glanced over at Anna and smiled, trying to imagine what outlandish curiosity was rolling around in Kim's head.

"I know what you're thinking. I don't usually ask first." Kim turned her back to the trio at the end of the pool and lowered her voice. "Actually it's about both of you. I was wondering how you guys were getting along?"

She was taken aback by the serious tone, expecting the usual nosy inquiry about their sex life, which Kim usually directed at Anna just to watch her become flustered. "We're fine. Why would you ask such a thing?"

"I know my sister. She's out of sorts about something, and it isn't just work."

Lily bit her lip and glanced back to check on the boys, hoping her casual demeanor would set Kim's worries to rest. Yes, something big was going on, but she and Anna had made a pact not to tell anyone about it until the time was right—if it ever was. "She's under a lot of stress. They all are. I'm sure you see it in Hal too."

Kim eyed her with skepticism. "Is she sick?"

"No! Where did you get an idea like that?"

"I stopped by the dealership a couple of weeks ago to see Hal and I poked my head in Anna's office. She barely said hello and next thing I know she's driving off the lot with you in the middle of the day. Call me stupid but that has either marriage counselor or doctor's appointment written all over it."

That must have been their secret visit a couple of weeks ago to see Dr. Beth Ostrov, the fertility specialist Kim and Hal had used after struggling for eleven years to get pregnant. But her afternoon with Anna had also included a side trip to Andy's new school, which provided the perfect cover story. "We had an appointment to meet Andy's kindergarten teacher."

"Oh." Kim studied her fingernails impassively. "So neither of you is dying from some dreaded disease?"

"No, and we're not getting a divorce."

"It never hurts to double-check these things." Just like that Kim relaxed, her worries put to rest. "So what's Andy's teacher like?"

Lily scrunched her nose. "Mrs. Dooley...not quite what we'd hoped for. She's an older woman, really strict. Sort of reminded me of his last foster mother in San Francisco. I haven't seen Anna so intimidated since the day we brought Andy home the first time."

Kim laughed. "I remember that. She was calling me every day freaking out. Now they're best buds."

"It's like having two kids." *Having two kids.* The irony of her words astonished her and she drew a deep, calming breath. It would happen when it happened. In the meantime, the bond that had grown between Anna and Andy was a comforting reminder that their family was already complete, even if their efforts to have more children failed. She nodded toward the end of the pool. "I wish those three would call it a day already. I don't know about Hal, but Anna needs to relax and forget about the office for a while."

As if on cue, Anna's voice rose and her pen slammed against the teak tabletop. Lily had witnessed these outbursts with mounting frequency, a sign of Anna's frustration with her stalled business.

"This is the worst I've ever seen her, and believe me that's saying something," Kim said. "Is she like this at home too, or is it just when she's with Hal and George?"

"We usually try not to bring our work home, but she's really feeling the pressure right now." When they had married three years earlier, they had promised not to let their jobs take over their lives. It sometimes took a conscious effort from both of them, and it had gotten more difficult for Anna as Premier Motors struggled against a falling economy. And even when she stopped thinking about work, it was only so she could worry about their failed efforts to have children.

"Hal said they'd have to cut their staff…and that they've been getting calls from investment companies trying to buy her out at a bargain-basement price. Anna won't even pick up the phone."

"Yeah, they know she took on a lot of debt when she acquired the other dealerships and now they're circling like sharks. What they don't realize is that Premier Motors isn't just a business to her. Success is a matter of pride. And now that she's president of the Chamber of Commerce, everyone's watching to see how she's going to handle the pressure. If she caves in to those vultures, she'll feel like a public failure."

"Like that's ever going to happen." Kim hooked the loose strand of hair over her ear and huffed. "Premier Motors belonged to her mother and grandfather and she won't ever let it go. Some of those people have been on the lot for thirty years. They're like family."

Which explained why Anna felt the weight of the world on her shoulders. Maybe it was the thing that bothered her most after all. Having a baby had seemed like a good idea last fall. Not so much now with all the added pressures. "And she feels guilty because she can't save all their jobs."

"I'm glad she has you to lean on, Lily."

"We'll get her through it," she vowed, to herself as much as to Kim. "How's Hal doing? I bet he has second thoughts about leaving his cushy accounting firm for the car business."

"No way. Two of his old bosses just went to jail for cooking their clients' books. Hal thinks it's only the tip of the iceberg. He may have a lot on his mind with the dealership, but at least he sleeps like a baby at night…not like any of my babies, though. They hardly sleep at all." Kim scooted forward and slid into the pool. "I think one of us should go over there and break up that party. I nominate you."

* * *

Anna folded back the sheet as Chester lumbered onto his spot at the foot of Andy's bed. The basset hound had bowled them over with his usual exuberance the moment they walked in from their day at the Big House. "Did you sleep on the couch all day, boy?" She ruffled his floppy ears as he thumped his tail in reply.

Though they had never actually formalized the routine, Lily usually took charge of getting Andy up in the morning and Anna supervised his bath and tucked him in at night. It had become a highlight of her day, and possibly the only time she could truly forget her worries. She chuckled sheepishly, remembering how she had avoided being alone with Andy when he first came to live there. Now she couldn't wait for bedtime. The feelings of love that welled up inside her in these quiet minutes made her wonder how she had ever lived without him in her life.

He emerged from the bathroom in his favorite racecar pajamas, his curly brown hair still wet from his bath. "Mama says I swim just like a fish. Jonah swims faster than I do, but I can hold my breath underwater longer." There was a faint rasp in his voice, which usually preceded an episode of asthma. That happened regularly when he laughed too much or played too long, as he had today. Lily was confident he would outgrow it soon, but not soon enough for Anna. She hated how it always forced him to keep his excitement in check, no matter the occasion.

"I hear wheezing, pal. That means it's time to calm down and take it easy. Do you want to sit with me in the rocking chair?"

"Whatever."

"What kind of answer is that?"

Andy shrugged. "Jonah says it."

Anna shook her head and let out a small sigh. At least it was better than the last word her nephew had taught him. "I've got an even better idea." Foregoing the chair, she scooped him up and guided his head against her shoulder. She dreaded the day when one of them decided he was too big to be held like this. "Just close your eyes and try to relax."

Ever so slowly, she paced the room as he gradually went limp in her arms. Then she walked the floor two more times for good measure before placing him in his bed. With a kiss to his forehead and a scratch under Chester's chin, she whispered goodnight and tiptoed from the room. On the landing she briefly toyed with the idea of returning to her work downstairs but changed her mind. Lily was already in the shower, signaling her intention to call it a day even though it was only eight thirty. With Andy in bed, they could take advantage of quiet time together to unwind, something that had eluded them of late. Relaxing wasn't easy with all they had hanging over their head.

She entered their spacious master bath just as Lily turned off the shower. Condensation on the glass door robbed Anna of the view but she knew Lily's naked body by heart. "Too bad you're finished. I was about to join you."

"You're such a tease," Lily said, holding the shower door for Anna to enter. "I wasn't expecting to see you so soon. Andy must have been worn out."

"He was. Good thing he likes to sleep, unlike my sister's children."

"Let's hope our luck holds with the next one," Lily said, a nervous smile playing on her lips. Those were the first words uttered by either of them today about their plans. It was hard not to talk about it, but talking sometimes made them worry even more. Their doctor said it was common for struggling couples to become stressed, and she suggested they put the topic off-limits whenever they were trying to relax. Talking about it wouldn't change their results and would only increase their anxiety.

Anna couldn't ignore the remark though, not with their emotions simmering so close to the surface as they awaited the next day's definitive blood test. Lily's anguish about her failure to get pregnant after their first two attempts was acute, so much that when the doctor casually reminded them they had other options, Anna had stridently offered to carry their child if this third effort came up short. She still couldn't believe those words had left her mouth. It wasn't that she wasn't willing to do it if that's what it took—she just didn't want to be pregnant now when she already had so many other demands on her attention. She knew it was a selfish attitude and that's why she kept it to herself. "One of these days, we're going to be the luckiest people on earth."

Lily pressed her palms against the door of the shower and kissed the glass. "I've been telling myself all day that I already am." She quickly dried her short blond hair and disappeared from the room.

It didn't surprise her that Lily had been preoccupied at the Big House, especially since she had spent so much of the day talking with Kim...probably about baby Alice. Her own thoughts had bounced between work and babies throughout the day. With their third pregnancy test only a few hours away, she finished her shower and hurried through her ablutions, determined to give Lily her undivided attention.

To her surprise, she found their bedroom aglow in soft candlelight. Lily sat on the edge of the bed wearing her favorite sleepwear, a worn purple tank top that draped to her thighs.

Anna stopped in the doorway of the bathroom and folded her arms. "What's this?"

"Probably not what you think. Get over here and lose the robe."

"I love it when you go all dominatrix on me."

Lily chuckled. "That'll be the day." She guided Anna into a prone position across the bed and straddled her backside. Then she dug her fingers into the small of her back and began to knead.

Anna moaned with pleasure, turning on the mental clock that usually kept track of these things so she could return the gesture in kind.

"I know what you're thinking, Amazon. Forget it, this is all about you." Lily's hands trickled outward and brushed the sides of her breasts with feather-like strokes. "Well, not all of it." She massaged the knots in Anna's neck, producing a sensation that was alternately torture and bliss.

Anna tucked her chin to expose the long muscle. "You're killing me…but oh, what a way to go."

"Give it a minute. If it hurts, it's probably because you need it."

"You mean because you *knead* it."

Lily answered her pun with a deep, two-handed pinch to her trapezius.

"Ow!"

"Just try to relax. If nothing else, it will feel good when I stop."

Anna drew a deep breath and tried to empty her head of everything except the physical sensations. It was as if she could feel the muscle fibers separating as Lily pried them apart. "No offense but that feels better than sex."

Lily chuckled. "Good thing I don't happen to believe you, or I'd take that personally."

Anna opened one eye and stole a peek at the clock. "When did we start going to bed at nine o'clock?"

"Maybe it was when you started waking up at four a.m. so you could get a head start on worrying about your day."

There was no denying that. What Lily probably didn't know was that she often awoke several times in the night, her mind bombarded with worries about both their fertility efforts and her business. Sometimes it was all she could do to resist getting out of bed to walk the floor and try to clear her thoughts. Over the past two weeks, she had come up with a plan that should take care of her work problems—gutting Premier Motors to its barest operating essentials, from where all forward business spelled profit instead of loss. Encouraged by Hal's projections, she nonetheless dreaded what the moves would mean to her staff and their families.

"Stop thinking about work."

"How did you know that?"

"Because you always think about work." Lily pressed hard on both sides of her spine and popped her back in three places.

"Not always," Anna grunted. "I've been thinking about our baby too. I can tell you've been worrying about it. You aren't the only one who can read minds."

"Not worried, just anxious. I wish it was tomorrow already."

"It'll get here soon enough." She wanted to point out they might already be pregnant, but it would only underscore the other two times she had said that and it turned out to be false. "It'll happen, sweetheart, whatever it takes."

In the quiet minutes that followed, Lily's touch subtly changed from a therapeutic massage to a loving caress, and Anna became aware of pubic curls brushing her backside. She concentrated on the point of contact, trying to decide if the tantalizing touch was intentional or mere coincidence.

"You have the most gorgeous body," Lily whispered, sliding aside to cup Anna's bottom. Then her lips left a moist trail from hip to shoulder, and she settled alongside.

The heat rose between Anna's legs as Lily stroked her backside and thighs, and she drew her knee upward to open herself. As fingers slid through her wetness from behind, she nestled backward into the warm body and surrendered. Lily took her time, never lingering in one place for more than a few strokes as her lips continued their gentle caress of her shoulder. From her occasional murmurs, she was focused solely on Anna's satisfaction, and once the tiny spasms began, so was Anna.

"That's it, baby. Let it go."

She shuddered and covered Lily's hand with hers to hold it in place, savoring the intimate connection that was always part of their lovemaking. Only one thing felt better—giving the same pleasure to Lily.

Already aroused, Lily responded quickly. Anna got her wish, her fingers deep inside as Lily's climax rippled out. Spent, she hovered on the precipice of sleep, stirring only when Lily rose briefly to snuff out the candles.

* * *

Lily let out a breath as the nurse withdrew the fat needle and dabbed her elbow with a cotton swab. Only ten days had passed since the implantation procedure, not enough time to feel changes in her body, but this blood test would reveal if their efforts had been successful. This time they had used one egg from her and another from Anna. Dr. Ostrov thought that might improve their odds, since using Anna's eggs alone hadn't yet resulted in implantation. If this one failed they had to consider the possibility that her uterus wasn't suited for pregnancy, though she had never had any gynecological problems to suggest that was the case.

"It'll take a few minutes to run this," the woman said. "Dr. Ostrov said you should wait in her office."

With Anna's help, Lily slipped back into the dark brown jacket of her suit, which she had worn for an afternoon court appearance. Determined not to let anyone know about their fertility efforts until they were successful, she had taken a couple of hours of sick leave under the auspices of a routine checkup. Considering how many times she had done that since last winter, her co-workers at the Braxton Street Legal Aid Clinic probably shared Kim's suspicions about a dreaded disease.

Anna had no meetings today, so she was dressed casually in black slacks and an aqua shirt that made her blue eyes shine. Her stomach growled loudly as they stepped into the hallway and she glanced around nervously to see if anyone else had heard.

"I warned you not to skip breakfast."

"I was too nervous. I would have thrown up." She handed Lily her handbag. "Take this. I need to make a pit stop."

With deliberate slowness, Lily strolled to the end of the wide green hallway, pausing to study several embryonic images taken at various stages of cellular development, artfully matted and framed. It was a fitting collection for a practice that specialized in fertility issues, and she was grateful they hadn't chosen portraits of smiling mothers and their perfect babies. Not all fertility aspirations ended so happily.

In Dr. Ostrov's office, diplomas lined the wall behind the spotless cherry desk. Medical school at the University of Washington and a residency at UC-San Francisco Medical Center made for a distinguished pedigree. Lily pegged her for mid-forties, even though her short curly hair was completely gray. From her trim and fit figure, she probably lived the healthy lifestyle she prescribed for her patients.

Too nervous to sit, Lily went to the tenth-floor window and looked down on the hospital's emergency room. It wasn't much in the way of a view, but she doubted Beth spent much time in her office gazing out the window.

Their expectations were tempered this time, as if their next attempt—a fourth, in which Anna would be implanted—was already a foregone conclusion. That thought filled her with frustration. She wanted to carry their child, but when Anna had offered to do it next time she realized how eager Anna was to have a baby now.

Her stomach tightened with anticipation as the door opened, but it was Anna, not the doctor. "No sign of Beth yet," Lily said.

"It took about twenty minutes last time." That was five

months ago after their second try, when they both had felt the odds were in their favor.

"Twenty minutes that seemed like twenty days."

"I'll gladly sit here that long if it means good news."

All morning Lily had sensed Anna's resolve. Neither of them had wavered about wanting another child, and the sooner the better. "I need to ask you something important, but it's okay to say no."

Anna chuckled and slumped into one of the chairs in front of Beth's desk. "You should know by now the answer is whatever you need it to be."

Lily perched on the edge of the other chair and twirled her wedding ring nervously. "It's kind of scary to me to realize how much I want this. I don't just mean us having a baby. I mean me. I know Beth said if it didn't work this time we should think about letting you be the one to get pregnant. I just...I really want you to let me keep trying, at least another couple of times."

The look on Anna's face was pure surprise. "You're kidding." Then she shook her head with obvious disbelief and started to laugh. "All this time, I've been having nightmares because I said I'd go next, and here you've been freaking out because you didn't want me to."

"Nightmares? I thought you were in a hurry to have children. You said you didn't want to be the oldest mom at graduation."

Anna laughed even harder. "This is LA. If I'm worried about looking too old, I'll get my face pinned back."

"Over my dead body! No one touches that face." Their silliness was a welcome relief to the angst that had been building for days. Even if today's test came up empty, Anna was willing to give her more chances, and that felt like release of a pressure valve. "I can't believe I've been worrying this whole time. I didn't want you to get frustrated about how long it might take. That's what we get for not talking to each other."

"We studied all the options, Lily. The way I see it I'm just a backup plan. I only offered because I didn't want you to get discouraged about it."

That was the Anna Kaklis she knew and loved, the one who would go to any lengths to make her happy. "I don't care what any of those other people say. I think you're the most amazing woman in the world."

"What other people?" Anna quirked her eyebrows with suspicion just as Dr. Ostrov burst through the door, her open lab coat trailing behind her like a cape.

Lily tried to read her face. No frown, but that didn't necessarily mean anything. She might just be trying to keep an optimistic outlook.

She dropped a folder on her desk and collapsed into her high-backed leather chair declaring, "I love my job."

Both of them sat up ramrod straight, their hands tightly entwined. "What are you saying?"

"Technically speaking, I'm saying your hCG was thirty-six." She then broke out into a wide grin. "Not so technically, I'm saying the third time's a charm. You're pregnant."

Anna's eyes went wide and she covered her mouth to muffle a quiet scream. "We did it!"

"Indeed we did," Beth said, folding her hands atop the manila folder. "Feel free to pretend I'm not here for a minute. That's what most couples do right about now."

Lily realized she was grinning wildly, and she leaned into Anna's eager kiss. This was it, the answer to their dreams.

"The blood test is just the first step," Beth continued. "All we know right now is that the embryo implanted and that kicked up your hCG. Actually, it could be two embryos."

"Two?" Lily asked. They had known from the beginning that twins were a possibility because they were using two eggs to increase their odds. But since Anna's eggs hadn't implanted before, Lily had automatically assumed this baby was from her egg. "You think it's possible Anna's would have implanted too?"

"Her eggs were as healthy as any I've seen. As far as I'm concerned this baby could belong to either of you."

"But why didn't it—"

"Just the odds."

"It doesn't matter. This baby belongs to both of us," Anna declared exuberantly.

"That's the spirit. We'll do the blood tests every couple of weeks just to make sure things are happening on schedule. In the meantime I want you on a regimen of vitamins and exercise, and this is where you have to start watching your diet…lots of fruits and vegetables." Beth paged through the folder again. "You don't drink so that's not an issue…no medications. As of right now I don't want you taking anything without getting my okay, not even for an upset stomach or headache. Got it?"

"Got it." She crossed her heart for emphasis, realizing that Anna was squeezing her other hand so hard the knuckles had started to turn white.

"What else?" Anna asked, her voice changing to business mode. "Does she have any other restrictions? Should she take it easy? Quit work?"

Lily had a feeling that if it were up to Anna she would stay home in bed starting this afternoon. She had planned to continue working as long as she could, but after the trouble they'd had getting pregnant in the first place, it occurred to her Beth might want to take a more cautious approach.

"I don't advise taking up a new sport or active hobby, but most women are fine doing the things they've always done." She slid a pamphlet across her desk. "Here are some things you should watch for in the first trimester. Your body will change a lot in the next few weeks, probably even more than in the final months of pregnancy."

It was surreal to think of her body as different now, especially since it didn't feel different at all. She didn't mind the prospect of changes, not even the ones Kim had complained about when she was pregnant. Anything was worth it to get the baby they wanted.

"What's our due date?" Anna asked.

Beth nodded toward the pamphlet in Lily's hand. "I wrote it down for you. First of June. I also circled December first because fourteen weeks is what we consider the end of the greatest risk period. Some couples like to wait until then to tell everyone, but it's totally up to you. My guess is you'll be showing a little by then." She abruptly stood and clapped her hands together with a smile. "Now if you'll excuse me, I need to go make some more babies. I'll see you back here in two weeks for another blood test."

Lily sat frozen in her seat until Anna gave her a tug. "I can't believe it. We're actually pregnant."

"Let's take the day off and go home to celebrate." Given the demands at Premier Motors, it was an incredibly generous offer.

"I can't. I have to be in court this afternoon. My client is getting a much-needed divorce. I'll take a rain check though."

Anna sighed, but by her wide grin she was anything but disappointed. "I hope Andy doesn't mind being put to bed at six thirty. I think a private celebration is in order."

"If I get home first I'll make him swim laps until he's exhausted."

After making a stop at the desk to schedule their next appointment, they continued to the garage, where they had parked side by side. Anna held the door of Lily's X3 SUV. "I won't tell anyone today, but folks are going to wonder why I'm smiling so much when we're losing money."

Fear gripped Lily for the first time. "I think we should wait until December, like Beth said. I don't think I could stand losing—"

Anna cut her off with a kiss. "We won't lose anything, sweetheart. Our baby will be perfect."

Typical Anna, strong and confident. Lily hoped the same for their baby, and that it would have her crystal blue eyes as well.

Chapter 2

Lily jiggled the connector cable to her monitor, bringing her document back to life. The equipment at the Braxton Street Legal Aid Clinic was ancient by the standards of most law firms. More than once she had considered buying her own computer for the office, something compatible with the one she used at home. Over the summer she had written a small grant to upgrade their office computer system, but with the recession most foundations were sitting on their funds.

The intercom button on her phone beeped. "Lily, Tony wants to see you in his office."

Their workload had exploded in the past year with the rise in foreclosures and evictions, to say nothing of all of the people clamoring for benefits. She had managed to carve out a specialized caseload of family issues, mostly custody and adoption cases, and divorce. As always her concern was for the welfare of the children.

She pushed her stocking feet into her pumps, buttoned the cuffs on her striped Oxford shirt and smoothed her navy skirt. It was her typical office attire, comfortable enough for a casual day behind her desk, yet with a matching jacket dressy enough should she be called to court. No sign of a growing belly so far, though she was now eight weeks along. It thrilled her to think she might be showing in only another month, and neither she nor Anna had broken their pact not to tell anyone, somehow keeping their secret for six weeks.

Walking past the reception area to Tony's office, she noted the unusual clutter on Pauline's desk. Clearly they all were swamped.

"You need to see me, chief?"

Tony glanced up from his desk, where he was studying several open case files. "Yeah, give me a sec."

Last year, soon after his forty-second birthday, he had started wearing reading glasses, and they now sat perched upon his nose. His thin sandy hair was standing up as though he had mussed it in exasperation and his tie hung loosely around his neck.

Lily took advantage of the chance to stretch her legs, foregoing the offered chair to gaze out the window onto busy Braxton Street. She had the same view from her office but couldn't see it from her desk unless she stood.

With a deep sigh, Tony picked up a file and joined her at the window. Over the past three years, marriage and family had cut into his active lifestyle, and Colleen's home cooking had deposited a spare tire around his waist. They now had three children, two from her previous marriage and the baby they had welcomed just last year. Lily was bursting to share the news of her pregnancy, but was determined to hold off for a few weeks more until their tests checked out. No doubt Tony would panic, just as he had when fellow attorney Lauren had gotten pregnant a couple of years earlier. She had taken only two months maternity leave. Lily planned to ask for six.

"You'll never guess who called this morning." He handed her the file. "Maria Esperanza."

Lily knew Maria all too well. In her seven years at the clinic, she had handled two divorces of Maria's from husband Miguel, four criminal complaints involving domestic violence, and no fewer than seven custody hearings for the couple's two children, Roberto and Sofia. "It never ends for those two. What is it this time?"

"First she wants a restraining order. Then she wants Miguel's visitation revoked permanently. She claims he threatened her with a gun…said he was going to make her sorry one of these days."

Miguel already had two assault convictions for battering his wife on his record, and had done eight months in the county jail for the second offense. "If he has a gun, that's a violation of his probation. I can have him picked up and thrown in jail by dinnertime."

"Assuming she's even telling the truth. You know how she is, Lily. She'll say anything to get the judge mad at Miguel."

Not only that, she also had a history of hiding the kids when her ex-husband showed up for visitation, an act that had provoked his violent side. But a threat with a gun definitely raised the stakes. "I've never worried before that he'd hurt his kids, but sometimes I think he gets so angry at Maria that I wouldn't put it past him. Are the police involved?"

"No, not yet."

"Why don't I start with Pete Simpkins? He was still Miguel's attorney last I heard. Maybe I can get him to call the probation officer to go over and search for a gun."

"Works for me." He handed her the file and pushed his hands in his pockets, clearly troubled.

"Something else, Tony?"

He looked down at his feet for a few seconds before finally meeting her eye. "The Cryder Foundation didn't renew us for next year."

The Cryder grant was specifically set aside for children and family legal services, and it covered most of Lily's salary. She had written the application herself last summer touting the number of people that had benefitted from the foundation's previous support. "Did they say why?"

He shrugged. "Like everyone else, their portfolios crashed. They hardly funded anyone this cycle, but they invited us to apply again next spring."

She had worked at the law clinic long enough to know her job was secure, though it likely meant she would be handed more criminal cases, since their contract with the public defender's office was one of their main sources of funding. "You're sending me back to jail, aren't you?"

"I'm afraid so. I know how much you hate it, so I promise I'll at least try to get you all the juvie cases."

She definitely preferred juvenile justice to adult crime. The last thing she wanted was to find herself defending the likes of Miguel Esperanza.

* * *

Anna touched her cheeks with blush before the mirror on the back of her office door. For a six whole weeks she had done her best to keep her expression calm and serious in front of her staff, but in the privacy of her office it was all she could do not to whistle with joy. Their second blood test had confirmed the embryo's growth, which made them breathe easier. They could hardly wait for the first sonogram, only two weeks away.

In the meantime, she had her hands full with Premier Motors. The sooner she got the dealerships back on track, the more time she would have for Lily and their family. Today's meeting was the critical first step toward turning her business around.

The whispers had started already, from the office and sales staff all the way out to the service department. It wasn't every day she gathered the executives and managers from all four dealerships in one place. She needed their support for this transition as much as they needed her decisive leadership. She rolled up the sleeves of her white cotton shirt, hoping to convey her readiness to work just as hard as she was asking them to do.

In the conference room she took her place at the head of the table, flanked on one side by Hal, her chief financial officer, and on the other by her father, who was vice president of operations at the Beverly Hills Volkswagen dealership. Next to him sat Brad Stanley, who held the same position at the BMW dealership. Their Palm Springs counterparts were next, along with the company's vice president for human resources, Nancy Gravitt, who had helped iron out the final details of their plan. Sales, service and office managers from all four lots were seated around the perimeter of the room.

"Perfect attendance. I like that." Anna pasted on a confident smile and tried to make eye contact with everyone present. "I know you're all expecting bad news today, but I hope when you come away from this meeting you'll feel I've given you just the opposite."

There was no discernible change in their worried expressions. People were anxious and rightly so.

"You all know our bean counter, Hal Phillips. He and I have been working with Nancy on a reorganization plan we think will pull Premier Motors back into the black. We were lucky to have also the advice of my father, George Kaklis, who has successfully steered this company through forty years of ups and downs." Invoking her father's role in developing the strategy for their turnaround would help win support among some of the old-timers in the room, people who had come up through the ranks in the car business back when he headed the company. "That said, I want you to know these are my decisions, and mine alone. If you have grievances, bring them to me."

The last thing she wanted was sniping about favoritism among her executive staff. She had done her utmost to assure each dealership of its importance to the Premier Motors brand.

"I don't have to tell you that the auto industry is suffering right now. The good news is that our German brands have hit bottom already and started making a comeback, unlike our competitors in Detroit. And let's face it—BMWs will always sell in Southern California. The sad fact, though, is we're down almost thirty percent in sales of new and used cars, and people are putting off bringing their cars in for parts and service. Quite a few of our salespeople have already left us in search of greener pastures, but they were all on commission so that didn't save us any outlay. The real problem is that we haven't kept pace in our office and service departments. We currently have one hundred-eighty full-timers excluding sales staff, and we need to get that down to one-thirty. The math is easy—that's fifty jobs, and the losses have to be spread across our entire workforce."

She paused to catch her breath and realized they were catching theirs too. No doubt all were mentally calculating what such cuts might mean to their respective departments.

"Those of you who know me understand what a difficult decision it is for me personally to part with people I care about, people I've worked with every day for years. That's why the main objective of this plan is to avoid forced layoffs. Instead we'll be offering early retirement to all employees fifty-five and older with at least ten years service, and severance packages to everyone else based on salary and length of service. Nancy has all the specifics, and now I'm going to turn the meeting over to her."

As Nancy spelled out the details, Anna studied the attentive faces of her executive and managerial staff, not surprised they seemed relieved her initial plan wouldn't include involuntary terminations. Morale was low enough with the decline in sales. It was an attractive package, but one she hoped no one in the room would accept. It had taken a couple of years after the acquisitions to get all the right top-level people into place. Without them she was sure to find herself working long hours again.

With the baby coming she had more reasons than ever to want a competent management team. When the recession started she began working more frequently on the weekends, and that cut into her family time. At least Andy enjoyed coming to the dealership with her on Saturdays. She wondered if this new child would share their appreciation for cars.

Hal cleared his throat and gave her a peculiar look.

Anna straightened abruptly in her chair and wiped the errant smile from her face, realizing with horror that everyone in the room seemed to be awaiting her word. "Excuse me, could you repeat that?"

It was Roger Goforth, the service manager at the Palm Springs VW dealership. "I asked what happens if you don't get fifty volunteers. It's a tough time to expect people to give up their jobs."

"I appreciate that, Roger. That's why we've tried to make this a generous offer." Indeed, she had pushed the package ten percent higher than Hal's recommendation so she wouldn't have to feel guilty about forced terminations. "But we don't have a choice about these numbers. If we can't hit our quotas throughout the company we'll have to resort to layoffs, and those people won't be eligible for severance because they'll be entitled to unemployment."

It sounded threatening when she put it that way, and by the fear on her managers' faces they thought so too.

"Look, I know people are scared. But we have to present this as an opportunity for folks to take that step they've been thinking about, like going back to school or starting a small business of their own." She was glad to see several heads nodding in approval. "Some people might want to feel like they have control over what happens to them, that they aren't just sitting back waiting for whatever life hands them."

After Nancy finished her remarks, Anna took a handful of questions. Then she adjourned the meeting and waited until all but her brother-in-law had left the room.

"What was that about?" Hal asked. "You looked like you were off in dreamland."

"Guilty as charged." It was no use playing dumb since he had caught her in a full-on smile, but she couldn't tell their secret. "I was thinking how nice it would be once we get things back to normal here so we can get home to our families on the weekend."

He looked at her sheepishly. "I have a confession to make. I've been sneaking out of here after lunch on Saturdays for the past month."

"You straighten your desk and turn out the lights in your office, Hal. You call that sneaking?" Since joining her business four years ago he had become her right hand, the person she depended on most. That didn't mean she expected him to work the same long hours she did. "My sister would kill me if you didn't show up at home once in a while."

"I'm surprised Lily doesn't come down here and drag you home."

"I'm a little surprised too." Anna smiled again, thinking once their baby arrived, someone might have to drag her to work.

* * *

Lily cinched the backpack around her waist as Anna gathered the remnants of their picnic lunch. Andy had already started down the trail. With luck he would make it all the way back to the car on foot, sparing them the chore of carrying him piggyback, along with his child-sized backpack. These mountain hikes were few and far between, but still one of Lily's favorite ways to spend time together as a family. Even Anna, born and raised in Beverly Hills, had come to appreciate what nature had to offer.

Having Anna along on a Saturday hike was a rare treat these days. She had been spending more weekends at work, but seemed to be breathing easier now that some of her employees were coming forward to claim severance and retirement benefits.

She smiled to recall their first hike together, a short jaunt to the falls at Temescal Gateway Park. Anna had joked that no one should have to walk up a mountain when there were perfectly good four-wheel-drive vehicles to get you there. Now she was an old hand at hiking, decked out in sturdy trail shoes, knee-length nylon pants with zippered pouches on the side, a long-sleeved T-shirt with built-in sunblock, and her dark ponytail tucked through the opening of her favorite Dodgers cap.

"What are you thinking about?" Anna asked, falling into step beside her.

"The first time you came hiking with me."

"I remember that. You made me sleep in a tent, and then you laughed at me when I fell out of the canoe."

"Oh, the weekend at Kidz Kamp. Actually, I was thinking about the time it was just you and me and we went to Temescal."

"When you dragged me twenty miles to that waterfall? I thought I was having a heart attack."

"It was only three miles and I didn't drag you…although I do remember you asking me to fetch the car for you. It's hard to believe you're the same person."

"Ha! And when I met you, you were driving a hundred-year-old Toyota. Which reminds me, we put a brand-new X6 in the showroom the other day, white with tan interior. Had your name all over it."

"My name? You're the one who needs a new car."

"No way. My Z8's a classic."

"A classic that holds only two people." She almost laughed at the look of panic on Anna's face. After her family, Anna loved that car better than anything else on earth. "You can't put Andy and a baby in a two-seater convertible."

"I don't have to. We have your car for that."

"But think of all the times you have to pick up Andy when I get hung up at work. What would you do if I called and said I was stuck in court? There's no way you could put both Andy and the baby in your car."

"But it so happens I own four car dealerships. In an emergency,

I'm sure I could find something to drive."

She had to admit Anna had a point, but having four dealerships wouldn't help if she was stranded at home with two children and a Z8. It would take some time to bring Anna around to getting something more practical, a nudge here and there instead of a push all at once.

Andy had gone well in front but stopped to wait while they caught up. Four miles round trip was a long way for a five-year-old.

"Let me carry your backpack, pal," Anna said, looping one of its straps over her shoulder.

Andy gladly relinquished his pack, which carried only a small canteen, a compass and the less popular remnants of his Halloween candy. Lily estimated it would buy them another half mile before he gave out and asked to be carried. At least by then they would be close to the car.

"Andy, are you having a good time?" she asked.

"Uh-huh. I like it when I get to pee outside."

Anna looked at her and they rolled their eyes in unison.

"Don't get used to it," Lily said sternly. "You aren't supposed to do that unless you're with us and you ask permission."

"Not even with Uncle Hal?"

"I guess you can do it if Uncle Hal gives you permission but no one else."

"What about Grandpa?"

Lily could see they had opened a can of worms and there was no good way to explain to a five-year-old why some situations were okay and others were not. Besides, George never said no to any of his grandchildren. "No one else. Just your mom and me, and Uncle Hal."

He made a face before skipping ahead again. If there was one thing about Andy they could count on, it was that he generally accepted the rules they imposed on him about his behavior. That was a blessing, especially considering his background in foster care. Unlike other children his age, he had never really tested the limits of his independence, so they were reluctant to rein him in unless it was absolutely necessary.

Anna squeezed her hand and bumped their shoulders together affectionately. "Maybe we'll have a little girl."

Lily chuckled. "And what makes you think she'll be any different? I bet she'll want to pee in the woods too. And besides, in a few months I'll probably be running behind a bush with Andy."

"I wonder how many more times you'll feel like doing this," Anna mused.

"Beth said I could keep up my normal activities. Who knows? Maybe I'll even have the baby up here on this mountain."

"Don't even think such a thing." Anna laced their fingers together as they slowed to a stroll behind Andy. "You have to go into labor in the middle of the night just like everyone else."

"Lucky it's me that's pregnant, because you'd probably give birth in the service department."

"At least she'd be covered under warranty."

"We'd have to give her a German name, like Heidi."

Anna gave her a sidelong look. "You really think it's a girl?"

"No idea, but I read they could probably tell us if we go for a second-trimester sonogram." They had gone back and forth over whether or not to learn the sex of their child, with each changing her mind a half dozen times.

"I'm still not sure I want to know," Anna said. "I kind of like the idea of being surprised, but then sometimes I think if I knew what sex it was, it wouldn't be so abstract. People always say 'the baby this' or 'the baby that' like it's a thing instead of a person. I hate that."

Lily nodded along. "And I think it would be easier for Andy if he knew whether he was getting a brother or a sister. And speaking of Andy…"

He had tired of walking and was sitting on a rock to wait until they caught up. "These old bones won't go another step," he said dramatically, mimicking one of his grandpa's favorite expressions.

Without a word of protest or cajoling Anna hoisted him onto her back and began to gallop down the trail. Lily adored how the two of them seemed to worship each other, and she couldn't wait to see them interacting with the—she caught herself doing exactly what Anna said she hated—with his brother or sister. She fished her camera from her side pocket and snapped a photo, envisioning it in the rotation of the screensaver on her office computer.

By the time she caught up, Andy was already in the car and Anna was leaning against the front fender, arms folded. "What took you so long?"

"I'm a mere mortal, show-off." She poked Anna in the stomach playfully. "I appreciate you hauling him all the way down here. I don't think I could have done it."

Anna grinned and glanced back at Andy, who was buckled in and ready to go. "I'll make you a deal," she said, her voice too low for him to hear. "You carry this one the first nine months and I'll take it from there."

▲ ▲ ▲

"I knew it. I'm starting to show," Lily said, running her hands over her belly as she twisted from side to side before the mirror in the master bath. "I wear those pants all the time and they've never been tight around the waist until today. Can you see it?"

Anna appreciated each and every opportunity to gaze upon Lily's naked body but could honestly say she had never studied it with non-sexual motives. She focused on the tummy, which looked as flat and firm as ever. "Not really."

"Oh, come on." She turned in profile and rested her hands on her hips. "See there? It's curved outward right below my belly button."

"If you say so."

"If I say so?"

The sharpness of the retort took Anna by surprise. "All I'm saying is I don't notice it the way you do. As far as I'm concerned, you look terrific as always."

"In other words, I won't look so good once I get fat."

"I didn't say that."

Lily snatched her robe from a peg on the back of the bathroom door and cinched it about her waist. "Not in so many words, but your meaning was quite clear, thank you. I look terrific as long as my stomach is flat, but not so much when it starts to stick out. Glad to know I have that to look forward to."

Anna stood with her mouth agape as Lily stormed out of the bathroom. In slow motion, she cocked her head to see herself in the mirror, not at all surprised at the look of shock on her face. That wasn't like Lily at all, neither the sudden anger nor the silly insecurity about her appearance. She couldn't possibly think being pregnant would make her unattractive. That had to be a mood swing, maybe some kind of hormone eruption brought about by fatigue from their long day's hike. The pamphlet Beth had given them had warned that her emotions would be all over the place during the first trimester.

She took her time brushing her teeth, hoping the few extra minutes would help Lily cool down. Then she donned her robe and drew a deep breath for courage just in case the tantrum wasn't finished. Finding their bedroom empty she followed the source of light to the family room downstairs.

The room lived up to its name, since they spent most of their home time with Andy here, watching TV or surfing the Internet while he played on the area rug in the middle of the hardwood floor. His box of toys, mostly small cars and the erector set he used to build streets and towns, sat at the near end of the L-shaped sectional sofa. In the corner was a wide-screen TV, mounted above a cabinet that held dozens of children's movies. French doors on one wall led out to the patio. Directly across from the sofa, one door led to a half-bath, another to the small office where she and Lily managed their mail and worked at the desk. The family room was also their main avenue for entering and leaving the house, since the door led across the uncovered driveway to the two-car garage. It was a cozy room, and perhaps would be too cozy once their family grew.

Lily was stretched out on the long side of the sofa with her head on a pillow, watching TV. Anna could have sat at the other end by herself, but chose instead to push the envelope by sliding under the pillow and pulling it away, leaving Lily's head in her lap. "Is everything okay?"

"I guess," Lily answered meekly. "I just got excited when I thought I'd popped out a little, but then you said you couldn't see it. I wanted you to get excited too."

Anna breathed a silent sigh of relief. "I am excited. And that business about not looking good when your tummy gets bigger? Ridiculous. You'll always be the most beautiful person in the world to me, and nothing will ever change that. In fact, I bet you get more beautiful every day. My sister did."

"She didn't think so." Lily sniffed loudly and wiped her eyes with the back of her hand. "My hiking pants were tighter than usual, I swear."

"I believe you." Anna swept a lock of short blond hair from her forehead tenderly. "Looks like it's time to go shopping for some stretchy clothes."

That suggestion drew an exasperated groan. "I'd rather scoop dog poop than shop for clothes."

"Lucky for you, there's always lots of dog poop in the side yard."

Without a word Lily rolled toward her and burrowed into the opening of her robe.

Anna thought at first it might be an amorous advance, but then Lily blew a loud raspberry into her belly, and all she could do was laugh, grateful the tension had passed. "You know what would feel good right now?" she asked, tipping her head toward the French doors.

"Count me in," Lily answered, hopping up to grab bath towels from hooks on the back of the bathroom door.

Only minutes later they were in the churning water of the hot tub. Anna pulled Lily into her lap, determined to erase any doubts about how she felt about her body.

* * *

"...and there's nothing quite like realizing your own kid is afraid of you because you're a drunk," Norman said from the tabletop podium, his chin dipping in obvious shame. "That was the bottom for me and I knew the only way I was coming up was to stop drinking. This program—these twelve steps—I work them every day. If I didn't I couldn't bear to look my son in the eye."

Lily liked Norman, a moderately successful film producer who had joined her regular Alcoholics Anonymous group a couple of years ago and already was a meeting leader and sponsor. Unassuming and friendly, he had none of the pretense she generally associated with Hollywood types. Here in this room, no one was special.

"Anyone else have a story?" he asked, relinquishing the podium to return to his seat in the small meeting room in the basement of St. Simon Catholic Church. Two dozen men and women, mostly professionals in their thirties or forties, pondered his call.

Lily's attendance at the meetings had fallen to about once a month, which was more than enough to sustain her resolve not to drink. She rarely talked in front of the group but their topic tonight—how they came to admit their lives were unmanageable—resonated with her, stirring painful memories of her brief separation from Anna four years ago. She had been thinking about those days because they were such a contrast to the joy in her life now.

"I'm Lily and I'm an alcoholic," she began, taking the podium to recite the traditional introduction. "Like Norman, I work the steps every day to keep my life manageable. It's amazing when I think back to how out of control I used to be, and even then I wouldn't admit I was an alcoholic. I'd lost my license, my job, my home…and worst of all, the companionship of the only person who mattered to me, my partner. I was almost halfway through a twenty-eight day program before it finally dawned on me that maybe…just maybe…being a drunk had something to do with all that. I guess it took a couple of weeks of sobriety to clear my head enough to see it, but once I did, I knew this program was the only path back to being in control."

Virginia, a woman in her fifties who had befriended her at Redwood Hills and become her sponsor, nodded along in support from her seat on the second row. Her long dark hair and clear blue eyes had captured Lily's attention back then, since it was easy to imagine Anna aging just as beautifully.

"There's no comparison to my life now and my life then. I'm in control because alcohol no longer dictates my choices or priorities. I was luckier than a lot of people here because the losses I suffered weren't permanent. I got my job back, and my partner and I are stronger together than ever. And now we have a son who means more to me than life itself. I hear Norman talk about his son and it scares me to think that could have been me, and that if circumstances had been different my son might have suffered from my drinking. How can you justify bringing pain to a five-year-old because you chose to be a drunk? Thanks to this program and the people in it I don't have to answer that."

Virginia corralled her in the parking lot after the meeting. "Something good is going on in your life."

Lily planted her tongue in her cheek and shook her head. "It's uncanny how you do that."

"You only speak up when you're struggling with something or feeling good about it. Tonight was obviously the latter."

"I get so focused on myself that I sometimes forget the Twelfth Step."

"Helping others," she said, nodding along. "It does help when you speak up, and I like it because I can hear how confident you are. It makes me not worry when I haven't seen you for a while."

"I've been swamped," she said sheepishly. "But life is good, Virginia. And everything I said was true. Good things happen when you're in control."

"So what's happening? Anything special?"

It was too soon to share the news of their baby, but not the sentiment. "Nothing…just that I love my family. I've been thinking about them a lot lately, and it's impossible for me to come to one of these meetings and not acknowledge how important the steps have been for getting us where we are today."

"I like hearing that from you. I worried last year when you didn't take that job that you might have regrets about it, but it sounds like things have worked out for the best."

No question it would have been nearly impossible to hold down a job as executive director of the county's guardian *ad litem* program and also juggle the demands of a newborn. Lily summed up her perspective with aplomb. "Things have a way of working out."

Chapter 3

Lily had almost finished her lunch when Sandy Henke shuffled between the tables in the crowded café and took the chair across from her. Sandy's brown sweater, worn over tan polyester slacks that forgave her abundant hips, set off the strawberry highlights in her wavy blond hair. At forty-two, she had nearly twenty years with the California Department of Social Services, and balanced an active caseload of more than two dozen children. If the size of her black canvas satchel was any indication, she had already had a busy morning.

"Sorry I'm late. I had to get Doris to sign off on this affidavit." She drew a manila folder from her satchel and passed it across the table. "I can't believe those two are back in court again. Someone should just kidnap their two kids and whisk them away."

Not only was Sandy her best friend, she was also the caseworker for the Esperanzas' two children, Sofia and Roberto.

"Maria's finally gotten her feet on the ground," Lily said.

"She's working full-time at a daycare and the kids are keeping up at school. Miguel's the one making trouble." She scanned the folder quickly to make sure it had everything she needed. The affidavit documented four social service interventions that came about because of Miguel's violent outbursts. "This is perfect."

"Good. Maybe this time they'll nail his ass once and for all."

"Who knows if it'll be enough? Pete Simpkins called and said his PO didn't find a gun, so our only shot is to get the judge to look at Miguel's history and connect the dots. He's threatened her before and followed through."

"You think she might be lying about the gun?"

"If she is, she's gotten very good at it. She seems really afraid this time." Lily pushed her plate away, suddenly nauseous at the smell of tuna salad, which until today had been one of her favorites. "I keep remembering all those horror stories about men who kill their own children just to get back at their wives. It gives me chills to think of Miguel doing something like that."

"Guys like him give me the serious creeps anyway. Let's hope he just moves on." Sandy ordered a glass of ice from the waitress, then drew a can from her satchel and began to shake it.

"Don't tell me you're back on that diet."

"I need to do something," she whined, pouring her drink over the ice. "The holidays are right around the corner and I can barely get into my clothes as it is."

Lily knew that feeling, though she didn't share Sandy's angst. She had taken Anna's advice and picked up a few new things that didn't pinch her waist. "What are you guys doing for Thanksgiving?"

"Bakersfield," Sandy grunted as if it were a terminal diagnosis. It was no secret she detested her partner's mother, and the feeling was mutual. "But at least I'll have my annual visit out of the way."

"I always feel so sorry for you when you talk about your mother-in-law. Anna's dad is a piece of work, but I have to admit I love the old coot."

"That's because George Kaklis is a normal parent who wants

his daughter to be happy. Suzanne's mother can't stand that she's gay, and she never misses an opportunity to let us both know it."

"Then why do you put yourself through it? Just tell Suzanne you don't want to go."

Sandy augmented her diet shake with a handful of potato chips from Lily's plate. "I think Suzanne actually likes antagonizing her. She wants to rub her mother's nose in it, and she needs my help to do it."

Lily couldn't begin to imagine such a rift in the Kaklis family, but she knew all too well from growing up in foster care that giving birth to someone didn't mean love automatically followed. "It sucks to spend a holiday like that. You guys should book a cabin somewhere and take off for a weekend together."

"That sounds romantic. Unfortunately, I'm married to a woman whose idea of romance is not farting when my friends are around."

She clinked her water glass against what was left of Sandy's shake. "And for that she has my eternal gratitude."

* * *

Anna pressed two fingers to her forehead as she studied her printouts one last time. "I refuse to have a migraine on such a glorious day," she said under her breath, trying to temper her excitement. It was the last day for employees to accept the offers of early retirement or severance, and she had exceeded her quota by three with five hours to go, which gave them a little extra wiggle room to recover from the downturn. It wasn't a cheap solution—a one-time payout of a million and a half dollars—but it meant Premier Motors should be operating in the black by the first quarter of the next fiscal year. She was tempted to gather her whole family at Empyre's to celebrate, but it struck her as unseemly to be so cheerful after bribing people to give up their jobs.

The list of departures included a few she would genuinely miss, such as Javier and Rudy, two of her detailers who planned to pool their payouts and set up their own business. Others she might not miss as much…Janet in payroll, who hadn't smiled since Reagan was president, or TJ, the service representative whose cologne could asphyxiate at thirty yards. Only one of her managers had bailed, Roger Goforth of the Palm Springs VW service department, and she already had a replacement in mind.

Her intercom phone beeped to announce a message. "Anna, are you in?" It was Carmen Soto, the receptionist.

"That depends on who wants to know."

"Me, silly."

Anna's laugh was a low rumble. Carmen had worked at Premier Motors for over thirty years, and was probably the only one on staff besides Hal who could get away with calling her "silly," except today when her good mood was practically invincible. "I'm always in for you."

Moments later, Carmen appeared in her office, her macramé belt swishing against her denim skirt. At fifty-eight years old, she was a self-described child of the Sixties who always dressed the part. To Anna, that made her a breath of fresh air among the Beverly Hills fashion plates.

"Please tell me that isn't what I think it is," Anna said, suddenly noticing the single sheet of paper in her hand.

"It isn't another summons for jury duty if that's what you're afraid of." Without waiting for an invitation Carmen plopped into the chair across from her desk. "I've decided to accept your generous retirement offer."

"Oh, no, you don't. I've just hit quota. I'm not accepting any more."

"Bullshit."

"Don't go calling 'bullshit' on me. You can't leave this place until I do."

Now it was Carmen's turn to laugh. From her deep pocket

she withdrew a new paperback and plunked it in the middle of Anna's desk. From the blood dripping off the title font, it appeared to be a thriller, the type that filled the racks at airports and grocery stores. "Did you know your mother loved to read murder mysteries? She and I used to trade back and forth, and we'd read them on our lunch break."

Anna hadn't thought of her mother in weeks, but when she did, it was often in the context of the old days at Premier Motors, before her mother died of breast cancer at age thirty-four. "I honestly don't remember that much about my mom, but I can almost picture her with one of these."

"That's the first in a series. The heroine is Nora Scot, ME."

"A medical examiner?"

"Affirmative. And it just happens to be an anagram of Carmen Soto."

Anna blinked and studied the book jacket until realization dawned. "You wrote this?"

Carmen nodded and smiled with pride. "I've been reading these for years and finally got up the nerve to try one myself."

"You're a published author!"

"It's not exactly a million-dollar enterprise...just barely five figures if you want to know the truth, but I'm having the time of my life. I go to mystery writer conventions, and I meet readers and sign their books. You can't imagine how delightful it is. If your mother were still living, I bet she'd be my biggest fan."

"Then I guess that job falls to me," Anna said with an indulgent sigh before striding around her desk to give her old friend a congratulatory hug. "Does this mean you're going to write mysteries full time?"

"When I'm not too busy being retired," Carmen said over her shoulder as she started out. When she reached the doorway, she stopped. "Speaking of your mother...I saw a lot of her in the way you handled this downsizing. She always tried her best to put people first too."

"That's nice to hear. It makes me proud."

"You'd make her proud…which is exactly what all of us want from our kids."

* * *

Judge Maynard "Rusty" Evans, his orange hair and black robe looking like holdovers from Halloween, scanned the docket before him, his face flashing annoyance. Periodically he frowned down from the bench over his half-glasses, first at Lily and her client, then at Pete Simpkins and his.

"I see the Esperanzas are back with us. Has anyone looked into getting these two assigned parking in the garage?" He glared at Miguel, then at Maria. "What's this? Ten times? Twenty times? I see you two more than I see my wife."

Lily bowed her head to hide her smirk. By her count she had appeared in court nineteen times in all with Maria Esperanza as her client, over half of those in Rusty Evans's court. He nearly always sided with Maria when it came to the welfare of the children, but the other judges were less dependable. At least Judge Halden had seen fit to grant an emergency restraining order last month barring Miguel from coming within a hundred yards of Maria.

"I can hardly wait for the next thrilling chapter. Why don't we begin with you, Ms. Stewart?"

Lily cleared her throat and looked at him awkwardly. She appreciated that old habits were hard to break, but she had married and changed her legal name nearly three years ago.

"My apologies. Ms. Kaklis."

She had carefully crafted her opening statement to hit all of the arguments most likely to sway this particular judge, even adding a few to inoculate against the counter arguments Pete was likely to make on Miguel's behalf. "Your Honor, three weeks ago on October twentieth, my client, Maria Esperanza, sought and was granted a temporary restraining order against her ex-husband, Miguel Esperanza, who is here in this courtroom today." As she submitted her document into evidence, she picked up what she thought was a hint of disdain on Judge Evans's face as he looked at Miguel. That would work in her favor.

"The cause of that order, detailed in an official report to the Los Angeles Police Department, was an allegation that Mr. Esperanza had appeared at her home, brandished a gun and threatened—in his words—to make her sorry for all the trouble she had caused him." She submitted this report also, along with Miguel's numerous arrest records. "On four occasions, Mr. Esperanza has committed violence against my client, each time resulting in arrest. He has two convictions for domestic battery and eight months incarceration in the county jail, for which he was paroled one week prior to the alleged incident."

The judge cast another scolding look at Miguel.

"Today we are asking the court to make the restraining order permanent, to bar Mr. Esperanza from coming within one hundred yards of her residence, her workplace or those of her family members. We also request that he be barred from contacting her by mail or delivery, by phone, by e-mail or by any other means. In addition, Your Honor, we are seeking permanent revocation of Mr. Esperanza's visitation rights with their two minor children, Sofia and Roberto."

She held up the paper Sandy had given her at lunch, hoping to drive home her point that Miguel was a violent man who could not be trusted with the welfare of his children. "I submit to this court a sworn affidavit from Ms. Sandra Henke, the children's social worker, who documents interventions pursuant to each arrest, two of which resulted in visitation restrictions for Mr. Esperanza pending completion of parenting and anger management classes. Though no physical abuse against the children was alleged, Sofia and Roberto subsequently received therapeutic services for psychological and behavioral problems thought to have resulted from their proximity to violence in the home. Their most recent assessment, conducted during Mr. Esperanza's incarceration, found both children to be healthy and well-adjusted, and performing satisfactorily in school. Given Mr. Esperanza's past behavior in which he threatened and committed violence, we ask the court to permanently safeguard these children and allow them to continue their progress by granting Mrs. Esperanza's request."

She returned to her seat beside Maria, confident she had presented the best case against Miguel given the facts. There was speculation, but no actual documentation, that Miguel had very little interaction with his daughter and routinely dropped her at his parents' home. His primary interest was Roberto— specifically to encourage machismo in his timid son. If she had been able to argue that his parental influence would likely result in another generation of abuse, her case would have been a slam dunk. Instead she had to hope Rusty Evans would read between the lines.

Pete Simpkins took the podium and pensively viewed his notes as if delaying his remarks for dramatic effect. She had known Pete for seven years, since his early days in the public defender's office. Now he worked for one of the smaller downtown firms, but continued to represent Miguel Esperanza as a pro bono client. At nearly six and a half feet tall, he towered over her, which usually brought a chuckle from the judge whenever they approached the bench side-by-side. These days he was sporting a stylish beard that squared his jaw and made him seem less mild-mannered. Though she generally thought of him as a friend, she rarely saw him outside their adversarial meetings in the courtroom.

"Today, Counselor?"

"Yes, Your Honor. I'm sorry. Thank you for hearing this case today."

Judge Evans lifted his hands in the air. "What can I say, Mr. Simpkins? It's my job."

Pete chuckled uneasily, as if realizing he had scored no points for his polite gesture. "Your Honor, as you know, the LAPD and the Department of Corrections take the terms of one's probation very seriously. Subsequent to these allegations by Mrs. Esperanza, my client's probation officer and the LAPD initiated a comprehensive search for a gun in my client's possession, namely the one she reported to police. No such weapon was discovered at my client's home, his parents' home or in his motor vehicle. Furthermore, there is no record of a sale and we have discovered no other witnesses who can attest to having seen Mr. Esperanza in the possession of a handgun." He cast a dubious glance at Maria before continuing. "Ms. Kaklis is correct that my client has been arrested four times for domestic disturbances, and convicted twice of criminal behavior. However, Mrs. Esperanza declined to press charges on one of those occasions, and in the other my client was cleared of the charges for lack of evidence."

Lily shot to her feet. "Objection. Counselor's claim misstates the facts. Charges were dismissed on one occasion against Mr. Esperanza, but he was not cleared."

"Sustained."

"Apologies, Your Honor. Charges were dismissed for insufficient evidence. We contend that Mrs. Esperanza has a history of making unsubstantiated claims. That seems to be the case here as well."

She was frankly surprised that Pete had made such a rookie mistake in saying his client was cleared, and also that he seemed to be studying his notes as if seeing them for the first time. It wasn't like him to come to court unprepared.

"As for the question of visitation, Mrs. Esperanza has made numerous efforts—some in violation of this court's orders—to interfere with my client's visitation rights. In the absence of irrefutable evidence that his presence in their lives is detrimental to their well-being, there is no justification for curtailing parental rights."

It was by far the weakest case Pete had ever made, and she almost wondered if he was sandbagging. The Esperanzas would try anyone's patience, and it wouldn't surprise her if this was Pete's way—even subconsciously—of washing his hands of Miguel.

Judge Evans took a long time to respond and when he did, he sounded flummoxed. "You're right, Mr. Simpkins. In the absence of corroborating evidence it would seem only fair to dismiss these allegations. Yet when I look at the whole picture I see a man who has been convicted twice of abusing his wife, proof positive that he is capable of such behavior. While I would like to give Mr. Esperanza the benefit of the doubt that he has been sufficiently rehabilitated by his incarceration, I can also understand why Mrs. Esperanza fears for her safety. As they have no further business with one another that would require direct contact, I see no harm in granting her petition for a permanent restraining order."

Lily patted Maria's hand underneath the table, though she feared from the judge's frustrated tone that their hope for revocation of visitation request was on thin ice.

"I am hesitant, however, to arbitrarily end the relationship between a father and his children. While I am pleased to see that Sofia and Roberto have progressed under their mother's exclusive care, I would like to give Mr. Esperanza an opportunity to prove he can now be a positive influence in their lives." Judge Evans removed his glasses and shook them at Miguel. "You cannot do that, sir, if you are making threats and possessing weapons in violation of your probation."

Miguel nodded meekly without looking up, a sign that Pete hadn't prepped his client any more than he had prepped his case. The lack of eye contact wouldn't sit well with a judge like Rusty Evans.

"You will have supervised visitation only for the next six months, at which time I'll review the recommendations of social services. Miss two sessions or violate this restraining order and I'll terminate visitation altogether." He slapped his gavel. "We're done here."

* * *

Anna was met at the door by Chester's deep bark and the lingering smell of a dinner she had probably missed. Following her nose to the kitchen, she found Lily and Andy still seated at the small breakfast nook in the bay window. The family ate most meals here, since Anna had commandeered the dining room table three months ago for her spreadsheets and ledgers.

"We tried to wait, but you know how this guy is about his macaroni and cheese," Lily said, tipping her head in the direction of their son, who was happily wolfing down his favorite dish.

"That's okay. Sorry I'm late." Had she known about the macaroni, she would have lingered at the office for another hour or so. It was possibly her least favorite food, but she had to eat some or lose the moral high ground in convincing Andy to eat vegetables. "Yum, asparagus."

Right on cue he made a face, though he plucked the stalk on his plate with his fingers and gamely took another bite.

"There's glazed salmon in the oven," Lily said. "I'll get it."

She sat patiently as Lily prepared her plate, which included a spoonful of the dreaded macaroni. "Thank you so much," she said drolly.

"What was going on at work? You sounded cranky when you called."

"Carmen's leaving. And if that's not bad enough, Brad Stanley came into my office just when I was walking out the door at a quarter till six to say he was taking the early retirement offer too. Now I have to find a new operations manager for the BMW dealership and I don't have a candidate with enough experience." Anna downed the macaroni in two bites and followed it with a large gulp of sparkling water. "And to think I almost got through this without losing anyone critical."

"I thought you always meant for Holly to move up," Lily said, a reference to the BMW sales manager, a close friend of Anna's

45

who kept Chester for them whenever they went out of town.

"I did, but not for another two or three years. She's only thirty-two years old."

"And you were what? Twenty-three?"

"I was a prodigy, just like Andy here." She mussed his hair, smiling at his confusion over the new word.

"What's a progidy?" he asked.

"A prodigy. It's someone who's very smart at a young age. When I was in kindergarten I knew all about cars, just like you."

"BMWs are the best!"

Anna gave Lily her "I told you so" look, and held up her hand to ward off another spoonful of macaroni. "Not for me. Give it to the boy genius."

"But I've heard you say Holly knows all about cars too."

"She probably knows all the new specs better than I do, but she'll have to understand the business side too if she's going to run operations. She's never done a budget or a work schedule, she doesn't deal with personnel, and she doesn't get off the lot to network with other businesses. You can't just throw somebody into a job like that head first. The only one I have in the company who's ready for that is Marco." Except that Marco, her sales manager at the Premier Volkswagen dealership loved VWs, not Beamers. She was hoping to move him up to head the VW operation when her father decided to call it quits for good, and it would crush him to switch brands.

Lily shrugged and began clearing the dishes. "So make Marco the operations manager for the VW lot and bring George back to take Brad's place."

She opened her mouth to object, but couldn't think why. It was the obvious solution. "I think that's a…I'm really embarrassed I didn't think of that myself. It's perfect."

"Except that you have to work with George every day, and I bet he won't like not being the boss."

Anna's head was already racing with ideas about how to implement the change. "He'll love it once he realizes his real job is to train Holly. That means he gets to sit in the VP desk and hand off everything he doesn't want to do, like the advertising runs, the Chamber of Commerce, firing people, customer complaints...it'll be the best job he ever had."

"In which case your biggest problem will be getting him out the door when you're ready for her to take over."

"May I be excused?" Andy asked, already squirming from the padded bench that lined the bay window on one side of the table. He hadn't yet learned to tell time, but knew he had only a short while to play after dinner before his bath and bed.

"You may," Anna answered, swinging her legs sideways for him to crawl under. "I'll be in there in a minute." This was also her time with Andy, the few minutes she usually set aside every day to play with him before bed. As soon as he was gone, she carried her plate to the sink and set it down to wrap her arms around Lily from behind. "What would I ever do without you? You cook. You clean. You give me all your great ideas." She dropped her hands to Lily's belly and whispered, "And you even have our baby."

"Yes, I'm the deluxe, all-purpose model, available wherever fine women are sold."

Anna chuckled and nuzzled her neck. "How was court today?"

"Split decision." Lily finished loading the dishwasher and wiped down the kitchen sink as she brought Anna up to date. "So if Miguel misses two visits, he forfeits the kids for good. I predict that will happen within six months, and Maria's troubles will be over." She crossed her arms and leaned against the counter. "I've been representing Maria in family court for seven years. I can't even imagine what I'll do with all my free time once it's over."

Anna had a suggestion, one they had talked about several months ago, but Lily hadn't been keen on it at the time. Perhaps she would feel different now that their baby was on the way. "Maybe you'll decide to stay home with the baby after all."

Lily gave her a pointed look and she threw up her hands in instant retreat.

"Not that I'm saying you should, just that you could."

"The last time I left the law clinic it took me almost two years to get my office back," Lily said sharply, a reference to her suspension for an alcohol-related incident over three years ago. The anger in her voice seemed to come from nowhere.

Anna didn't dare chalk it up to hormones—at least not aloud. "Honey, I wasn't saying I thought you should. You know you can do whatever you want and I'll back you a hundred percent."

"Mom!" Andy called from the family room.

Lily threw the dishtowel onto the counter and muttered as she walked away, "Why don't you stay home with the baby? At least you can be gone as long as you want and still come back as the boss."

As Anna absorbed the tirade, she weighed her options. Something told her it would be best not to go chasing after her in order to smooth things over, as that might only prolong the quarrel. Instead she went into the family room to play with Andy, who had already emptied the contents of his toy box onto the floor.

"Is Mama mad at me?" His sad voice almost broke her heart.

"Of course not. She just isn't feeling well right now, but she'll be better soon."

After thirty minutes of playtime, they straightened the room and went upstairs to find the door to the master suite closed. Anna helped Andy through his bath and into bed, but held off on reading his bedtime story.

She found Lily sitting on the bed, still fully dressed, paging through a stack of old magazines. "Andy was worried that you were mad at him. I thought you might want to read him a story just to let him know things are okay, but if you'd rather not I'll go back in there and do it."

Wordlessly, Lily tossed her magazine aside and walked out of the room. It wasn't a gracious response, but at least she was making amends with Andy. Anna returned to the family room and cruised the television offerings before settling on the Lakers game.

Soon after, Lily appeared in the doorway. "I did it again, didn't I? Flew off the handle over something silly."

Anna was glad for the admission, since sweeping it under the rug made it more likely to happen again. She wondered how much of it was hormones, and how much was resistance to staying home once the baby was born. "It isn't silly to want to go back to work. This is your career and you've worked hard to get where you are."

Lily slumped in a heap at the far end of the couch and swung her legs up so they intertwined with Anna's. "It wasn't even about that, really. I was just picking a fight because I was in the mood for it. If it hadn't been work, it probably would have been something else."

"That's really unusual for you," she said teasingly. "Could it be that you're...I don't know, pregnant?"

A gentle kick was her answer. "How come you don't ever lose your temper?"

"I'm perfect. Haven't you noticed?"

"I have. It's very intimidating."

"Come here." Anna held out her arms and Lily backed into the embrace, resting against her chest. "We'll manage just fine if you want to go back to work. Hiring a full-time nanny to keep the house and be here when Andy gets home from school is probably a good idea."

Lily sighed. "Do we really want nannies raising our kids?"

"We'd still raise them. We just have to find someone who understands our values, somebody Andy really likes."

"I don't know, Anna. Maybe it isn't fair to the kids for both of us to work all day. We'll miss half their lives."

She couldn't tell if Lily was truly conflicted or still in her contrary mood, but now was just as good a time as any to air their thoughts. "Your mom worked full-time, and so did mine. We turned out okay."

"That's not a fair comparison, though. My mom was a teacher

at the same place where I happened to go to school, so I was with her all the time. And you grew up at the car dealership. I can't very well take the kids down to my office."

"Okay, so you could go back to work part-time, like when Andy first came to live with us. And you're right, I'm the boss. If I want to set up a playpen in my office for little…Ruby…I can."

"Ruby?"

Anna found herself grinning. "Yeah, what's wrong with Ruby?"

"Where did that come from?"

"I don't know. I just said it. Ruby Kaklis."

"What if it's a boy?"

"Then you get to name him."

"Ralph."

"Anything but Ralph."

Lily gently trailed her fingernails along Anna's long arms, and finally lifted her hands to kiss the backs of her knuckles. "I'm sorry I went off on you. Beth said all the hormones would settle down after the first trimester."

"It's okay. I'd rather be on the receiving end of an occasional tantrum than having my emotions go haywire or throwing up every day like you."

"You left out having to pee every six minutes."

Anna tightened her embrace and rested her chin on Lily's shoulder. "I love you for all the things you're going through for us. I wasn't sure I'd be a good mom, but Andy came along and showed me how easy it was. Now I can't wait for this baby."

"And I can't wait to see you be a mom again."

"Ruby."

"Ralph."

Chapter 4

Lily blinked and tried to move, vaguely aware that her arm was pinned by a small body draped across it. Andy had come to her bedside at two a.m. after a bad dream, and when he couldn't get back to sleep in his own bed she had brought him to theirs. Anna had barely stirred until Lily nudged her awake to slip into her nightshirt.

The pamphlet Beth had given her warned that she wouldn't have much energy while her body adjusted to pregnancy. Truer words were never written, but she took it as a welcome sign her pregnancy was proceeding normally. Naps had become her guilty pleasure—before dinner, after dinner and at any given moment over the weekend when she managed to get in even a semi-horizontal position.

Inch by inch she worked herself free of Andy and sat up to see him pressed against Anna's back, his curly brown hair tickling her shoulder. It was a Kodak moment, but more than that it was an opportunity for her to escape downstairs for a few minutes of solitude.

Not complete solitude though, she remembered as Chester's thud on the floor signaled his interest in breakfast. She picked up her slippers and tiptoed to the doorway, where she paused one last time to look back at the slumbering pair. It was unusual for Andy to sleep with them. He normally slept soundly in his own bed, but neither she nor Anna thought it was a big deal for him to join them once in a while. It always felt good to have him there, and he probably would outgrow the need long before they tired of it.

As she cinched her robe she was reminded of yet another first trimester side effect—breasts so tender she could hardly stand to button her shirt. At least she hadn't suffered with morning sickness today. There were few things she hated as much as throwing up.

Chester rushed ahead down the sweeping staircase to sit by the back door, where he thumped his tail wildly.

"Hold on there, fella." She lifted the panel of the doggie door and he disappeared through the hole.

On the kitchen counter was a packet containing Andy's school pictures, adorable with his missing front tooth. She selected one and wrote a note in a greeting card to send it off. By the time she found the stamps in the drawer, Chester had reappeared and insisted she fill his bowl.

He was vibrant for an eight-year-old house dog, owing his reversion to puppyhood to Andy, who romped with him through the park, the neighborhood, and up and down the stairs. It made her sad to think of Chester leaving them someday, as he was a living, breathing reminder of her mother, who had been gone for three years. She would have given anything had her mom lived to see their baby. Eleanor Stewart would have made one terrific grandmother. Tears welled up as she envisioned the sight.

"Must have coffee." Anna stumbled into the kitchen and caught her crying. "Baby, what's wrong?"

The floodgates opened and Lily found herself bawling onto Anna's shoulder. *More hormones.* In the last couple of weeks her anger had abated only to be replaced by uncontrollable sadness, or even just silly crying over laundry commercials. "Just wishing Mom was here."

Anna shushed her gently and drew her into an embrace. They stood that way for several minutes until the sobs subsided.

Then as quickly as she had rushed into Anna's arms, she stepped away and fanned herself with both hands. "All done. You wanted coffee?"

"I'll get it."

"What are you doing up so early? The way you two were sleeping, I figured I had time to go up Mount Baldy and back."

"Andy was drooling on my shoulder."

"At least he didn't pee on you this time." In fact, Andy hadn't wet the bed for several months.

"So what happened last night? Did he have a bad dream?" Anna helped herself to a cup of coffee and topped off Lily's mug.

"Something like that. Jonah told him there were mean old ladies that lived under his bed, so naturally the first person Andy thought of was his teacher."

"Mrs. Dooley? Why is my nephew so ornery? Never mind, I'm sure he gets it from his mother. It was probably a good thing Kim and I didn't meet until I was fourteen. Otherwise she would've ruined Santa and the Easter bunny."

"Instead she tormented you for twenty years by talking about sex."

Anna chuckled. "At least she knows all about the in vitro procedures so we won't have to endure the questions about how we did it. But she'll go nuts wanting to know who our sperm donor was."

Since Andy's father was of Mexican heritage, they had chosen a Latino man, a graduate student in the sciences who played competitive sports. They liked the idea that their children might appear to be siblings.

Anna picked up the greeting card. "Karen Haney?"

Karen was Lily's birth mother, a woman she had despised until only recently. When the judge granted her and Anna's petition to adopt Andy—officially ending Karen's participation in his life—he had requested the parties work something out informally with each other. "School pictures," she said matter-of-factly. That was all the discussion of Karen Haney she wanted. "Only three more days and we'll have our first pictures of the baby. Hard to believe it's eleven weeks already."

"When did she say we'd know if it's Ruby or Ralph?"

"Not till sixteen weeks. That's almost Christmas. But Beth said we should be safe to start telling people we're pregnant the week after Thanksgiving. I can't wait to see the looks on their faces, especially your father's." George would be especially excited if their baby turned out to be Anna's, though Lily had her doubts despite what Beth had said about the possibilities. From the moment she had learned she was pregnant, she hadn't been able to shake the feeling that she was carrying a child of her own blood. As much as that thrilled her, it also made her sad it wasn't Anna's.

"How do you think Andy will react?"

"Considering he practically worships Jonah, I think he'll be thrilled. Being a big brother gives them one more thing in common." Lily filled their mugs again. "When do you think we should tell him?"

"Not until the last minute. Keep in mind that he told me everything I was getting for my birthday as soon as you two got back from the mall. There's no way he'll be able to keep this a secret."

Lily dissolved into a fit of laughter, just as she did each time she recalled Andy's exuberant shouts about what was in the bag as she tried to sneak into the house with Anna's birthday gifts. It was understandable, though, since in his years in foster care he'd had little exposure to the concept of surprising someone. "You're right. We should tell him about two seconds before we tell everyone else."

"And then hold a hand over his mouth." Anna opened the *LA Times* and spread out the advertising page for Premier Motors alongside that of her Orange County competitor. "Cleve Shaw's swimming in debt. He called me the other day to see if I'd take some of his inventory, but I couldn't help. I bet he sells out before the end of the year."

"I thought you said the German cars were coming back already."

"They are, but he owns a GM dealership too. It's dragging him down."

"Are you tempted to make him an offer?"

"With what? It'll be two years before we're able to pay down the debt on Palm Springs, and that's only if this last round of cuts stops the skid." She folded the paper and pushed it aside. "Not going to talk about work today. What's on our agenda?"

"Nothing that takes a lot of energy, I hope."

"Maybe when sleepyhead wakes up we'll go do something fun," Anna suggested.

Lily opened the ad section again. "Like drive around town and check out the minivans?"

The look of horror on Anna's face was priceless.

* * *

Lily took a deep breath, hoping to quiet her roiling stomach. This time it wasn't the morning sickness, which she now knew had nothing to do with morning. She had barely slept the night before in anticipation of their first sonogram, and she couldn't keep her foot from bouncing as they waited.

In contrast to her own fidgeting, Anna was cool as a cucumber. There she sat, legs crossed and paging through a magazine as if she didn't have a care in the world.

Though they were alone in the waiting room, Lily whispered, "How can you be so casual about all this?"

"Who's casual? I've read this last paragraph nine times and I still couldn't tell you what it said." Then she cracked a smile and clutched Lily's hand. "Trust me, I'm as excited as you are."

"I can't believe we're actually about to meet our baby."

"Ruby."

"Stop saying that. It might be Ralph and he'll have a complex all his life because you really wanted a girl. Besides, we aren't going to know the sex today."

Anna sighed and closed her magazine. "I promise not to give our baby a complex if you'll stop calling him Ralph."

"Deal." A wave of giddiness bubbled up inside her and she nearly lifted out of her chair. "I'm excited. How can you just sit there?"

"What else can I do? I didn't bring a car to play with."

It so happened Lily carried one in her purse in case she found herself waiting somewhere with Andy, and she produced it only to see Anna roll her eyes. "You asked."

The minutes seemed like hours, but finally the receptionist, a young Latina woman, appeared and led them to an examination room. Her nametag read Marisol, and she seemed as excited as they were. Bubbling nonstop about their hectic morning in the clinic, she fished a gown from a drawer, slapped it into Lily's hands and rushed out the door, closing it behind her.

"Is it my imagination or are the women who work here happier than Disney characters?" Lily asked.

"They make dreams come true. That's got to be the best job in the world." Anna took her skirt and folded it neatly. "Can you imagine how exciting this was for Kim and Hal after trying for eleven years?"

"I don't know how they stood it. We almost went crazy after just eight months." Left unsaid was that Kim had also suffered two miscarriages. Lily could hardly bear to think about losing this baby, but it was in the back of her mind every second of every day. Only three more weeks and they would be past the period of greatest risk.

She had just gotten seated at the end of the examination table when a sharp knock sounded on the door. It was Seon-Lee, the blood technician, a thin Asian woman who, like Marisol, was all smiles. "I vant to drink your blood."

Lily laughed and held out her arm. Looking at Anna, she asked, "Do you get the feeling this woman likes her job too?"

Anna had already looked away, squeamish at the sight of the needle going into Lily's arm. It was hard to imagine how she would handle cutting the cord in the delivery room.

Beth entered just as Seon-Lee was finishing up. "Today's the big day, ladies. How's the morning sickness?"

"Nauseating."

The doctor grinned broadly, instantly forming crow's feet beside her deep-set brown eyes. "Yep, you're definitely pregnant, all right. Let me start with a quick pelvic check. You know the drill."

Lily found the stirrups with her heels and sucked in a deep breath as Beth entered her with a gloved hand.

"Normal, normal, normal." And just like that she was finished, snapping off the glove and tossing it into a bin. "Let's have a listen, shall we?"

Lily tried not to breathe as the fetal stethoscope slid from point to point around her abdomen. Beth frowned and repositioned the device several times, apparently oblivious to Lily's rising panic.

Anna had left her chair to stand beside them. "Is everything all right?"

"Yes, indeed. As a matter of fact, it's pretty fantastic." She positioned the piece and offered the ear buds to Anna. "Go ahead. Hear it for yourself."

Anna did and her face lit up in a brilliant smile. "Oh, my God. That's our baby."

Lily could hardly wait for her turn. "I want to hear it too."

She curled forward so the ends of the stethoscope would reach her ears and heard the furious fluttering for herself. "It's so fast."

Beth folded the instrument and set it aside. "Like I said... normal. The fetal heartbeat is about one-sixty." She then smeared Lily's belly with cold gel, one hand hovering near the dial on her display. "Let's have a peek, shall we?"

"Are we looking for anything in particular?" Anna asked, her eyes transfixed on the blank screen.

"Nah, this is just a routine check. Sometimes we do these to verify the due date, but we know exactly when the embryo implanted so there's no guesswork there. Once in a while something will pop up that we have to keep an eye on, but we don't have any risk factors here so I'm not expecting anything hinky."

Though Lily appreciated the reassuring tone, this was anything but routine to her. She gripped Anna's hand and took a deep breath in anticipation of the image coming to life. Wavy green lines appeared against a black background as Beth slid the transducer across her belly.

And suddenly there it was—their baby, its head dwarfing its tiny body.

"Congratulations, ladies. It's now officially a fetus." As her left hand waved the transducer, her right moved a pointer to various spots on the screen. A small white image near the center of the kidney-shaped mass pulsated. "See the heart?"

Lily stared mesmerized at the rhythmic swelling and falling, fascinated at the proof of life.

"Is that a foot?" Anna gestured to a hook-like appendage jutting from the bottom of the curve-shaped blob.

"It...is...indeed," Beth answered tentatively, wiggling the transducer to try to bring the image into focus. "Let's see if..."

Lily held her breath for Beth to finish her thought but she didn't. Her eyes remained riveted to the screen as the wand crossed her stomach, revealing a new angle from near the top of the baby's head.

Beth's forehead wrinkled pensively. "Usually I can look straight down from here, but your baby's turned to the side a little bit."

"Is that okay?" Lily asked, aware of the shake in her voice but unable to control it. She reached for Anna's hand and gripped it tightly.

"Sure, they wiggle a lot. Better get used to it." Beth moved the pointer to the edge of the womb. "The placenta's forming normally, and"—she marked two points on the screen to measure—"it's a bit longer than we usually see at eleven weeks… almost four and a half centimeters."

Anna chuckled and gave her hand a confident squeeze. "No way Lily's going to make a big baby. I bet this one's mine."

"I always said it could be, but the size at this point isn't usually predictive of birth weight. We'll see some rapid growth over the next few weeks, but the real weight gain and lengthening happens in the third trimester. If you want this for your Christmas cards, I can have Marisol print it out for you."

"That would be the perfect way to tell people," Lily said, her stomach still roiling from Beth's hesitation.

"So what are you girls doing for Thanksgiving? Big turkey plans?"

"We were planning to go skiing in Tahoe with the family," Anna replied, "but there's no snow in the forecast this year."

"So we're going to Tahoe to not ski," Lily added. "Which means we'll eat too much, watch UCLA smear Cal in football—I hope—and chase three kids through the house."

Beth turned off the display and wiped Lily's belly with a towel. "If it makes you feel any better, I probably would've advised you not to ski anyway. Not that hurtling down the mountain is bad for you. It's the sudden stops." She pulled a digital voice recorder from her pocket and spewed what seemed like hundreds of words in a matter of only seconds. "Schedule with Marisol to come back in three weeks. I'd like to have another look."

"That's only fourteen weeks," Lily said anxiously, sitting up and pulling the shift across her waist. "I thought the second one was supposed to be at sixteen."

"It usually is, but when these bashful babies turn away from us, I like to go in for another look so I can see from the top down."

Her reasoning did little to assuage Lily's concern, since Beth had said a sonogram wasn't absolutely necessary in the first place. Now all of a sudden it was imperative she have another in only three weeks.

A knock sounded and Seon-Lee leaned into the room with a sheet of paper. Beth looked it over and grinned wryly. "From the looks of your blood results, I'd say Thanksgiving looks like a good time to share your little secret with the family." With her characteristic broad smile, she congratulated them one last time and left the examination room.

Lily stared numbly at the closed door. Even with Beth's promise they were safe to tell their family and friends, she couldn't shake the feeling that something was amiss.

Piece by piece, Anna held out her clothes so she could get dressed. There was nothing about her look that suggested concern.

"Did you get the feeling there was something Beth wasn't telling us?" Lily asked as she wriggled into her skirt.

"What do you mean?"

"Like she kept…I don't know, not finishing her sentences or something. I don't get the big deal about the baby turning and having to see the top of its head. I think there's something wrong."

"If she was worried about something, would she have said it was okay to tell people?" Anna gripped her shoulders firmly. "Would she be printing off pictures of our baby to send to our friends on a Christmas card? I don't think so."

Lily let out a deep sigh as Anna drew her into a hug. She resisted at first, almost refusing to be mollified. But as she let herself relax, the moment took on the familiar feel of countless others they had shared when sadness and doubt had consumed her—the day her mother died, the night she came to the house to make amends for her problems with alcohol, and all the weeks she ached to bring Andy into their home. Each time Anna had reached out to give her strength.

And she always made everything okay.

* * *

Anna loved the way her sporty Z8 turned heads, even on the lot at Premier Volkswagen, where her staff had seen it hundreds of times. If it was possible to fall in love with a car—and as far as she was concerned, it was—the Z8 was a machine that could steal your heart. Only a few thousand of the concept cars existed, produced almost a decade ago over a three-year span to celebrate the 507, BMW's classic roadster. She almost hated taking it out on rainy days like this one, but the detailers back at her BMW lot would clean it up the minute she returned.

The very idea of giving up her Z8 for a sedan was laughable. Auto collectors had offered her up to three hundred thousand dollars for this vintage vehicle, but she wouldn't bite. At least they understood its worth. To Lily, it was just a car to go from Point A to B, but to Anna it was the pinnacle of both design and performance in automation. If they had room for a third car in the garage, she would gladly pick up another, something that would hold a car seat for the baby and a booster seat for Andy. Though he no longer required a booster according to California law, he still liked using one whenever he was relegated to the backseat so he could see out the windows without straining. He wasn't the sort of child who busied himself with toys or games in the car. He wanted to watch the traffic so he could see what others were driving. Anna understood that perfectly because she had been the same way as a child.

She pulled into her usual space next to her father's Imperial Blue 760Li sedan and turned off the engine, making no move to climb out into the rain. The events of the morning had taken a toll and she needed a moment to regroup. Beth's request that Lily return for a second sonogram had scared her half to death, but when she saw how frightened Lily was she had tamped down her own fears and gathered herself. Lily seemed to feed off her reaction to things, and staying calm would go a long way toward keeping her worries at bay. Once they parted in the parking garage Anna dropped the façade and mentally ticked off the things that had set her on edge—Beth's puzzled demeanor as she fumbled to find their baby's heartbeat, her apparent surprise at the size and shape of the image they were seeing, and the way she seemed to hesitate when they asked questions. None of it added up to panic, especially since she had given them the go-ahead to share the news of their pregnancy, but something was...what word had she used...hinky.

The rain let up for several seconds and she made a mad dash to the back door of the showroom, unable to avoid splashing through a large puddle that had gathered directly behind her car. With soggy feet, she carefully crossed the tile floor of the showroom, where Marco Gonzalez, her VW sales manager, had arranged their flashiest lineup—the CC, which was Volkswagen's largest sedan, the Beetle convertible, the SUV Taureg, and...a minivan?

"Hey, Anna." Marco greeted her with a broad smile. With his short dark hair and brown eyes, he cut a handsome figure in his starched white shirt and striped BMW tie. He set the perfect example of professionalism for his sales staff with his appearance, expertise and friendly manner, and Anna often imagined Andy would develop that same look when he got older. Marco was only thirty-four years old, but he had grown quickly into his job soon after Anna acquired the dealership and ushered the rude, lazy Tommy Russell out the door. She had been impressed with Marco's enthusiasm and passion for cars, and especially by his hunger to learn everything he could about the car business. For the past three years he had matured under her father's tutelage, and now it was time to move him up.

"Marco, what's this?" she asked, gesturing toward a white Routan, Volkswagen's seven-passenger minivan. "Since when do we park minivans in the showroom?"

"Since this is the vehicle more people want to see and they don't want to get wet looking at it."

"People are buying these?" She poked her head in through the open side door and looked around. "You could carry a whole soccer team in here."

"That's the idea. Families like them because the kids can spread out. Look." He pressed a button on the rear console and a screen lowered just behind the front seats. "Just load a favorite movie right here and all the kicking and whining stops. My wife and I are thinking about getting one too."

"Why? You only have two kids. You could go anywhere in the CC, or you could get one of the SUVs. You like driving too much to get a minivan. They're so...pedestrian." Which was another way of saying she would rather walk.

"Maybe, but to quote Lourdes, 'Not everything is about me,'" he said with a laugh. "She likes the idea of giving the kids their own space so they won't be picking at each other all the time. Plus, she can carpool two more kids, which means she won't have to drive as often. I'm sold on it. We're just waiting for a red one with all the features we want."

Anna shook her head. Marco was a great salesman, one of her best, but she wasn't buying his pitch. Who could possibly get a kick out of driving a box over the freeways of Southern California? "I need to talk something over with Dad, and then I'd like for the three of us to go to lunch. Can you do that?"

"You're the boss, Anna. I can do whatever you need."

She wound through the hallways to her father's small windowless office in the back, where he sat with his feet up, a phone pinched under his chin. He held up a finger and motioned for her to have a seat. She did, and kicked off her wet shoes. Her father's help in stabilizing the Volkswagen dealership had been invaluable, especially since she had fired most of the management within days of the acquisition. It was clear he enjoyed getting back to the nuts and bolts of running a business, and that he wasn't at all cut out for retirement. However, he was getting much more out of his leisure time now that he had grandchildren to occupy his afternoons and weekends away from the office.

He dropped the receiver in its cradle and scowled at the phone. "No, I don't want to take advantage of your slash in wholesale prices. I get ten calls a day like that."

"Me too. Half the used car dealers in town are liquidating their inventories. I'd be happy to cherry-pick two or three a week, but I don't need their junk."

"So what brings you over to the poor side of the tracks?"

She chuckled at his choice of words, as there was hardly such a thing as poor in Beverly Hills. "I've been hearing rumors that my ops manager's been cutting out early. Thought I'd come check it out."

"Bunch of tattletales. I tell you, you can't trust anyone these days."

"So while you run off to play with the other little boys, Marco has to cover for you. I might as well make him the ops manager."

"He's as capable as anyone. Does this mean you're firing me?"

"Yeah, I think I am." Her tone was unmistakably tongue-in-cheek. "Fact is, I need you back on the BMW lot next week to start teaching Holly Ganesh how to run the business. I want to move her up in two or three years and she needs to know all the things you've taught Marco."

Her father stood and puffed out his chest righteously, as if playing hard-to-get. "And what if my attention is needed elsewhere...say, about three o'clock on weekday afternoons?" Clearly, he didn't want to give up his newfound pleasure of playing with Jonah and Andy on those days Martine picked them up after school.

"Hard to say. Sometimes our afternoons get so busy people might not even notice if you slip out." She plucked a mint from the candy jar on his desk. "Seriously, Dad, we might need a few more hands on deck for a while now that we're down to a skeleton crew. If you could take over the ad management for the used cars—"

"I'll do anything but go to the Chamber of Commerce meetings. They put me on committees and make me work."

She tossed her candy wrapper at him but he batted it away. "I can't believe you won't go even when your own daughter is president. But that's all right. I don't want your sour disposition out there representing us anyway."

"Now you're talking. When do I start?"

"How about the Monday after we all get back from Tahoe?"

"So we finally get to have Thanksgiving together in Tahoe again and there's no snow. How's that for irony?"

They hadn't gone together as a family since the year before she and Lily had become a couple, when Kim and Hal's friend had briefly derailed their budding romance with an unwelcome kiss that Lily had misunderstood. "We have kids to keep us busy now. Are you and Mom still planning to drive up on Sunday morning?"

"You know Martine. She wants to be sure the refrigerator is stocked when everyone else arrives. God forbid anyone should go hungry." He patted his stomach with both hands, and Anna noticed a slight paunch on her usually trim father. That certainly jibed with Andy's report that he ate cookies and ice cream nearly every day he visited with his grandpa.

"No one stuffs a turkey like Mom. It'll be fun having everyone under one roof for a few days." Now that they had the go-ahead from Beth to share their good news, she was sure it would be a holiday to remember, especially for her father. "I think we should make Tahoe an annual tradition, something the kids can look back on and feel nostalgic about…like when we used to sail to Catalina."

Her reference drew a wistful smile across her father's lined face. She had only vague memories of the three of them as a family, but one vivid recollection was sailing on their cabin cruiser, which her father had sold upon her mother's death. He hadn't sailed since, not even with Hal, who had clung to his beloved boat until the month before Jonah was born.

"I've been a very lucky man," he said softly. "I married out of my league twice, and thanks to both of my wives, I have two of the most wonderful daughters any man could want. They brought me another son and daughter, and three healthy grandchildren to make sure I never get old. I'd love to make Tahoe a Thanksgiving tradition, but I'd be lying if I said I was doing it for the children."

"I know what you mean. I've been worried sick this past year about the dealerships going down the tubes, but then I'd spend a few hours with Lily and Andy and realize as long as I have them I'll be all right, no matter what happens at work. Having everyone together in Tahoe will make a nice celebration."

He nodded silently as if his head were a million miles away, and then abruptly slapped his desk and rubbed his hands together. "So let's go tell Marco the good news. The Old Man is finally getting out of his way." He hooked her hand to his elbow and led her up the hallway to the showroom. "By the way, did you see the new Routan? You should rent one of these when you fly into Reno. It'll hold seven, you know."

Anna almost stopped in her tracks. If she hadn't known better, she would have sworn it was a conspiracy.

Chapter 5

Lily locked her cruise control onto seventy and settled back into the sturdy leather seat of her X3. As she switched lanes on Interstate 5, the bump beneath her wheels jostled Kim awake in the passenger seat, and she shook her head as if fighting off the urge to doze.

"I don't mind if you want to catch some Zs. Looks like your daughter is," Lily said, motioning over her shoulder at baby Alice in her car seat.

The three of them had gotten an early start on the eight-hour drive to Tahoe. Anna, Hal and the boys would arrive ahead of them by plane this afternoon, but Alice was fighting an ear infection and the last thing she needed was a ride in the pressurized cabin.

Kim slapped her cheeks lightly several times. "No, I need adult conversation more than I need sleep. I hardly get either one these days."

"I'm all yours. What would you like to talk about?"

"I appreciate you making this trip with me, especially since you're driving. As you can see, I can't trust myself not to nod off."

"I don't mind. I enjoy driving but I never get to do it with Anna in the car. Can you imagine her letting someone else take the wheel?"

"Knowing my sister, she'll probably try to talk the pilot out of his seat this afternoon. By the way, I've noticed she's in a lot better mood these days. Hal, too. Things must have smoothed out at work."

"Yeah, they finally got all that downsizing behind them. But if I know Anna, she'll give herself this weekend off and then start worrying on Monday about her Christmas sales and the year-end inventory."

"Pffft!" Kim shook her head. "Can you believe it's Christmas already? It was just what, last month that we were taking down the tree?"

The year seemed longer to Lily, probably because they had spent eight months trying to get pregnant. And she was sure the next six months would take their sweet time as she and Anna waited for their baby. "Are you guys having a big Christmas this year?"

"Call us crazy but we decided to get Jonah a puppy. I have no delusions that a four-year-old can take care of a dog, but we need to keep channeling his energy into physical activity before he gets hooked on those computer games and videos that Hal's father's been sending him. Dr. Engle thinks he'll sleep better if he gets more exercise."

"I can vouch for that idea. Chester gives Andy a great workout and vice versa. You should see how they conk out together every night."

"I don't think either of my kids have ever conked out, except maybe in their car seats. I may as well buy two more and throw out their beds."

Too bad she and Anna hadn't already shared their news

because this conversation would be much more fun if she could actually compare her upcoming experiences to Kim's. She could hardly wait until tomorrow, when their plan was to tell everyone just as they were sitting down to Thanksgiving dinner. Then they could spend the rest of the weekend celebrating. It was getting harder to hide it, not only because of their excitement, but also because Lily was distinctly starting to show. The elastic waist of her dress slacks was covered by a long sweater, and she was surprised Kim hadn't already commented on her being overdressed for a day in the car.

The miles passed quietly and Lily caught her passenger jarring herself awake again. "We're making good time. Maybe you can stretch out and have a nap when we get there."

"That'll be the day." Kim looked over her shoulder at her still-sleeping daughter. "Eight hours in the car with Alice will pass a lot faster than one on a plane with Jonah. We got the best end of this deal."

Lily was pretty sure Anna could keep Andy in his seat, though he was as excited about flying as his cousin. That didn't mean he wouldn't be bouncing off the walls later—it was always like that when the boys played together—and that was trouble if it triggered an asthma attack. "I think it's great how well Jonah and Andy get along."

"It's been that way since the first day they met. Jonah can't wait to start school next year so he can be like his idol."

"Ha! If you ask me, it's the other way around. Andy goes on about Jonah this and Jonah that. I think it's been really good for him because most of the kids he was around in foster care were older and had a tendency to get in trouble."

"I hate to tell you this, but my kid's not exactly a model citizen." Kim looked at her watch. "In fact, Hal's probably telling the air marshals right about now that it's only Silly Putty and not C3 explosives."

There was a lot of truth to what Kim was saying. Jonah was hyper, loud and unpredictable at times, but he was also sweet and delightfully entertaining. "But thanks to Jonah, Andy isn't nearly as shy as we were afraid he'd be. He's made lots of friends at kindergarten and we never hear of him getting into any trouble. Of course, that's because he's terrified of his teacher."

"The infamous Mrs. Dooley. I hope Jonah gets her next year. I'm telling you, one of them will come away changed forever but my money's on the teacher."

Lily wasn't so sure. If anyone could tame Jonah it would be Mrs. Dooley. Even Anna was afraid of her.

Alice sputtered in the back seat and began to cry.

"Would you mind pulling into the next rest area? I think someone's hungry." Kim cajoled her daughter with singsong words for several more miles until Lily found the exit.

She had watched Kim nurse her children dozens of times but not since learning she was pregnant. Her eyes were riveted to the sight of Alice's small mouth closing around her mom's nipple. "That has to be one of the most beautiful sights in the world."

"Try telling that to the people I worked with down at the real estate office. The first time I brought Jonah in you would've thought I'd excused myself to masturbate."

Lily tried to imagine the reaction of her co-workers at the law clinic. Tony's wife Colleen had nursed their baby at work, but in the privacy of her office. It hadn't been a big deal to anyone, though she didn't envision bringing her baby to the office for more than just a visit, as Lauren had done. "Do you ever miss work?"

"Not the work part," she said with a snort. "But like I always say, I miss being around grownups. Funny thing, though. Last summer I had to take that recertification class for my broker's license. I'd been dying to get out of the house and I even got Mom to come over and stay with the kids every day so I wouldn't worry about them. I couldn't stand it!" Her voice grew more animated as she spoke. "By Wednesday morning I was texting her every twenty minutes to find out what they were doing. I couldn't wait to get home and see them." Kim shifted her daughter from one breast to the other. "And to do this. I think I need this even more than she does."

Lily looked on with both envy and anticipation. Giving nourishment with one's body seemed such an exquisite act. "How much longer do you think you'll nurse Alice?"

"Hard to say. I like it. She likes it. Maybe another six months or so. Jonah practically weaned himself after he learned to walk. He couldn't sit still long enough to nurse. Alice is on the run all the time too, but she's constantly looking over her shoulder to make sure I'm right behind her."

Lily listened as Kim expanded on the differences between her children and it occurred to her she had thought very little about what her child would be like. So far she and Anna had been caught up in the excitement of being pregnant and giving birth. "It's amazing you can have two such different children."

"Isn't it? I think we can shape them a little but for the most part they already know who they are. We're just along for the ride." She put Alice back into her car seat and they got underway again. "How did you like staying home with Andy?"

"It was perfect. Dropped him off at preschool every morning and picked him up at one. The only fly in the ointment was when I had to be in court, but Anna loved those days because she could go get him and bring him back to the dealership. I think it was her way of making sure he stayed focused on the car business."

"Don't look now, but I think it worked."

* * *

Anna turned the duffel bag upside down and shook it, spilling its contents onto the twin bed. "No wonder that was so heavy," she muttered to herself, surveying the spread. Her suggestion to Andy that he bring only his favorite toy cars had yielded over two dozen, all of which no doubt would be scattered throughout the

71

villa when it was time to pack up on Sunday morning.

The boys were finally calmed down from the trip thanks to the DVDs Martine had brought along. Knowing Andy, he was probably asleep on the couch already. She was tempted to join him in a nap but didn't dare risk Lily finding her sacked out, since the hormones still made her mood unpredictable. Best to stay on her toes and try to have everything in place when Lily arrived.

There already had been one major change in plans, this one with regard to sleeping arrangements. She and Lily had been slated for the room with the queen-sized bed, where they were to sleep with Andy. Hal and Kim had offered to take this room with the twin beds. Their plan was to put Jonah and Alice in separate beds and sleep on a full-sized inflatable mattress on the floor in between. Andy and Jonah, however, were so taken with the novelty of the air bed that they begged to sleep together on it and Anna relented. After all, it was her idea to make Thanksgiving memories for the children. She and Lily could stand a few nights sleeping across the room from one another.

Lily's last phone call had come from Truckee, which meant they would be pulling in at any moment. She had finished stowing their things neatly in the closet and dresser when the crunch of gravel signaled an arriving car. From the upstairs window, she watched as Lily and Kim exited the X3, looking surprisingly chipper given their long day on the road. "See? Plenty of room for all of us," she said to herself. Her idea to borrow a car from the dealership on those rare occasions when she needed to ferry both children was workable, even if complicated by the need to have quick access to a car seat. Too bad Lily didn't like driving a stick shift or they could simply switch vehicles on those days.

Before dashing out the door to greet them she confirmed that Andy had indeed fallen asleep on the couch. Jonah, though, was still going strong and had already shot down the porch stairs to meet his mom. Anna raced ahead and intercepted Kim to snatch Alice from her arms, inhaling her magnificent baby scent. "Nice ride, ladies?"

"Not bad at all," her sister replied. "I can't think of the last time I got to sit still that long."

"I supplied the nice, long adult chat," Lily said, scurrying around the car to deliver a quick peck on the lips. "Have fun with the boys?"

"I did, but Southwest Airlines will never be the same."

Kim thrust the diaper bag into her hand as Hal swooped in for a hug. "Here, lady with the baby. You're going to need this too."

"Better get your practice now," Lily whispered with a grin as they started up the steps.

Anna shuddered. She felt the same about baby poop as she did about blood, and frankly dreaded all the dirty diapers in her future. However, Alice's sweet baby smells were marginally worth the trouble of an occasional stinky diaper, especially since she laughed and jabbered at every interaction. The whole point proved moot as soon as they walked through the door and Martine whisked Alice from her arms. That freed Anna to point out the sleeping Andy and lead Lily upstairs to their bedroom.

"I thought we were supposed to have the other room."

"*Were* being the operative word." Anna explained the switch and added in her most suggestive tone that she wasn't averse to sharing a twin bed.

"What do you say we share this one right now?" Without even looking back, Lily gave the door a kick and abruptly pushed Anna backward onto one of the beds. She then fell on top, crushing her with a kiss as her hands roughly brushed Anna's body. "I've missed you."

"So I gather," Anna replied, reluctantly clutching Lily's wandering hands. It wasn't unusual for Lily to be aggressive but it was surprising to see her take such forceful command in a house with so many people. "But knowing my father's walking around underneath us at this very moment sort of dampens the mood, if you know what I mean."

Lily's face fell. "Point taken. At least kiss me one more time before we go back downstairs."

Anna complied, taking time to savor their closeness. As much as she wanted to release their passions, she didn't dare with her family nearby. If they stayed absent too long Kim would surely make some raucous remark at dinner...not that she wouldn't do that anyway.

"I want to tell everyone tonight," Lily said. "Right now."

"I thought we were going to wait until we all sat down to Thanksgiving dinner tomorrow."

"I can't hold this in another minute. Kim talked about babies all the way up here and I was practically hyperventilating."

"But we haven't told Andy yet."

"So go wake him up!" Lily emphasized her eagerness by shaking Anna's shoulders.

"Okay, okay."

Hal and Kim were settling into their room, Martine was preparing dinner and Jonah was playing a board game with his grandfather.

Anna scooped Andy into her arms and jostled him awake. "Have a nice nap, pal?"

He grunted and laid his head on her shoulder as she carried him up the stairs.

"Look who's here."

Lily tenderly brushed his hair off his forehead, and seeing his waking smile, held out her arms to take him. "Hey, sleepyhead."

He was a bear to rouse in the morning but naps seemed to leave him feeling as if he had missed something, and accordingly he snapped himself awake. Today he had missed his mama's arrival, and he fell into her arms to tell her at once of his adventures on the plane. Anna winced when he got to the part about riding with Jonah on the luggage carousel.

"It was only five seconds—tops!" She and Hal had turned their heads to collect bags. "It crossed our minds to act like we didn't know them."

"And then we rode on the suitcases," Andy added. "Mom pulled me and Uncle Hal pulled Jonah."

Lily looked at her pointedly. "How will I be able to trust you with a stroller?"

"What can I say? I'm the fun parent." She followed them to the bed, where Lily had positioned Andy on her lap.

"Andy, speaking of fun, Mom and I have something fun to tell you. Would you like to hear our big news?"

He wiggled from her lap and began to stomp from side to side on the air mattress at their feet.

Anna tugged at his arm until his feet stilled. "Andy, this is important. Mama and I called you up here to tell you something special and we want you to listen. Will you come back and sit in her lap?"

It wasn't like him to be insolent, but after a day with his cousin all bets were off. They had recently seen signs of a mild stubborn streak, which they agreed was typical for a five-year-old testing his limits, but nothing to cause alarm. If either of them grew stern, as in an urgent situation or when his behavior was affecting others, he would grudgingly fall in line, but their preferred approach was to make their expectations clear and ignore his antics until he came around.

Once he settled again on her knee, Lily ran her fingers through his curly hair. "Andy, when you first came to live with us your mom and I were so happy because we had a new person to love. Remember that?"

Anna wagged her finger between her and Lily. "And you were happy because you had both of us to love. And then there's Grandpa, Grandma, Aunt Kim, Uncle Hal..."

"And Jonah," he added.

"Who else?"

"Alice."

Anna nodded, recalling all the tips they had read on how to break the news of a new baby to a child his age. What mattered most was that he not feel displaced. "And we have enough love for everybody in our family without ever running out."

"That's right," Lily said. "The more people you have, the more love you feel. Your mom and I wanted even more love in our family, so we decided we'd have a little baby too, a baby that can be your little brother or sister."

He showed no reaction at first except to demonstrate that he had been listening. "Alice is Jonah's little sister."

"That's right. We don't know yet if we're going to get a baby girl like Alice or a baby boy. But we do know that all three of us are going to have someone else to love as much as we love each other."

Anna poked him in the rib. "How about that, pal? You get to be a big brother just like Jonah."

That brought a wide grin. "Can we go get it now?"

Lily chuckled. "Not just yet, Andy. Our baby is right here inside my tummy. It has to grow until it gets big enough, then it will pop out. But you'll be able to see it on the outside soon because my tummy will get bigger and bigger."

"You'll be big and fat like Henry Hippo," he said, referencing a character from one of his favorite books.

"Let's hope I'm not that big."

"Nobody else knows about our baby yet," Anna said. "That means now we get to go downstairs and tell the whole family. Everybody's going to be happy, just like they were when we told them you were coming to live with us forever. You remember that?"

He tugged on his bottom lip thoughtfully and shook his head. "What's the baby's name?"

Lily shot her a warning look. "We haven't named it yet. Your mom and I have some ideas and I bet you will too. Once we find out if it's a boy or a girl, we'll talk it over, okay?"

When they were satisfied they had answered all of Andy's questions, they moved downstairs and assembled the family in the great room. Kim held Alice and cuddled with Hal in the center of the sofa. George sat squeezed into an armchair with

Jonah, who had refused to sit on his lap. Martine perched on the arm of the sofa, one eye still on the kitchen where something simmered on the stove.

"We have a little news we'd like to share," Anna said, pacing casually in front of the hearth where Lily sat with Andy on her lap. "We were planning to wait until we all sat down to Thanksgiving dinner but thought we'd just get this out of the way so we can focus on Mom's delicious turkey tomorrow."

"Right, it's not a big deal or anything," Lily added with a comical air of nonchalance, "just a little update on what's been happening in our world."

Anna continued, "I told Dad last week I thought we should make Thanksgiving in Tahoe a family tradition—or anywhere else as long as we're all together. Something very special happens when we all gather under one roof, whether it's here, or at the Big House, or even at our usual table at Empyre's. That's because being with all of you gives me the warmest feeling in the whole world and I know Lily feels the same way."

"And so does Andy." Lily nudged him and he covered his face coyly. "When I lost my mom I thought it was the end of the world, but you guys picked me up and gave me a new home, and then you turned around and did the same thing for Andy. I don't even want to think about where we'd be if it hadn't been for the Kaklis clan."

George cleared his throat. "You've picked us up too, you know. Martine and I always say we're very lucky that our daughters chose such wonderful people to bring into our family. And giving us these beautiful children...what parent could ask for more than that?"

Anna quietly marveled at how much her father's sentimentality had grown over recent years—ever since the earthquake that had nearly claimed her life—as though he was determined to leave nothing important unsaid. Judging from how he had welcomed all three of his grandchildren, news of a fourth would put him over the moon.

"So yes," she went on, "I'd like it if we'd all plan to keep this holiday for each other. There's nothing I'm more grateful for than my family, and I like having us all together so I can say that."

"But next year…seriously, guys," Lily interjected, "can we get a bigger place? We don't have enough room for the baby here."

"Right, it doesn't have to be huge. We don't mind sharing a room with the boys, but it would be a lot easier on everybody if we all had our own space." Anna fought to keep a straight face as she took in the perplexed expressions on her family's faces. "That way if our baby cries at night, we won't have to step over anyone to get to the crib."

Several seconds of stunned silence passed before Kim finally spoke. "You need a…which one of you…"

"Lily's having a baby."

"Oh…my…God!" Kim practically flung Alice into Hal's arms and leapt off the couch squealing, unable to decide whether to hug Anna or Lily first. They saved her the trouble and met in a group hug that was quickly joined by the others.

Anna waited until everyone had settled down to address their barrage of questions. "I'll tell you everything we know, which isn't much. Our due date is June first. We've seen the sonogram but it's too early to know the sex, but Beth says things look—and I quote—normal, normal, normal."

"Who's the father?" Kim blurted.

She nodded at Lily's questioning glance. They had agreed to keep most of the details private, but that didn't include their family or their closest friends.

"Anonymous," Lily answered. "We didn't want people looking at our two children and thinking they weren't related, so we tried to imagine what Andy's father looked like. Beth had a huge database of donors and we chose a Latino man, a college student majoring in science who plays sports."

"But here's the real fun. We aren't even sure who the mother is." Anna went on to explain the procedure, including their two failed attempts. "We probably won't know until it's born. If it comes out holding a cheeseburger, it's Lily's."

"And if it drives out, it's Anna's."

For Andy, the excitement was over and he slithered onto the floor to resume playing with Jonah, who was boasting that he was already a big brother. With their family meeting finished, Anna noted Kim's beckoning look and followed her upstairs.

"I can't believe Lily rode all the way up here without telling me. Now I know why she was asking me all those questions about whether or not I missed working."

"What did she say? We've been talking about that. Lily says she wants to go back to work after the baby comes, which means we'll probably have to hire a nanny. You got any leads?"

"Trust me, that's not going to happen no matter how much she insists on it now. I can see it all over her. Once that baby comes she won't be able to walk out the door without it. She could hardly tear herself away from Andy."

"But you always say it makes you nuts to be home with the kids all day."

"That's where you come in. You need to come home from work on time." Kim emphasized her point by poking Anna in the chest. "You need to eat whatever Lily wants for dinner and watch what she wants on TV. Don't think just because you've been at work all day that you're the only one who has a right to be tired. Wash the dishes. Walk the dog. Play with Andy. And don't wait for Lily to ask you to do it."

"This may come as a shock to you, but I do those things already."

"Whatever you're doing now, double it. No, triple it. And don't wait until the baby comes. Start right now. Treat her like a queen and make her comfort your top priority. And whatever you do, don't disagree with her."

"Oh, I figured that out weeks ago. How long are these mood swings going to last?"

"Potentially forever, and don't call them mood swings," she said sharply. "That's patronizing, like you think she's being ridiculous but it's okay because of her hormones. What Lily needs more than anything else is for you to feel every single backache, cramp and hemorrhoid as if it were your own. Everything good is a reason to eat ice cream and everything bad is your fault. Got it?"

Anna nodded tentatively as she took in her sister's version of pregnancy and child care, acknowledging a whole new respect for what her brother-in-law had endured as he awaited the birth of his children. "If I promise to treat all of that advice like a holy book, can I ask you a serious question?"

Kim looked at her pointedly, as if to emphasize that every word had been serious.

"Did you ever get scared when you were pregnant that something would go wrong?"

"All the time, and with good reason. We had two miscarriages."

"What about later, like with Jonah and Alice?"

"That was different. We were taking all of our cues from Beth. Once she was satisfied we were out of the woods, we tried to quit worrying."

Anna wished it were that easy for her, but she wasn't the type to simply close her eyes and trust the professionals, particularly since she wasn't entirely convinced Beth thought they were out of the woods.

* * *

Lily's stomach knotted when their destination came into view, the In-N-Out Burger in San Ramon off I-680. Karen Parker Haney, her birth mother and the woman who had fought her for custody of Andy last fall, waited inside. Since setting up this meeting yesterday, Lily had second-guessed herself a dozen times. Was it fair to ask Andy to interact with a total stranger?

"Have you decided?" Anna asked, her voice barely above a

whisper. They had talked before leaving Tahoe about whether or not to tell Karen about the baby.

"I don't see any reason to tell her. She's not a part of our life other than this." Lily wanted no part of Anna's observation that their baby was just as much Karen's grandchild as Andy was. She had never considered Karen related to her in any way so she wasn't about to concede that this child was. Then Anna had tossed a trump card onto the pile, suggesting their children's common relationship with Karen might make them feel more like siblings.

"Can I have a milkshake?" Andy asked as they pulled into a parking space.

"Sure you can, pal," Anna answered. "Remember what we talked about? We're meeting that woman we saw at the courthouse in San Francisco last year. You probably don't remember her but she remembers you. Your mama and I want you to be nice to her, tell her how you're doing in school and things like that. Okay?"

Andy mumbled his agreement as he worked his seat belt free.

In the privacy of their bathroom that morning, Lily had insisted to Anna that Andy didn't have to be nice if he didn't want to be, but she had lost that argument. They were training him that adults were to be respected and it wasn't a good idea to send him mixed messages by telling him it was okay to be disrespectful to Karen. Besides, Anna had argued that Andy couldn't possibly understand the circumstances the way Lily did, and even if he could there was nothing good that could come from instilling ill will toward Karen.

When they entered the restaurant Lily spotted Karen instantly. She was wearing a raincoat—unusual for such a sunny day—but the reason became apparent when Lily saw her high heels and fishnet stockings. The coat was covering the leotard and miniskirt Karen wore to her job as a cocktail waitress at the Holiday Inn lounge. The woman smiled and gave a small wave in their direction, and Lily sucked in a deep breath. She could stand anything for thirty minutes, even this.

As planned, Anna split off to break the ice with Karen while Lily and Andy stood in line to order their food. Anna's reasoning was that Andy would be more relaxed if he thought they already knew each other. The plan paid off when he sat down across from Karen and responded to her greeting without hesitation.

"Hello, Karen," Lily said stiffly, almost laughing to realize their strategy hadn't worked on her, since she wasn't relaxed at all.

"Lily, thank you so much for calling me. I can't tell you how much it means to me to have this chance to see Andy, and you and Anna too. It's amazing how much he's grown." She turned to Andy and smiled broadly. "You're getting to be such a big boy."

"I'm thirty-eight pounds."

"Your mama sent me your picture. Looks like your tooth has grown back."

He opened his mouth wide to reveal a chewed-up cheeseburger, and wiggled one of his canines with his finger. "This one's loose now."

"I see that. Do you still play with your dog?" When he nodded vigorously she went on, "I found a book I thought you'd like. It's all about dogs and there's a picture of one just like Chester." She pushed the book across the table and opened it to a page that told all about basset hounds. From what Lily could surmise, the book was aimed at the fifth or sixth grade level, certainly not at someone in kindergarten who couldn't read at all. "I was going to send you this for Christmas but since I already had it and was going to see you today, I thought you would enjoy getting it early."

The book was clearly used, purchased probably at a thrift store, or perhaps a yard sale, but that did nothing to diminish Karen's obvious pride in her gift or Andy's apparent appreciation. Momentarily forgetting his lunch, he leaned forward on his knees to flip through the pages..

"I hear you're in kindergarten now. How do you like school?"

Andy settled back in his chair and between bites of burger and fries talked animatedly about his favorite activities—music, art and lunch.

"Do you like your teacher?"

His frozen look said it all, causing Anna to laugh. "That's okay. I'm afraid of her too, pal."

As they rambled on about Mrs. Dooley, Lily's thoughts wandered back to the book. Whether Andy realized it or not, he had just learned a lesson that a gift from the heart was valuable, no matter how much it cost. What surprised her, though, was the feeling that she had learned it also.

The time passed quickly and before she knew it they were finished and headed en masse for the car. She didn't object at all when Karen asked Andy for a hug, or when Andy obliged without wavering. She placed a hand over her tummy, deciding it was silly and immature not to say something about their baby. "Andy, why don't you tell Karen the big news? Remember what we told everyone the other day?"

"I'm getting a new brother or sister. Mama's going to eat everything and get really fat until the baby pops out."

Lily rolled her eyes and chuckled. "With my luck it'll happen exactly like that."

Karen's eyes brimmed with tears. "Lily, I'm so happy for you. All of you. I hope you'll…" Her words trailed off and she waved a hand in front of her face, as if she didn't dare ask for more.

"We'll send you a note when the baby's born." She couldn't bring herself to promise more than that.

When they got underway again Anna reached over and patted her knee. "That was very nice what you did, telling her about the baby."

She shrugged and looked out the window, not willing to admit she had done anything out of sentiment or the kindness of her heart. Sometimes it took turning things over in her head before she came to the right conclusion. "I decided you were right about giving our children something else in common. Now would you mind if we stopped by the cemetery in San Jose? I'd like for Andy to meet his other grandmother."

Chapter 6

Ever mindful of Kim's orders to treat Lily like a queen, Anna pulled out the chair in Sandy and Suzanne's dimly lit dining room and waited for Lily to sit. Sandy had prepared a feast of lasagna, salad and garlic bread. This was the first time in weeks they had socialized with their friends, since it was hard to give up a night alone at home when Andy stayed over with Jonah.

Suzanne took the chair next to Anna and immediately began serving the lasagna. "I bet you're starving. Your stomach thinks it's ten o'clock."

"Not really," Anna said. "I wasn't in DC long enough for my body to transition to East Coast time. We finished up our meetings last night and I went to bed at eight o'clock." At the national meeting of Chamber of Commerce organizations, the US Secretary of Commerce had given a pep talk that seemed only to underscore just how out of touch the administration was on the woes of the economic recession outside the Beltway. All in all, it was a wasted trip made worse by the fact she had missed going with Lily for her second sonogram.

At least the test had gone well, since Beth apparently had seen what she wanted to see from the other angle. Lily certainly seemed a lot calmer than she had the week before.

Sandy dished up four bowls of salad. "You guys in the car business must be dying. Every time I read the paper, there's a dealership closing somewhere."

"Those guys aren't selling BMWs and Volkswagens. I think we'll come out of it, but we had a gut check last month with downsizing."

"Speaking of gut, this lasagna is good," Suzanne said, smacking her lips. "Can I just say how happy I am you didn't put turkey in it? I've eaten turkey sandwiches, turkey potpie, turkey noodle soup and turkey salad. I don't care if I ever see another turkey again."

"You're the one who brought home a twenty-pound bird for two people."

"That's what the hospital gave me. Considering it's the only perk I get for working there, I'd think you'd be more grateful. At least I didn't make you go to Bakersfield."

Sandy clasped her hands and said a silent prayer of thanks skyward. "I am grateful, and that's why I wanted to take advantage of every ounce you brought home. You should be happy to have a girlfriend who is so creative in the kitchen."

Suzanne chuckled and looked over her glasses at Anna and Lily. "I'm happy because my girlfriend is creative in every room of the house."

"Too much information, Suzanne," Lily blurted, holding up her forefingers in the shape of an X.

Anna seized the opportunity to change the subject back to food. "Sandy, this is delicious, and I have to admit I'm also glad it isn't turkey. I wouldn't mind you giving this recipe to Lily."

Lily chuckled. "There's a reason we eat out on Italian night. Sandy makes her own pasta and there's no way mine's going to be anywhere near as good as this."

Sandy suddenly gasped. "Did you hear about Rusty Evans? He broke his foot."

"Yeah, just what we need, something to make him—"

"More cranky. I know. He was bad enough that time he had surgery on his wrist. There he was trying to bang his gavel with his left hand and he—"

"...threw it on the floor!"

Anna loved watching the interaction between Lily and her best friend. They finished each other's sentences, knew each other's likes and dislikes and shared the kind of easy affection Anna had known only with her sister Kim. She wasn't at all jealous of their friendship, but given they worked so closely together, she often felt she was on the outside looking in. It was easy to understand how Lily had become a champion of disadvantaged families, but Sandy had grown up in a privileged household, the daughter of a successful real estate developer. "Sandy, I've always wondered about something. How did you end up in social work?"

"Long story," she said, carving off another small slice of lasagna. Still watching her weight, she had insisted on only a small slice the first time around, but this second one made her total serving equal to the others. "I was an English lit major at Cal State Northridge when I met Suzanne."

"I'll take it from there," Suzanne mumbled, still chewing a mouthful of salad. "When I met Sandy there wasn't a doubt in my mind that I'd love her till the day I died. So naturally I wanted to take her home to meet the family in Bakersfield. Big mistake."

"A week later they cut her off completely. Can you believe that?"

"I almost had to drop out of school. But then Sandy asked me to share her apartment and she wouldn't let me pay any rent. I wasn't looking for a sugar mama, but I was in love and not about to say no."

"And I watched her work so hard," Sandy said, looking proudly at her partner. "She was so devoted to what she was doing at the hospital, and I felt like such a snob for sticking my nose into Chaucer and thinking I could make a difference in someone's life by teaching them the finer points of *The Miller's Tale*. I had taken a sociology class that I thought was interesting, so I went back and applied to the school of social work. It took me an extra year to finish but I've never looked back." She punctuated her remark with a quick kiss on Suzanne's ear.

"Aw, that's a very sweet story. Is any of it true?" Anna asked.

Suzanne kicked her gently under the table. "Every word."

"I'm kidding. I've told Lily before that I'm very proud of the kind of work she does. That goes for both of you too. You guys make me feel guilty sometimes about the luxury car thing."

"Don't forget that you provide jobs for a hundred and thirty people," Lily said.

"Down from a hundred and eighty only a couple of months ago."

"The recession isn't your fault, Anna, and you didn't just lay people off. You gave them severance and a chance to do something else. That's way more generous than most people would have done."

Anna followed Sandy's lead and kissed Lily on the cheek. "That's because you've rubbed off on me."

Suzanne made an X with her fingers and huffed. "Now who's giving too much information?"

Like true friends they followed their hosts into the kitchen and helped clean up. Then the four of them took the party outside to the hot tub, where the December air was crisp and the sky filled with stars. From the dim light of the kitchen window, Anna caught Lily's wink as she turned her back to her friends and undressed. Moments later they lowered themselves into the steaming pool, and swapped places so Lily could have the jets on her lower back, which had been bothering her for a few days.

"Oh, by the way, I almost forgot," Lily said casually. "We're having a baby in June."

Sandy faltered for several seconds, opening and closing her

mouth. "Excuse me. I thought I heard you say…"

"I'm pregnant."

"Aaaaaaaah!" Sandy screamed. "I'd hug you but I'm naked."

Lily spilled out their story to her friends' delight, including the news of the sonogram the day before. "We don't know the sex yet, and unless Beth orders another sonogram we won't find out until it's born."

"I always thought you guys would make great parents," Sandy said. "I never could get Suzanne to even think about it."

"I thought about it. I just didn't like the idea. But I like it a lot for you guys. This kid's going to be as lucky as Andy, and he's the damned luckiest kid I ever saw."

Anna liked Suzanne, but found her brash and insensitive sometimes. Then she would say something like that and make up for everything all at once.

* * *

Andy burst through the door and made a beeline for the living room, where a majestic ten-foot Christmas tree twinkled in the otherwise darkened house. "He didn't come!"

Lily leaned in the doorway and sighed. "I don't think our plan worked." They had stayed at Hal and Kim's long after Christmas Eve dinner, hoping an evening of playing with Jonah would wear the boys out. It was now nearly two hours past Andy's usual bedtime and he seemed to be gathering steam for a fresh round of mayhem.

Anna approached from behind and rested her chin on her shoulder. "Something tells me it's going to be a long night."

"I'll get him upstairs and settle him down." She started for the stairs, feeling her own wave of exhaustion. It had been a long day, starting with a half-day in the office that ended with a holiday luncheon. She had taken that opportunity to share with her co-workers the news of her baby, after which Tony paid Lauren twenty bucks to settle a bet. Lauren had noticed not her belly, but her change in wardrobe. "Let's go, Andy. Bath and a story. Now."

Her commands didn't seem to deter him, as he raced immediately into the dining room and kitchen just to be sure Santa hadn't already paid them a visit. Chester was hot on his heels, barking with enthusiasm.

"No Santa in there either," he announced as he returned to the living room, dropping to his knees to count the presents under the tree. "One…two… A lot of these are mine!"

Lily had gotten him a set of adventure books and DVDs along with a UCLA Bruins football jersey. Anna got him several new car posters for his room. Those gifts were wrapped and under the tree already. Santa's stuff was hidden in the pool shed.

"Go with Mama, pal. Santa doesn't come until after everyone falls asleep."

"I have to do the milk and cookies!"

"Okay, let's do it then."

Lily waited patiently at the bottom of the stairs until the ritual was finished and then escorted Andy to his room. Her task was to make enough noise as they readied for bed so he wouldn't hear Anna ferrying his Santa presents into the living room.

Andy jabbered through his bath about Santa and the reindeer before finally climbing into bed for a story. Apropos of the occasion, Lily chose *The Night Before Christmas*, which turned out to be a bad move because it stimulated even more questions.

"How will Santa know where our house is?"

She smoothed his hair gently in an effort to lull him to sleep. "Remember? We put lights all along the sidewalk so he can find our house."

"And he'll come down the chimley?"

"That's right, but not until you go to sleep."

He burrowed into his bed, but it was clear from his worried look that he still had concerns. "Do you think Santa will come here before he goes to Jonah's house?"

"It's hard to say. But I'm sure he'll come to both houses, so I guess it doesn't really matter which one he goes to first."

"But Jonah said he might run out of toys."

She gritted her teeth at her nephew's mischief. "Shhh…Santa always has enough toys. If he runs out he just sends his elves back to the North Pole to get more. Quit worrying and go to sleep."

They had discovered a trick for calming him when his asthma acted up—running a hand gently over his tummy and chest—and she employed that now. After only a couple of minutes he began to fade, his eyes finally closing once and for all as he drifted off to sleep. She gave him an extra minute or two for good measure and tiptoed out of the room just as Anna reached the top of the stairs.

"Did you get him to sleep?"

She nodded. "How does it look?"

"Go see for yourself."

The twinkling tree afforded enough light to show off the exciting display. The gleaming BMX bicycle had been at the top of Andy's wish list when the Christmas season rolled around. She had suggested a bike with more features, like a basket, a bell and streamers for the handlebars, but Anna insisted the Mach 1 Jr. was a better mechanical design that Andy would appreciate because of his fascination with cars.

He would love the construction set too because he could use it in conjunction with his small toy cars. There was a paint set to encourage his artistic side and a toy guitar to develop his music aptitude. All in all, a collection of practical gifts he would enjoy.

On the coffee table were remnants of the peanut butter cookies and milk Andy had left for Santa. Nice that Santa happened to like Anna's favorite.

When she heard water running in the master bathroom, she hurried back to the laundry room where she had hidden Anna's present the night before. It was a rectangular box nearly three feet high, wrapped brightly in gold foil with a dark blue velvet ribbon. Once she had it positioned next to the tree she checked on Andy one last time and headed for bed, leaving the bedroom door ajar in case someone decided to sneak downstairs early.

The sight that greeted her brought a smile. Anna, with an obvious inkling of how sexy she looked, sat on the end of their king-sized bed wearing a knee-length baseball shirt and a Santa hat. "Did you happen to bring the mistletoe?"

"An unnecessary formality." Lily straddled her lap and urged her backward onto the bed. Their kiss was just the right mix of tenderness and heat to share their love but not enough to send them into a lustful romp, which was off-limits with the door open.

"It's been quite a year," Anna said, turning off the light to settle beneath the comforter. Her long arms drew Lily close. "Seems like it was only yesterday we did this Santa stuff."

"Kim said that too. We started all the fertility shots last January…"

"And we took Andy to Munich to see where the BMWs are born…and spent a whole week in July camping out at Silverwood Lake."

"He started school. You went through all that downsizing at work."

"It's been a pretty good year now that I think about it. We worried a lot but things worked out just the way we planned."

"And before you know it we'll be lying here talking about Santa again and wondering where the year went." Lily drew Anna's hand to her lips and kissed it. "Did I ever get around to asking what you wanted for Christmas?"

"I have everything I need under this roof…you, Andy…" Her hand crept lower to caress Lily's tummy. "A healthy baby on the way. I don't how you could possibly top this."

"I could always get you a minivan to replace that little sports car."

* * *

There was nothing quite like a child's delight on Christmas morning, Anna decided. She had every intention of instilling charitable values in her son as he grew older, but for now would savor his innocent belief that a jolly man from the North Pole squeezed down their chimney overnight and deposited this bounty. Andy was already wearing his new football jersey over his pajamas and couldn't wait to ride his bike, play his guitar, paint a picture or build a town for his cars. He also clamored to read the books, watch the DVDs and eat the candy that had been stuffed into his stocking.

Lily snapped a picture as he slung the guitar strap over his shoulder and began to sing. "Reminds me of your cooking," she said, covering her mouth as she leaned over.

"Pffft, what cooking?"

"Exactly."

"A little louder, Andy. Mama's having trouble hearing you." Anna stuck out her tongue at Lily. "Give me that camera and go open your presents."

She snapped away as Lily unwrapped an elaborate foot massager, bubble bath, scented massage oils and a gift certificate for two at a day spa in Palm Springs. "Someone thinks I'm going to need a little relaxation."

"Your comfort is my reason for living." Since her talk with Kim in Tahoe, she had been on a mission to find the most pampering gifts on the market. Remembering how her sister had complained of not being able to tie her own shoes, she had helped Andy pick out two pairs of sturdy slip-ons Lily could wear to work.

"Okay, your turn." Lily snatched the camera from her hands and directed her toward the large box in the corner. "Let's see if Santa thinks you've been a good girl."

Anna ripped off the paper to find a car seat. "Very nice. I

can keep it at my office," she added, hoping to fend off further discussion of selling her beloved sports car.

"I predict that will last a couple of months, three at the most. Then you'll get tired of running back and forth to fetch a car. You'll be begging me to drive my new minivan."

"You know me better than that. Those things are hideous."

"They're practical, and they're safer than riding around in something no bigger than a roller skate."

Invoking safety was below the belt. "I've never had an accident, unless you count someone spilling a milkshake all over my console. And I'm sure all the studies would say the safest cars are the ones we feel most comfortable driving." She looked to Andy for support. "Mama wants me to get rid of the Z8. Does that sound like a good idea to you?"

"You can give it me," he answered without missing a beat.

"Now you're talking. I'll drive it until the day I hand it over to you."

Lily sneered at her cynically and she answered with her most innocent smile.

* * *

At the rate Jonah was tearing through the Big House in pursuit of his new puppy, Kim and Hal's strategy for wearing him out was almost certain to pay off. It was no surprise to see Andy following along with equal excitement as the black-and-white mutt dashed from room to room. Martine, on the other hand, was anxious about her fragile antiques, lamps and sculptures, and insisted they confine their chase to the family room and kitchen.

"Can we get a puppy too?" Andy asked the moment he sat down for a breather.

"We already have a dog," Lily said.

"But he isn't a puppy like Peanut!"

"Peanut will only be a puppy for a little while. Then he'll grow up and be a dog just like Chester." Except judging from the size of Peanut's feet at only ten weeks, he would be twice as big as their basset hound and probably three times bigger than what Kim and Hal had in mind when they suggested Jonah call him Peanut. Someone at the animal shelter was probably still laughing hysterically at their gullibility when he insisted this dog wouldn't grow much more.

Anna slid onto the sofa and scooped Andy into her lap. "Mama's right, pal. If we got a puppy, you might not play with Chester as much and it would hurt his feelings. You wouldn't want that, would you?"

He shook his head but looked unconvinced. "I could play with both of them the same."

Lily had anticipated Andy's interest in the puppy, but was pretty sure he would forget about it once he got back home with his new bike and other toys. "There isn't enough room for two dogs on your bed and you know how much Chester likes sleeping there. And what if you threw the ball and the puppy got it before Chester could? That wouldn't make him very happy, would it?"

Anna hugged him fiercely. "You can play with Peanut whenever you go to Jonah's, just like he plays with Chester when he comes to our house. Did you tell Jonah about your new bike?"

That sent him scampering into the kitchen after Jonah, creating a space next to Anna that Lily filled. "He'll settle down when we start to open gifts," Lily said.

"Yeah, but it won't last long. Something tells me Peanut will steal the day."

"Maybe not. We have a lot of presents to open from each other. Who knows? There might be something special in there."

"More special than a puppy? It better have four wheels and a V-8 under the hood."

When Christmas dinner was finished the family gathered around the tree to exchange gifts. Lily gave Hal their pre-arranged signal and he disappeared briefly, returning with a large box she had dropped off last week and hidden in one of the guest rooms at the Big House.

The children's gifts came first. For the sake of harmony, George and Martine gave both boys the same thing, inflatable kayaks for the pool. Alice got a small pony on wheels that she could scoot throughout the house.

Kim's gift to Lily was a cookbook—for Anna—called *Cooking for Morons*.

"Very funny," Anna said. "I'll have you know I made a perfectly good lasagna last week, so there!"

Lily shielded her mouth from Anna and whispered loudly, "She warmed it up. Sandy sent it home with us after we went over there to eat."

"I didn't just warm it up. I added a little parmesan cheese on top," she countered indignantly. "You guys never give me any credit."

"You're right, honey. It was delicious…especially that little sprinkle of parmesan. And that bag of salad…" She kissed her fingertips with flair. "Magnifico!"

Andy gave his grandparents his school picture, framed and ready to hang in the den beneath the ones of his mother and aunt. Lily voiced her satisfaction that his class had gone for pictures before lunch, since he had arrived home that afternoon sporting a mustard stain on his new sweater vest.

Not to be outdone, Jonah presented a photo from his preschool, and topped Andy's gift by adding a studio photo of him holding his sister. They were beautiful children, Lily had to admit, and she didn't blame Kim and Hal one bit for showing them off. From his fallen face, Andy felt his gift had come up short.

"Come sit with me, Andy. There might be another surprise under the tree."

They worked their way through the gifts until only the large box remained. "This one's for Anna," George said. "From Lily."

Anna looked at her curiously. "What's this? We always do our gifts at home."

"Just a little something extra."

"Little?" The box was half again as large as the box that had held the car seat, and wrapped identically in gold foil with a velvet ribbon. Anna tore the paper tentatively and finally opened the top to peek inside. "There's another box inside this box."

By this time the boys were curious too, and they helped separate the two boxes. "Open it," Andy said, pulling the ribbon on the smaller package.

Inside, Anna found a second car seat. "I feel like I'm having a déjà vu. Is this supposed to be one for your car and one for my office?"

Lily shook her head. "Nope, for your car."

Anna sighed and looked at the others plaintively. "She's trying to talk me into selling the Z8 and getting a minivan. I told her no way, that if I needed to pick up Andy and the baby I'd just grab something off the lot. Seriously, can you guys picture me in a minivan?"

"I think it's a marvelous idea," Kim said. "You can swing by and pick up Jonah too…and eight of his closest friends."

"Don't you need a bus driver's license for that?" Hal teased. "And I think they have a union."

Even Martine got into the game. "You can wear a uniform! Dark slacks and a short-sleeved shirt with a necktie."

"You guys are hilarious. I'm not getting a minivan." Anna folded her arms and stubbornly jutted out her lower lip.

"Maybe I'll get a minivan," Lily said.

"I don't see why you'd need one. This baby seat will fit just fine in the X3."

"That one's yours."

"Then the other one, the one you gave me this morning."

"That one's yours too."

Anna's face contorted and she locked eyes with Lily, who was fighting a losing battle not to smile.

"Holy—" Kim slapped her hand over her mouth.

"Holy what? Why would I—" Her jaw dropped and her eyes went wide. "Oh, my God."

Lily nodded. "You'll need both of them. And two cribs…two high chairs…and a double stroller."

The next few moments were a blur as the room filled with shrieks and everyone reached out to claim a hug. When the chaos cleared, Anna was holding her in front of the tree grinning wildly. "Twins."

"Two of them."

"And you've known this how long?"

"Since the second sonogram. That's why Beth had me come back. She saw a shadow and it turned out one of our babies was hiding behind the other one." The last two weeks had been sheer torture as she planned her surprise. The idea had come to her as she wrapped the first car seat, which she had bought with every intention of letting Anna keep it in her office for emergencies. Now with two children on the way, the sports car was toast. "And there's more."

"Not more children."

"More news, smart aleck. Beth's pretty sure from the way they're situated that they aren't identical, which means…" She waited a few beats for realization to dawn. "One of them is mine and the other is yours."

Another round of cheers erupted and Andy wrapped his arms around their legs. "Why is everybody so happy?"

Lily knelt and put her arms on his shoulders. "Because we aren't just having one baby. We're having two. You might get two little brothers or two little sisters, or maybe even one of each."

There was a flicker of concern but it lasted only a second. Then he turned to Jonah and announced proudly, "I'll be a bigger brother than you."

Chapter 7

"Are you doing that on purpose?" Hal asked, leaning away to cast a look of annoyance.

Anna was momentarily perplexed, until realizing she had been crunching potato chips in his ear as she peered over his shoulder at the figures on his computer screen. That passed for lunch these days, as she never seemed to have time to get out of the office. Everyone was pulling a heavier load now that their staff was leaner, and she was back to handling all the advertising for the BMW lot.

"Sorry...type faster and I'll get out of your hair." She was anxiously awaiting his December report, their first full month since the downsizing. If they couldn't turn a profit with a skeleton crew and year-end sales that slashed prices to just over invoice, Premier Motors was going to hell in a handbasket.

"I think you're going to be happy with the numbers."

"Happiness is too much to hope for. I just want to exhale for a change."

He made some final adjustments to his spreadsheet and zeroed in on the profit/loss column. As he predicted, they finished in the black for the first time in eight months. "What'd I tell you?"

There it was, the first sign they were bouncing back. "It's not as much as I'd hoped."

"Southern California isn't out of the slide yet, Anna. As people get back to work, that number will grow. But for now you've stopped the bleeding, which is what the reduction in force was supposed to do. That's quite a feat in this economy." He continued with his calculations. "Whatever you do, don't look at the fourth quarter by itself. You'll have a heart attack."

The severance payouts had cost them almost two million dollars, but she had braced for the drop. Without them she would have leaked the money gradually through payroll and been forced into layoffs. "What's that number going to look like for January without the Christmas sales?"

"It'll probably be flat for a while, but we should be sailing again by the time your little ones get here in June."

Twins. She had been smiling nonstop for the last three weeks. They had known going in that twins were a strong possibility since they were implanting two eggs, but after their first two attempts had failed it seemed unlikely.

"How's Lily?"

"That depends on which minute you're talking about. She's got some energy back but she's still having her mood swings—except I'm not supposed to call them that because it's patronizing."

"Ah, yes. I remember it well." He swiveled in his chair as she perched on the edge of his desk. "You can't even head it off because sometimes it's just flat-out contrariness. Kim finally admitted to me that what she wanted was just to bitch. If I tried to make things better I was an insufferable pest, and if I left her alone I was a heartless bastard."

"Was there anything you could do that actually helped?"

"Keeping Jonah occupied seemed to help the most. It was

good for him too."

Anna recalled several times she had dropped in to find her sister relaxing on her own. "I think Andy would like that. By the way, we want to get an early start down to Palm Springs on Saturday. Can we drop Andy off around eight o'clock?"

Hal snorted. "Jonah will have been up two hours by then."

"Knowing Andy, he'll fall asleep in the car on the way over."

"It isn't fair."

"I know, but we're rolling the dice with these two on the way. With our luck, they'll sleep at opposite times and wake each other up." She slumped into the chair across from his desk. "Anything besides keeping Andy occupied?"

"I did a lot of little stuff that seemed to help, like bringing flowers or rubbing her feet while we watched TV. That was kind of a crapshoot though because sometimes she got sentimental and it made her cry."

"I don't know how you stood it."

He smiled. "The first time you hold your babies you'll forget all about the bumps in the road. And here's the kicker—no matter how much you do for Lily while she's pregnant, you won't ever feel like it's enough. I watched Kim suffer through all those fertility treatments and two miscarriages. Then she had all those aches and pains. It made me love her like crazy."

"I already feel like that and we're not even that far along." She felt pleased with herself for how she had stepped up to take over many of the things Lily used to do, like laundry and grocery shopping. Their only real sticking point had been the issue of a new car, which had turned from teasing banter to a sharp-tongued battle of wills. She could understand why Lily would find a minivan more appealing for carrying three children, but her continued insistence that Anna get rid of the Z8 was beyond reason. "Did you ever...never mind." After all the things Hal had just said, it was ridiculous to think he would understand where she was coming from over something as silly as a car.

"What?"

"I was just wondering…how did you feel about giving up your boat after Jonah was born?"

"It broke my heart, if you want to know the truth. But after Jonah came there was no way we were going to get out more than a couple of times a year. It didn't make sense to pay all those docking fees for something I couldn't even enjoy."

"But you loved it."

"I did, but I loved being a dad more. It was one of those bargains I made with myself, to trade one for the other."

That wasn't exactly the answer she was looking for. "But who said you had to trade? You could have had both."

"Come on, Anna. You know how it was when Andy came along. No more sleeping in on Sunday. No more making out on the couch. It's part of the decision to have kids."

Yes, their routines had changed, but their sex life hadn't suffered that much.

"But you know what I realized? I can get another boat someday. I can't get this time back with Jonah and Alice."

She should have known better than to look for support from her family when she and Lily disagreed because it seemed nearly everyone took Lily's side without even realizing there were sides to take. That meant she was being unreasonable. "Looks like I'll have to get rid of my Z8."

"No, you won't. Rent a garage and put it away for special days."

She groaned. "You mean save it for my midlife crisis."

"Right, swing by someday and pick me up and we'll go buy another boat."

* * *

Lily steeled herself as the massage therapist's knuckles bore into the tight knots at the base of her neck. He seemed to have a bead on all the places that held her tension, but there was no denying his precision work was chasing it from her body. When he lowered his hands to the small of her back she tipped her head sideways to look at Anna, who was lying on a table alongside her. Her back was bare also and the woman seemed to be pinching her, at least that's what Anna's grunts and whimpers suggested.

Nick and Una, the husband and wife team who specialized in couples massage, set a relaxing scene in their studio. Candles flickered around the room as a new age mixture of rainfall and flutes played softly from hidden speakers behind her.

Anna turned to meet her gaze. "This is heavenly."

"If heaven is anything like this, I'm going to be very good."

They had gotten an early start from LA, arriving at the spa at ten a.m. Their day of pampering had begun with manicures and pedicures, followed by facials and bikini waxes. Next was lunch on the veranda, then two hours of massage. The spa day was one of Anna's Christmas presents to her, and while the indulgent treatments were special, nothing compared to the treat of getting out of town on their own for a couple of days, something they hadn't done since last summer. With twins on the way, it was hard to imagine when they would get another chance, and Lily had no intention of wasting a second, especially tonight in their hotel room.

"What are you thinking about?"

She was glad for the dim light that hid her blush. "Later."

Anna rumbled with a knowing laugh. "You're thinking about later or you'll tell me later?"

"Both."

They quieted until Nick and Una left them.

"Are you enjoying your Christmas gift as much as I am?" Anna asked.

"If I enjoyed it any more I'd be unconscious. What's next?"

"Sauna for twenty minutes, then tepid showers. Last is the salon."

"And dinner?"

Anna smiled and stretched out her hand until they touched. "Room service."

They wrapped in robes for the walk across the common area, and exchanged them for bath towels to enter the sauna. A middle-aged woman and a teenage girl were already seated and, from the tension in the air, had just had an argument.

"For three thousand dollars, you'd think I could buy one day of not hearing what a disappointment I've been as a mother," the woman said, walking out the door with obvious disgust. The girl tossed her chin defiantly but the embarrassment of their public argument was plain on her face. Several awkward seconds passed and she gathered herself and followed in her mother's wake.

"Three thousand dollars?" Lily asked.

"Damn straight, so you'd better not bring up getting rid of my car."

Lily laughed, started to speak, and laughed again. "Believe it or not, it was the farthest thing from my mind. I've decided to let you keep your silly old car, but I still want a minivan and when we all go somewhere together, you have to drive it."

Anna clutched her chest as though she had been mortally wounded. "I'll have to keep a mask in the console so people won't know it's me. And little masks for all the children."

"Oh, no. Our children will be proud of the minivan, so proud they will beg to ride in it." She laughed at the exaggerated anguish on Anna's face. "We'll get one of those personalized license tags that says 'Kaklis 5' so everyone will know it's ours. And I'll decorate it with bumper stickers for our honor students."

"Kill me now."

* * *

Without opening her eyes, Anna began the morning in her usual way, reaching to her right to find Lily. Their decadent getaway had served its purpose, as they had shed a good bit of the stress that had been building over the past year. The indulgent treatments had worked like a reset button, certain to send them back to their lives refreshed and renewed.

"Please don't tell me we have to get up," Lily mumbled from beneath the comforter.

Anna wrapped her in an embrace, relishing the warmth of her smooth skin. "We have the room until one, so that means breakfast in bed."

"I already have the most delicious taste on my lips this morning."

"So you're not interested in French toast with confectioner's sugar and warm maple syrup?"

Lily made a small squeaking noise at the mention of her favorite breakfast. "With bacon?"

"I'll order it now." Lily nuzzled her neck as she placed their order, a move that proved very distracting. "Yes, and one French kiss…I mean toast, with a side order of…bacon. And coffee for two."

Lily burst out laughing when she hung up the phone. "Did you just order a French kiss?"

"I hope you're amused by my humiliation. I'm hiding in the bathroom when they get here."

"I think you're adorable when you blush. Now I know why Kim tortures you." She tried to get up but Anna held her firm.

"Don't think you're going to tease me like that and leave me cold."

"You looking for a quickie?"

"He said twenty-five minutes, and I'm already halfway there. How about you?"

Lily answered by straddling Anna's hips and clutching both of her breasts. "Not too quick. I like the view from here."

Anna relaxed for a moment under the attention but as her arousal grew, she gently nudged Lily alongside her and ran her hands along her torso, stopping to caress her growing tummy.

"You get more beautiful every day."

After only a token fight for dominance, Lily closed her eyes and inhaled sharply, a gesture Anna had come to recognize as surrender. Their tongues parried in a lavish kiss as Anna's hands roamed the familiar body she had claimed only hours ago. It was never enough.

"Go inside me," Lily whispered.

She parted the wet flesh and delved deep within, her pulse quickening at Lily's immediate response. Her fingers went still as she waited for Lily to dictate her need, which she made known by the rise and fall of her hips.

Lily's eyes danced beneath their lids as her expression changed from one of fleeting sensation to deep focus. Anna stared intently, knowing that when Lily tipped she would seek out her gaze. When she did, unspoken emotions passed between them, fortifying their connection and affirming her belief there was no one in the world meant for her but Lily.

"I love how you do that," Lily said between gasps.

"Do what?"

She took a few seconds to catch her breath. "Everything. After five years of making love with you, I still feel it in my body and soul." She rolled onto her side and burrowed into Anna's embrace, hiding her face as if embarrassed. "I know that probably sounds cheesy but I don't know how else to say it."

"It's not cheesy. I know what you mean, that it's not just a physical thing."

"Right...but the physical's nothing to sneeze at," Lily said, giggling into Anna's neck.

"So was it good for you?" Anna asked, pretending to smoke a cigarette.

"The best."

They were interrupted by a swift knock and announcement of room service. Lily dashed naked into the bathroom as Anna grabbed her robe and directed the waiter to wheel the table onto their balcony.

Lily dug into her French toast with zeal. "I can't believe I'm eating something this decadent. Beth told me I was eating for three now, but then she reminded me the other two weren't teenage boys. She wouldn't like this."

"Then we won't tell her. Besides, it's not like you do it every day. You've been very good about your diet and exercise. The only thing missing is rest."

"Can I help it if you keep me up all night?"

Though it had been said playfully, Anna felt a sting of remorse. For all its wondrous release, making love sapped her energy, so it certainly had double the effect on Lily. Beth had warned them that her sexual needs would ebb and flow, but what mattered most was communication. Though getting away for the weekend had been a lovely idea, it wasn't enough for Lily to relax overnight in a resort. "I want you to make time to get more rest. Seriously, starting tomorrow I'm going to pick up Andy in the afternoon and keep him with me down at the dealership every day. And I'll take care of dinner on weeknights, even if it means I have to learn to cook."

"Whoa! Where did that come from?"

"It bothers me to see you so tired. You're doing something extraordinary for both of us, and the least I can do is take some of the responsibilities off your plate. You should come home from work and soak in the tub...or take a nap, whatever relaxes you. I can't be pregnant with you, but I can be your partner."

Lily's eyes filled with tears. "You are so sweet."

"Don't cry!" This was exactly what Hal had warned would happen. "Save your tears for when I start to cook."

"But it's sweet that you'd do something like that. Cooking? That's a life change for you."

"Look, Lily." She slid both hands across the table and intertwined their fingers, hoping Lily's unpredictable mood swings were well behind them. "If I had my way, you'd quit your job tomorrow and stay home. You could sleep as late as you wanted, go for walks...do whatever helped you relax. Having a baby is a big deal. Having two is just…"

Lily didn't answer but from the set of her jaw, it was clear she wanted no part of this conversation.

"You don't have to say anything. I already know how you feel about working, and I'll support you completely. That's what this is about. If you're going to work all day, you need to rest at night. Period."

"Okay," she conceded, her jaw still firm. "Then I'll say it again. It's very sweet of you to do that, and I promise I'll relax more at home. But if you really want to support me, don't keep reminding me that you wish I'd quit my job. Those things don't go together."

"Fair enough." She could think it and not say it.

They followed breakfast with a long soak in the spa tub then reluctantly packed for home. As they accelerated onto the Five, Anna made a big show of shifting through the gears. "Just can't feel those Gs in a minivan."

"I already said you could keep it." Her cell phone chimed and she checked the number before answering. Her brow wrinkled immediately. "This can't be good."

* * *

As her case was announced Lily shuffled to the front of the courtroom, where the bailiff delivered Maria Esperanza to the defense table. In handcuffs and a stiff orange jumpsuit, she looked haggard, as though her last thirty hours had been pure hell. They probably had.

Judge James Anston, an African-American nearing retirement age, busily signed papers placed before him by his clerk, but looked up long enough to ask Lily for her plea.

"Not guilty, Your Honor."

Her counterpart from the District Attorney's Office was Rod

Samuels, who looked fresh out of law school in his off-the-rack black suit. From his cherubic face, she expected a voice that was much less austere. "The state requests remand."

"Your Honor, a first-degree murder charge is outrageous in these circumstances. My client had a restraining order that prohibited the victim from coming within a hundred yards and he clearly violated it."

"The state plans to prove this defendant lured the victim to her home, where she was lying in wait to kill him. Capital crimes are not eligible for bail."

Lily eyed Samuels with disbelief. "We believe the state's conclusions have been drawn prematurely, and in a factual vacuum. Once these facts come to light, we expect not simply a reduction of charges, but a dismissal. My client is the primary caretaker for her two small children and—"

"This is just the arraignment, Ms. Kaklis. We're not here to try the case," Judge Anston said. "Talk it over with the prosecution. If the state sees fit to reduce the charges, I'll consider the question of bail. Until then I'm remanding Mrs. Esperanza to the county jail to await trial"—he pored over his calendar—"on the twentieth of May."

There was little chance Lily could be in court on such a late date with her babies due less than two weeks later. If the case dragged out or got postponed until she delivered, it could result in a mistrial, and Maria would have to endure more time behind bars awaiting a new trial. "On behalf of my client, I request a speedy trial."

The judge looked at her with incredulity. "In Los Angeles? Four months *is* a speedy trial."

"May I approach?" She and Samuels spoke in hushed tones so their words would be off the record. "I'm pregnant with twins, Your Honor. My due date is June first, and twins are rarely carried full-term. May twentieth is a pretty iffy date."

Samuels glibly interjected, "Perhaps your client should seek new counsel."

"I've represented Mrs. Esperanza for seven years, much of that involving domestic abuse by the deceased, so I'm sure she would appreciate having me by her side for what we hope is the last time she has to fight to be free of her ex-husband."

The judge, whom she had known for years, looked at her with just a hint of a smile, clearly pleased by the news of her pregnancy. "I can move this back to July if you like."

"That wouldn't be fair to my client. She deserves the chance to swiftly answer these charges so her children can be returned to her."

He looked again at his calendar, shaking his head. "I just signed off on a plea deal that opens up the court for March first. That's five weeks. Can you be ready, Mr. Samuels?"

He visibly blanched. "A capital case requires meticulous preparation. We don't want to waste taxpayer dollars doing a substandard job, and we can't afford to let a murderer go unpunished."

"The state has already asserted it can prove murder in the first degree. It sounds now as if the assistant district attorney doubts his own evidence, which means my client should be released on reasonable bail."

"Sounds like a 'gotcha' to me, Mr. Samuels. Put up or shut up." He waited for an objection that didn't come, slapped his gavel and announced, "Trial begins March first. Next case."

Lily exited to a small conference room where guards had taken Maria, who was still handcuffed and now sitting in a metal chair. She dropped her legal tablet with a thud and nodded to the guard, who left and closed the door behind him.

"Tell me everything."

Maria's tears came instantly and she made no move to wipe them away. "Sofia and Bobby were playing in the front yard when he drove by the first time. They knew he wasn't supposed to be there and Sofia ran into the kitchen to tell me, so I called his cell phone."

"Why? Why didn't you call the police like I told you?"

"I told him I would if he came back again. I thought it would scare him away."

"Obviously it didn't," Lily said with frustration. "Instead it looks like you lured him there, just like they said."

"But I didn't," she wailed. "He said I was turning Sofia into a fucking whore and Bobby into a fag, and he wasn't going to let me do it."

"And what else, did he threaten them?"

Maria gave her a chilling look. "I knew what he meant. I don't care what anyone says, I knew he had a gun because I saw it."

Proving that in court was another matter entirely. "That's all the more reason you should have called the police. Why didn't you? Tell me exactly what you were thinking because it's a key part of your defense."

"I didn't see him when he drove by—only the children did— so I knew I wouldn't be able to answer the police's questions. They wouldn't have come. That's how they are."

From the Esperanzas' history of police encounters, Lily could easily prove that Maria knew exactly what kinds of questions to expect when filing a report, and she was likely correct that the police would not have responded on the word of her children. "What happened next?"

"I told the children to stay on the porch. Sofia did what I said, but Bobby went around to the driveway to play with his soccer ball. I could see him through the kitchen window. That's when I heard Sofia scream. I ran back to the living room and saw Miguel pushing her into his car."

Lily stopped writing and scanned the police report. "Wait, how much time passed between when you called him and when he came back?"

Maria shook her head, clearly agitated.

She slammed her palm on the desk. "Think, Maria! This is important."

"I don't know. Three or four minutes...maybe not that long."

The report indicated the time of the 911 call, but not the

time of the call that was logged on Miguel's cell phone. If Maria's version of the facts bore out, it bolstered the argument that he was already in her neighborhood when she called him. That torpedoed any argument she had lured him there. "And then?"

"Miguel slammed the door with Sofia in the backseat and yelled at her to stay there. Then he started screaming for Bobby. I went to the closet to get my gun."

"When did you get a gun? Is it registered?"

She shook her head without looking up, as if bracing for Lily's wrath.

"Damn it! What were you thinking, Maria?" She wanted to scream about how dangerous it was to have a gun in a house with children, but if not for that gun her children might be dead at the hand of their father. "Tell me about the gun. Where did you get it and when?"

"Sam…my sister's husband. He gave it to me after Miguel threatened me and we went to get the restraining order. He warned me Miguel wouldn't stay away and he was right."

"Is this your sister in Culver City? The one who has your kids right now?"

She nodded.

Lily tossed her pen on the table and slumped against the back of her chair, almost wishing she hadn't asked the question. For the sake of Sofia and Roberto, she had to follow through. "Does Sam keep a gun in his house too?"

Maria wouldn't look at her.

She opened her cell phone and held her finger over the keypad. "One call, Maria. I'll have Sandy Henke and the police tearing that house apart looking for it. Save me the trouble. You know we won't leave those children in a house with a gun."

"They don't have anywhere else to go," she wailed, running her hands through her hair. "He has another one. He keeps it locked in the closet. Please don't take my kids away from them." Sofia and Roberto had been placed a half dozen times with Maria's sister, and probably felt secure there.

"I don't want to move them, but Sam will have to get rid of his gun. It's not negotiable." She scooted back up to the table and poised her pen to write again. "Okay, when you saw Miguel with your own eyes, why didn't you call the police?"

"There wasn't time. He already had Sofia in the car and she was crying. If he had gotten Bobby he would have left and it would've been too late."

Lily scribbled furiously as Maria related the harrowing tale.

"I went out the back door and showed Miguel the gun and told him to leave. He laughed and called me a bitch…said I didn't have the guts to use it. So I shot at the ground just to scare him, but it jumped in my hand and the bullet almost hit his foot. He screamed and started toward me. His eyes were so wild, and he kept yelling that he was going to show me."

"Where was Bobby? Did he see any of this?"

Maria shook her head. "No, he was hiding behind the garbage cans…around the corner of the house."

Too bad, Lily thought. No witnesses meant all the weight would be on Maria's credibility. "What happened then?"

"I pointed the gun right at him and started backing up. He kept coming toward me so I pulled the trigger and shot him in the neck. Then his hand came out at me like this"—she made a reaching motion—"and I shot him again."

As she described the particulars, her voice grew more defiant, a sure sign she felt justified in her actions. It was exactly the attitude Lily wanted a jury to see.

"Maria, you'll have to tell that story over and over, because I'll need to know every single detail that pops into your head, even if you don't think it's important. The DA's going to focus on three things—why you called Miguel, why you already had a gun in your house and why you shot him when he wasn't physically threatening you. He's going to say you planned it, that you were still angry for all the times Miguel beat you, and that you didn't want him coming around the kids anymore. He can prove you called him and that a few minutes later he came to the house, and he'll argue that you lured him there to shoot him. No one else can testify to what he said, so they don't have to believe you. He'll also argue that you were lying about Miguel having a gun, and he'll say you didn't feel threatened at all, that you just wanted Miguel dead once and for all. That's what we're up against."

"He was going to kill my children. I know it."

In her gut, she agreed.

Chapter 8

Anna stared at the dismal budget figures. Chamber membership was down almost a third from when she had taken the reins as president. It wasn't only that businesses—including Premier Motors—were cutting back on discretionary spending during the recession. More than half of the losses were small businesses that had gone under.

"We need to shift our priorities to small business needs." Jack Stroman, who produced television commercials for local businesses, sat opposite Anna at the far end of the conference table. His placement was fitting, since his views were usually contrary as well. As chairman of the budget committee, he wasn't without sway. "I know it's self-serving, but the number one reason businesses join the Chamber is to network, not to support the community."

Geri Morgan, a longtime friend and ally, spoke up. "We had an election on those issues last year, Jack. The members were seeing positive results from our community investment."

"With all due respect, that was last year. Members want to see their dues coming back to them, not going to a bunch of *social enrichment* programs."

Anna bristled at his sarcastic intonation, but held her temper in check. She wasn't on the budget committee, but as president was here as their guest. She said evenly, "Those objectives need not be mutually exclusive. What we saw in seeding the community with job training and development grants was that people had more money to spend. The model that Dave developed is solid." She gestured to Dave Cahill, the owner of an office supply chain who had tapped her as his vice president two years ago so she could carry on his youth-oriented programs. "If we allow these community initiatives to fail, we'll forfeit not only our investment, but our future customer base as well. This is not the time to abandon our goals."

"If I may…" Dave was seated at the corner next to Jack, and had been silent throughout the contentious meeting. He seemed leaner than the last time she had seen him, and his handsome face was red and lined with worry. "Eighteen months ago, every single store in our chain posted record profits. Last Friday, I'm sad to say…Cahill Office Supply filed Chapter 7 bankruptcy."

An awkward silence followed for several seconds. They had lost dozens of big-name companies in the past year, but none from someone so high in their organization.

Dave went on, "Our business was dependent on other businesses thriving, not on whether or not we have afterschool programs and little league baseball. I can't tell you how many times I asked myself if things would have been different had I pushed more of the Chamber's resources into the kinds of things Jack's advocating we do now."

Delores Gottleib, an investment banker sitting next to Geri, checked her watch. "I call the question," she said, invoking the parliamentary procedure for voting on the motion. It was no doubt clear to her—and to everyone else in the room—the balance had shifted and there was no more need for debate.

When the meeting adjourned, Anna and Dave remained in their chairs as the room emptied.

"Sorry about the blindside," he said grimly. "I tried to call you with a heads-up this morning but you were on another call."

"I'm not worried about the blindside. I'm worried about you."

"I wish I could tell you it wasn't as bad as it looks, but it's actually worse. I did the stupidest thing a business person can do. When the slide started I tried to prop things up with my own money, which means Maureen and I will be filing personal bankruptcy too," he said, his voice cracking. "We took a second mortgage, so we'll probably lose the house...Michael will have to get student loans." He snorted. "Good luck with that."

"I don't know what to say. You don't deserve this."

"None of us do, but that's hardly the point. Bad luck finds us all."

"Maybe so, but I also believe you did everything right to build your business, and you can do everything right again. Re-file under Chapter 11 so you can reorganize. Downsize if you have to, whatever it takes to ride this out."

"That's the problem, Anna. I don't have what it takes anymore. I'm fifty-six years old with high blood pressure and cholesterol off the chart. Maureen wants to head to Arizona and start over with something on a smaller scale. I used to like keeping my own shop. Maybe I'll try my hand at that again."

After what she had just gone through with her own company's downsizing, Anna understood the appeal of scaling back. It would have been the easiest solution—selling off a couple of the dealerships to erase her company's massive debt—and it's exactly what she would have done had her staff reductions not resulted in a return to profit. At least she hadn't dipped into her personal wealth to float her company along, as Dave had.

Before parting they shared a warm hug, and she offered the best she could—the gift of confidence. "You'll land on your feet, my friend. I have no doubt about it."

Fellow attorney Lauren Miller leaned against the doorjamb where Lily sat alone in the conference room at the Braxton Street Legal Aid Clinic. "So how are you holding up?"

She heaved a sigh and slumped back in her armchair, folding her hands across her prominent stomach. "I have one more deposition this afternoon. That gives me two weeks to plan the defense."

"I can't believe you're still here working and not home already. Just the thought of having twins sends a shudder all the way through me."

Lily found that hard to believe. The way she saw it, Lauren was the epitome of a supermom. She had worked all the way to her due date with both of her children—not complaining for an instant about hormones, back pain or discomfort—and returned to a full caseload after only two months of maternity leave looking as beautiful and rested as ever. She made it all look easy, and Lily was determined to follow her lead.

"You feeling okay about your case?"

"Between you and me, this Samuels guy is a prick. He just transferred over to felonies last fall and he's trying to impress his bosses by turning this into a capital case. I like our chances against Murder One, but it makes me nervous as hell to roll the dice on Maria Esperanza's life."

"How's his case?"

"I think I can chip away at it enough to get reasonable doubt, but I'm not sure I can keep Maria out of prison if the judge comes back with instructions on a lesser offense. They're going to argue that she set him up, going all the way back to when she first reported that he had a gun."

"Because no one ever found a gun."

"Right, so it casts doubt on her story that she shot him because she was afraid he would hurt the children."

The intercom beeped and Pauline announced the arrival of the last witness, Miguel's brother Eduardo, and the assistant district attorney.

"Show them back, please." She smiled as Lauren crossed her fingers for luck, and closed the folder with all her notes. The last thing she wanted was for Samuels to preview her defense strategy.

As Pauline led the visitors in, Lily took a long pull on her water bottle, regretting that she hadn't remembered to run to the restroom. Once the trial began, sitting for hours in court would be sheer torture.

She welcomed Eduardo and asked him to sit directly across from her in a stiff wooden chair. Samuels she directed to a chair in the corner, where he could observe but not participate unless invited.

Lily went through the formalities of introductions, and turned on her recorder so Eduardo could give his personal information for the record.

"Mr. Esperanza, you are the brother of Miguel Esperanza, the deceased in this case. Is that correct?"

"The victim," he answered, his hostile tone a stark reminder that he was the opposition's witness.

"And what is your line of work?" she asked dryly, showing no hint of intimidation.

"I own an auto body shop."

Through a series of routine questions, Lily easily ascertained the testimony Eduardo was likely to give for the prosecution—that after serving time in jail, Miguel had turned his life around and become a devoted father who loved his children.

"When was the last time you saw your brother?"

"Two days before she murdered him," he spat.

"Mr. Samuels, you may want to advise Mr. Esperanza to check his attitude, or I'll be forced to treat him as a hostile witness. You know how juries feel when they think you're having to force a witness to tell the truth."

Samuels got up and mumbled into Eduardo's ear, after which Eduardo sat up straight and folded his hands on the table in an act of apparent contrition. "It was the Friday before he died."

"And what were the circumstances?"

"He came by the shop."

"Did he come to your shop often?"

"At least once a week. That piece of crap he drove, it was always breaking down."

"Breaking down? Yours is an auto body shop, right? You don't work on engines."

"It was falling apart. Like his mirrors fell off, his windshield cracked. That kind of stuff. The cops like to write up Latinos for little shit like that. They call it Driving While Brown," he added with a sneer. "And then it was his window. It was always coming off the track. He'd bring it in for us to take the door panel off. I showed him how to do it, and how we fixed glass and stuff. He liked it, working with his hands. I was thinking about giving him a job."

"So why didn't you?" She wanted to establish that even Eduardo had doubts about Miguel turning his life around.

"Business was slow. I barely had enough work for my crew."

"Did he ever bring his son Roberto to the shop?"

Eduardo nodded. "Yeah, he said he wanted him to hang around guys. Maria never let him do anything but school stuff, and play with Sofia and her girlfriends. So Miguel and Bobby would come and shoot the shit...I mean, talk with the crew. He wanted Bobby to get interested in cars or something."

"Mr. Esperanza, do you own a gun?"

The question seemed to surprise him. "It's not your business. I'm not accused of anything."

She looked again at Samuels, who directed him to answer.

"I have one. I keep it in the safe at the shop in case of robberies. I have a permit."

Lily already knew about the permit, but that wasn't the burning question as far as she was concerned. "Did Miguel have access to your gun?"

"No, absolutely not."

"Are you certain?"

"I'm certain what 'absolutely not' means. Are you?"

"Can you describe the gun?" she asked, ignoring his petulance.

"It's a twenty-two."

"Revolver or semiautomatic?"

"Revolver."

The handgun Maria had described in the possession of Miguel was a semiautomatic. "Do you have any unregistered guns?"

"No."

"Have you had any in the past?"

"No."

"Did you ever see Miguel with a gun?"

"No."

"But you didn't live together. Did you ever go to Miguel's house?"

"No, he was always moving around to different apartments."

"So if you never went to his house, how do you know he didn't have a gun?"

"Because he would've told me." He seemed satisfied with his answers and pressed to make his point. "My brother was a good man. He had one weakness and that was Maria. I tried to get him to move on, to go out with other girls, but he wouldn't have anyone else. I would've tried harder if I'd known she was going to murder him."

"Did you know your brother was driving by Maria's house?"

He paused, as if contemplating how to word his answer.

"Yes or no?"

He nodded, and she reminded him to answer aloud for the recorder. "He couldn't stay away from her. He was so hung up on that girl. I said to him, 'This girl's bad for you, man.' But it was her or nobody. I don't know why but he loved her, and he believed they'd get back together just like they always did."

In court, Lily would point out that such beliefs made stalkers out of men, and she would cite a dozen cases where spurned husbands killed their children to get back at their wives. Miguel had always exerted physical power to control what Maria did or whom she saw. Her two attempts to leave him had been met with force, and it was her success at living on her own with the children that made him finally snap.

"Did you know Maria had a restraining order?"

"Yes," he answered quietly.

"Did you ever consider reporting your brother to the police when you knew he was driving by her house?"

"They would have arrested him."

"And he'd be in jail...alive," she said, closing her folder. She needed to pee.

* * *

"It's not supposed to burn up like that," Andy said, pointing at the fire that had erupted beneath the saucepan full of rice.

The flames licked at Anna's fingers as she pulled the pot off the burner, where the boil-over had left a sticky mess. "I know that," she said sharply. "Don't you have homework? Something to watch on TV? Cars to play with?"

He shook his head. It was after six and what he wanted was dinner.

Lily's greeting from the family room was a mixed blessing. Anna hated to have her find dinner in disarray, but her expert hand would put everything back on track. With a quick kiss to Anna's cheek, she reached across the stove and turned down the dial. "Simmer is a two. Anything else will boil over."

"Two...got it. The book didn't say that." She held up *Cooking for Morons*. "I guess they underestimated my ignorance."

"It's no big deal. What else are we having?"

"Meatloaf," Anna said tentatively, peering through the oven door. "Except it looks like a brick sitting in a puddle of grease."

"All meatloaf looks like that. Just lift it out while it's hot and drain it."

"It looks disgusting."

"I bet it tastes wonderful." Lily put her arms around Anna's neck and gave her a proper kiss on the lips. "I'm so proud of you."

For the most part, Anna was proud of herself too…except for the boil-over. "I nearly burned the house down."

"But you didn't, and now you know…"

"Simmer is a two."

She had tossed a salad—something definitely within her comfort zone—and cut up strawberries for dessert. It wasn't exactly gourmet, but it followed Lily's simple menu of meat, vegetable, starch and fruit. She was keeping a vow to herself to take on the task of providing dinner on weeknights, venturing away from takeout for what was now the third time. She set the table as Lily looked over Andy's schoolwork.

"What's this?" Lily asked.

Anna spun around to see she had found the note from Mrs. Dooley. "She wants to see us on Monday morning."

"I can't go. I have to be in court for a divorce proceeding." She pulled Andy into her lap. "What's this about, bud?"

"I don't know." He rolled one of his toy cars across the kitchen table, not meeting her eye.

"That makes three of us," Anna said. "Why do people always do this on a Friday? Now we have the whole weekend to wonder what's up."

"I vote we not worry about it until Monday. I didn't bring any work home, and I hope the same goes for you." She gave Andy a warm hug. "And I hope you're done with your homework so you can relax with us too."

Andy enjoyed the meatloaf and rice, though not the salad. Anna was thrilled to have pleased him without resorting to the dreaded macaroni and cheese, and even more thrilled that Lily wanted to cook on the weekends. That gave her two days to gear up for next week.

Lily stepped up to talk quietly while she cleaned the kitchen. "Andy wet the bed again last night. That's six times in the last couple of months."

"Did you talk to him about it?"

"Just a little bit. He doesn't know why. I thought I'd take him to Dr. Engle for a checkup, but I don't want him to feel a lot of pressure about it." She looked back to double-check that Andy was out of earshot. "Have you noticed him acting different or anything?"

"No, I think he likes me picking him up after school, and we got some new training videos on the 6 series that he loves." He especially liked coming to the dealership now that her father was working there too.

"I don't think it has anything to do with you picking him up because you've only been doing it for a couple of weeks. He started wetting the bed again right after Christmas, remember?"

"You think it's the babies?"

Lily shook her head. "I don't know, but if it is, it's a delayed reaction. He was so excited after Thanksgiving that it was all he could talk about."

"But he's not talking about it anymore. Maybe someone at school said something and got him upset."

"Or that nephew of ours. I wouldn't put anything past Jonah." She hooked Anna's arm as they walked toward the family room. "Maybe we should talk to him again…ask him how he's feeling about it."

Anna nudged Andy from behind as he played with his toy cars. "Hey, pal. Go put your swim trunks on. Let's all get in the hot tub."

She didn't have to ask twice, as he was off in a footrace with Chester to his bedroom.

"You have the best ideas," Lily said as she changed into one of Anna's swimsuits, which fit her better because of its long stretchy waist. "This is the perfect way to end a week."

For a fleeting moment, Anna felt nostalgic for the days when she and Lily had the run of the house. They wouldn't have bothered with their suits, and probably would have made love in the water.

"Wait for me!" Andy called as he hurried down the stairs.

A wave of guilt pushed her reminiscence away. She wouldn't trade anything for the life they had with Andy, or the one their twins would bring.

"Andy, have you seen Mama's tummy? The babies are getting big."

"I know," he said just before he submerged in the warm, churning water. When he came back up, he began jabbering about his bike. He wanted to ride on Saturday and Lily quickly agreed.

"Have you thought anymore about your new brother or sister?"

"No."

"Do you wish for two brothers, two sisters or a brother and a sister?"

"Two...sisters, 'cause I won't have to share my cars."

Lily chuckled. "Sisters might play with cars too, Andy. Your mom played with cars when she was a little girl, and she grew up to sell BMWs. How would you like it if your brothers or sisters came to work with you in Mom's office when you all grew up?"

Anna added, "You might even get to be the boss, because you're the big brother."

"I want to be the boss like Grandpa." He went under again and came back up. "And I'll go live with him in the Big House."

"You mean when you get to be the boss?"

"When my brothers and sisters come."

Anna tugged him into her lap. "What's this, pal? You don't want to live here with Mama and me when the babies come?"

"No, because you'll play with them and not me."

"Where on earth did you get that idea?"

"You said we couldn't get a puppy like Peanut because then we wouldn't play with Chester." He explained his reasoning in earnest. "So when the babies come, that means you won't play with me anymore, but if I go live with Grandpa he can play with me."

Anna's heart nearly broke to hear how he had worked out his insecurities. How stupid she had been not to realize he would make such an association. "Andy, you goofball. Dogs aren't like little children. Mama and I will never stop playing with you."

Lily leaned over to nuzzle him. "That's right. Mom and I will have two more babies to play with, but guess what? So will you."

"And they're going to love you, pal."

The relief on his face was unmistakable, and he immediately set to talking about all the things they would do together. When she tucked him into bed, he seemed especially loving to Chester, the faithful hound who followed him everywhere. "Do you think Chester will like the babies too?"

The old hound liked everyone, but at his advancing age it was hard to imagine he would bond with the little ones the way he had with Andy. "I think he will, but I have a feeling you'll always be his best friend."

* * *

Anna walked timidly through the hallway of Andy's school with him by her side, feeling as though she had been summoned to the principal's office. When they reached his classroom she stopped and drew a deep breath. It was a conference, not an arraignment. Mrs. Dooley could not hurt her.

"Hello, Mrs. Dooley?"

"Ms. Kaklis, come in." Not hello. Not please. Just come in. At full height the woman came only to Anna's chin, but that mattered naught. The sternness of her voice was positively chilling.

Anna squeezed Andy's hand, as much to get his support as to give it.

Mrs. Dooley turned her sharp gaze on Andy. "Andres, in the book corner there is a story of a boy with your name. Find it." She gestured to an adult-sized straight-back chair positioned next to her desk and ordered Anna to sit.

Anna's feet could not have moved fast enough. She sat anxiously as the woman reviewed her notes, which were indecipherable upside down despite the perfect penmanship. "How can we help you with Andy?"

Mrs. Dooley removed her glasses and looked at her intently. "I have observed several changes recently in Andres."

"Yes, we've seen a few ourselves. In fact, just this weekend—"

"Let me show you something." She abruptly marched to a shelf of bins, one of which was marked Andres Kaklis. It was filled to the brim with pencils, crayons, markers and other art supplies.

"Wow, that's a lot of stuff."

"It's a month's supply—for the entire class."

She closed the bin and led Anna into the cloakroom, where a coat of Andy's she hadn't seen for weeks was slung over a box. "And there's this."

Anna bent down to examine the contents of the box. It was toy cars, over half of Andy's collection from home. "What's all this?"

"Your son collects things, as many things as he can get his hands on. He hides them away so other children can't use them. I've seen that before with school supplies, but I've never had a child bring his toys to school to hide them."

Anna recalled the story of when Lily first met Andy in foster care. He had rounded up all the toy cars in the house and hidden them under his bed. Given his return to bedwetting, it seemed his emotional setback was even greater than they thought. It saddened her to think how frightened he was at losing his newfound security.

"We've had some changes at home. My wife is pregnant with

twins and we just learned over the weekend that Andy has been worrying about what that meant for him."

Mrs. Dooley's dark eyes flashed with irritation and Anna bristled immediately that the woman might have taken offense at their lesbian relationship. Instead she huffed and lifted her face as if talking to the heavens. "Why on earth do parents think such things are of no consequence to their child's learning?" She glared at Anna and shook a finger. "When parents entrust their children to me, I expect them to be partners."

"But we are," Anna argued, realizing she had backed up against the wall of the cloakroom. "We read to him every night. We check his homework and put his pictures up all over the house. What more could we do?"

"Partnerships work two ways, Ms. Kaklis. Parents expect me to apprise them of every little thing their child does in school, but for some reason think what they do at home isn't any of my business. We have to communicate," she said, pounding her fist into her palm for emphasis. "How else can we help one another bring out his best?"

Anna's ire deflated at the teacher's words. Mrs. Dooley was undeniably intense, but she seemed to genuinely care about Andy's well-being. It was impossible not to feel lucky he had landed in her class. "We talked things out this weekend, and I think you'll see him start to settle down. He isn't usually a selfish child when it comes to sharing things. But when he was in foster care—"

"Foster care?"

Anna sighed. "Clearly we have much to talk about. I apologize that we haven't shared these things about our son, but we were worried he might be stigmatized by his past. Now that you and I have talked, I'm not worried about that anymore. I can see you have his best interests at heart."

They returned to the desk where Anna filled in the gaps of Andy's heart-wrenching story. Mrs. Dooley listened with great interest, and when he timidly approached her desk holding a book, she actually smiled.

"I see you found it. You'll be reading on your own before we know it. Now set it on my reading table and we'll start it after lunch."

Andy beamed with pride at her praise, showing off the gap where his canine tooth had been.

Anna caught his arm as he started across the room. "Hey, pal. Mrs. Dooley tells me the other children in your class are running out of pencils and crayons and things. How about you put those that you've saved in your bin back where the other children can share?" She winked at the teacher in a show of solidarity. "I also noticed you brought a lot of your cars to school. I'm going to take them home today. Toys aren't for school."

He nodded solemnly and she pulled him closer.

"Everything is going to be okay now. I just told Mrs. Dooley all about our new babies and how much fun we're going to have together when they get here."

"It's very exciting news, Andres. I'm certain you'll be a wonderful big brother."

As she walked toward the door with the teacher, Anna realized she was no longer intimidated. "Thank you very much for your interest in Andy. We promise to be better partners and keep you informed of the important things in his life, and we'll keep holding up our end with the reading and homework."

The teacher smiled. "Your son is a delight in the classroom, Ms. Kaklis. You and his other mother have done a terrific job, and I hope I'm lucky enough to have two more just like him in my class someday."

Anna walked to her car, beaming just like Andy from the teacher's praise.

* * *

Lily grabbed her insulated lunch bag from the bottom drawer of her desk and hurried out toward the park where Sandy

128

was waiting. She didn't care what people thought of the slip-on sneakers she wore with her business pantsuit. Those people could tie their own shoes without taking a header.

She collapsed on the bench, knees spread, feet planted. "Do you ever wonder why the legal profession attracts so many assholes?"

"All the freaking time. What's up?"

"I just got an e-mail from Rod Samuels. Now that he's denied Maria bail for five weeks, he's decided to reduce the charges to second-degree murder. He wants her to plead in exchange for ten years in prison, which is only five if she gets off for good behavior."

"Some people have nerve to burn. I hope you told him to shove it."

"I have to talk it over with Maria, but no matter what she says, I'm not going to answer him right away. That way he can think I'm considering it but he still has to prepare for trial all weekend. Then on Sunday night, I'll send him an e-mail just before I go to bed. 'Sorry, just saw this. No can do.'"

Sandy unzipped her lunch cooler and drew out a diet shake.

"I can't believe you're still drinking those things. How much weight have you lost?"

"Very funny. I'll have you know thanks to guzzling these shakes off and on for twenty-some years, I've lost about nine thousand pounds. Unfortunately I've gained about nine thousand-fifteen."

"Don't even tell me about weight. I've already gained twenty-four pounds and I'm not even in the third trimester yet. At this rate I'm going to look like an olive on a couple of toothpicks."

"Yeah, well you're having twins. You're supposed to gain weight. I've been on a diet for half my life and all I get is bigger." She eyed Lily's lunch bag with envy. "What have you got?"

Lily extracted the items one by one. "Turkey with sprouts on whole wheat...a tangerine...two cheese sticks...carrots, snap peas and cherry tomatoes...and three vanilla crème cookies."

Sandy looked up at the sky. "Can I please get pregnant?"

"Just don't let me be standing anywhere near Suzanne when you tell her."

"Come on, you wouldn't miss that scene for the world. Have you been back to the doctor?"

"Just for the usual. We decided to skip the sonogram that would have told us the sex." She opened the bag of veggies between them and gestured for Sandy to help herself.

"The suspense would kill me. You guys got a list of names yet?"

"Ruby and Ralph," she mumbled through a bite of sandwich. "Actually, that's our running joke. We've decided Anna gets to name the first girl and I get to name the first boy. And we're not telling each other what we've picked until they're born."

"Aren't you brave! I wouldn't trust Suzanne as far as I could throw her. We'd end up with a kid named after some alien on TV."

"I wanted to pick the boy's name because I had this nightmare she'd name him after her father. That's all I need, another George in my life."

Sandy's straw gurgled as she hit the bottom of her shake. "I could drink three of these and still not be full."

"Have some more of these veggies. I eat so many I feel like I could turn into a produce stand."

"I think there's something to that 'glow' thing. You look terrific. Your cheeks are all rosy and your hair's shiny." Sandy leaned closer to study her face. "If you have a wrinkle, I sure can't see it. Your skin's perfect. I think it's because you eat all that crap that's good for you…which means I could potentially look as good as you and not even have to be pregnant."

"Anna's taken over almost everything at home—even dinner—so besides all the good food, I'm relaxing a whole lot more. Not enough, if you listen to her and the doctor, though. Now that I'm going into the home stretch, Beth said I should consider taking an early leave from work."

"Sounds like a no-brainer to me."

Lily broke off half of her tangerine and gave it to her starving friend without comment. "I told her I wanted to hang on as long as I could so I'd have all of my maternity leave after the babies were born, but she put the fear of God into me. She said twins are almost always early, and I'd do them a favor if I took it easy and let them cook a little longer."

Sandy snapped a carrot in two and examined the ends. "Thanks for that visual while I'm eating raw food."

"I've got to hand it to Anna, though. She's wanted me to quit work from day one, and she didn't even gloat. Not one single 'I told you so.'"

"So you're out the door the second this trial wraps up?"

Lily nodded emphatically. "A woman of leisure."

Chapter 9

Anna released Alice's car seat from the seat belt, pausing as usual to inhale her glorious scent. Little boys were delightful in their own way, but she secretly hoped for one of these. The odds were good—three out of four—they would have at least one girl. She had even settled on a name.

As she fussed with the hooks and straps of the baby carrier, Andy helped Jonah with his car seat and both boys scooted out the other door, eager for the fun awaiting them on the Santa Monica Pier. "Can Jonah and me drive the cars?"

"You both can do everything if you're good listeners," Lily said gently. When the boys were together, it was especially important to set the rules early. They could be out of control in no time.

"And what happens if you're not?" Anna asked.

"Andy gets a whipping," Jonah said with a snicker.

"I do not!"

Lily shot her an incredulous look and turned back to Jonah. "What do you know about whippings?"

"Marcus—he's my friend—he gets them when he's bad."

"We don't give whippings. But if you aren't good listeners, you don't get to ride on the rides. Is that clear?" Lily pressed both boys to answer that they understood.

Anna situated the car seat onto the stroller and pushed it through the parking lot as Lily held hands with the boys. This would be their life soon, except one of them would walk with Andy while the other pushed a double stroller. Every single errand or trip to see family and friends would be like today, a gigantic production in which she had to double-check that everyone was secure, and that everything they could possibly need to raise children was loaded into the diaper bag.

First stop was the carousel, where Lily stood watch over Alice while Anna got the boys situated.

"Take the blue one, Mom," Andy shouted, pointing to the brightly painted horse closest to Jonah's. "I can ride by myself."

Had it been only Andy, she would have stepped off altogether and let him ride alone, but she didn't trust her nephew to stay put once the ride started. She loved Jonah dearly, all the while thanking her lucky stars for Andy's calm and quiet demeanor. At least Kim's puppy ploy had worked, according to Hal. Jonah was sleeping better, and so was everyone else…everyone but Peanut, who was getting a much needed break today.

Andy insisted on two rides so he could try a different horse, but then they moved on to the arcade. With all the bells and sirens of the video games blaring, Lily pushed the sleeping Alice on through to the rear exit. Anna herded the boys toward the age-appropriate games, but they lost interest the second Andy glimpsed the bumper cars through the open rear door.

She leaned over the rail and watched as Andy carefully selected his car, one exactly like all the others but for its blazing orange paint. Jonah was less discriminating, choosing the closest, which he used to ram Andy as soon as the power engaged. No matter how Andy maneuvered he could not escape his cousin's attacks, and when the ride finished he was in tears.

"It's part of the game, pal. That's why they call it bumper cars."

"But I wanted to drive."

She explained to Jonah that Andy enjoyed the cars for a different reason and sent them back for another, more peaceful turn. Behind her, Lily had struck up a conversation with another woman, obviously pregnant, whose small daughter was driving a bumper car as well. She felt a pang of envy—not jealousy—just a wish that she could share the kinship between the two women, even though they were total strangers to one another. Lily waved in her direction and in a matter of seconds the woman left her to stand at the rail.

With the boys engrossed in their ride, she joined Lily on the bench. "You made a friend."

"Not exactly." She kicked off her slip-on sneakers and shifted the stroller so that Alice's face was shaded. "We started talking about our due dates and I told her that Alice was actually my niece, and then I pointed to you and the boys. She asked if you were Alice's mother and I told her no, that you were my wife. Things went downhill from there."

Anna glared at the woman, who had plucked her daughter from the ride and was heading back through the arcade. "She actually said something about us?"

"No, she didn't say jack shit," she huffed, lowering her voice for the curse word. "She just got up and walked off."

"Wish I'd known. I would have blown you a kiss."

"And if you'd come over here, I would have shoved my tongue down your throat."

"Now you tell me." Lily had taught her not to waste energy on the bigotry of others, just to laugh it off and move on. "Say, did you happen to notice how nicely the X3 handled two car seats? Pretty nifty, huh?"

"Maybe that's what you should borrow when it's your turn to

pick up all the kids."

Anna had to hand it to her. Her mind was made up and she wasn't taking no for an answer, so it was no longer a question of if they would get a minivan, but when. Just this morning, Lily had cut out an ad for a Honda Odyssey from the *LA Times* and left it on her placemat at breakfast. "What's so special about the Odyssey?"

"I like the seat configuration. Andy can have the whole backseat to himself, or if he feels left out he can move up and sit between the babies."

"He turns six this summer. He can ride in the front seat then."

"Hmm…I hadn't thought about that."

"Have you seen the Routan?"

"No, who makes it?"

"D'oh! I do. There's probably one in the showroom down at the VW lot right now."

Lily's face brightened as Andy and Jonah emerged from the ride. She slipped on her shoes, and with a barely perceptible grunt, pushed herself off the bench. "As long as it has the SEL Premium package with running boards…I'm not particular about the color."

Anna took exactly four steps behind them before realizing she had been set up.

* * *

Lily gritted her teeth and rode out the contraction in her lower abdomen.

"All rise!"

The change in position was just what she needed, and her cramping dissipated. Braxton Hicks contractions they were called, perfectly normal for someone entering the third trimester. In her office she managed the pain by walking around for a few minutes, and at home she stretched out on her side. Neither of those were options in the courtroom.

Rod Samuels was wearing a new suit today. She knew—and so did everyone else in the courtroom—because the price tag bobbed from the armpit every time he raised his hand to make a point. Two of the women on the jury had traded smirks, which Lily chalked up in her column of intangibles. It wasn't something they would consider in deliberations, but every tiny detail left an impression, and this one would take him down a notch.

Though Maria had refused Samuels's offer of a guilty plea in exchange for a shorter sentence, the state had nonetheless reduced the charges to second-degree murder, and thus its burden of proof. No longer was Maria accused of luring Miguel to his death. Instead Samuels hoped to prove she had purchased the gun in anticipation of the opportunity to use it. He followed that conjecture with the trite charge she had "taken the law into her own hands" instead of calling the police.

The more she had reviewed the prosecution's case leading up to trial, the more irritated she had become that the state had filed any charges at all. Scuttlebutt around the courthouse was that Samuels had an uncle somewhere in the system who might have hastened his nephew's promotion to felonies. Rod was therefore anxious to prove himself, but in this case had clearly overreached with a first-degree murder charge. Someone in the DA's office had persuaded him to dial it back, but not far enough. She predicted he would come to her soon with a manslaughter offer, and if their first few days went well, she would advise Maria to decline that too.

His remarks were mercifully brief—in line with his evidence, she thought. Now it was her turn to stand in judgment before the jury. They likely wouldn't notice much about her suit, a dark brown jacket and skirt with a crème-colored top underneath. A mother-of-pearl sea horse, a Christmas gift from Andy, was pinned to her lapel, the only jewelry other than her wedding ring and gold post earrings. The only odd pieces to her ensemble were her shoes, sturdy black slip-on flats that clashed horribly with her otherwise professional look, but she wasn't worried it would cost her any points. The women on the jury would understand, and the men probably wouldn't notice.

"There is no instinct in nature stronger than a mother's need to protect her children, and nothing she won't do. Mr. Samuels would have you believe that's a crime, but you know better. He would have you believe Mrs. Esperanza intentionally exaggerated the risk to her children in order to fabricate an excuse to kill her former husband, but our evidence will show that she understood the risk all too well."

Lily paced before the jury box with her fingertips pressed together as if praying. It was a trick she had learned from Tony to keep from pointing or wagging her finger, something the jury might find condescending. "Undeniably..."—she lingered on the word to underscore her concession—"Mrs. Esperanza has made mistakes in judgment in her life, chief among them marrying Miguel Esperanza not once but twice. Their life together was punctuated with four domestic violence calls to the police. *Four*. That's a lot of experience to know what to expect from a police dispatcher and a responding officer. Mr. Samuels says she took the law into her own hands. I say she took her children's safety into her hands...like any good mother would do."

Point by point she named Miguel's violent offenses against Maria, which spanned seven years and concluded with his jail sentence. "While he was incarcerated, his children flourished. For the first time in their lives they were safe from the threat of his violence, and from watching that violence perpetrated against their mother. All that changed when he was paroled and reappeared at their home brandishing a gun and threatening to make his ex-wife sorry—think about that—*to make her sorry* for all the trouble she'd caused him." She paused for dramatic effect. "What would make a mother sorry? Simple...you harm her children."

She walked to the table to glance at notes she had made

during Samuels's opening remarks. It was important to head off his evidence in advance so the jurors would view it with skepticism. "Mr. Samuels intends to call police witnesses who will testify that Mrs. Esperanza reported recent threats by her ex-husband, threats that involved a handgun. He'll tell you they searched for a gun in Mr. Esperanza's home and car, but never found it. He will ask you to conclude that it didn't exist, that she cunningly concocted her story in order to set up a justification for one day killing him. But the fact that no gun was found didn't change her perspective because she had seen it with her own eyes. If it wasn't in his possession, then he had access to it through an acquaintance or he had hidden it very well from police. Either way it made her vulnerable...so vulnerable she sought and was granted a permanent restraining order, one that Miguel Esperanza blatantly violated on the day he was killed. He had subsequently lost visitation privileges with his children and was desperate to reassert his control...to make her sorry."

Maria sat at the defense table with her hands folded and chin poised defiantly. Now was not the time to show remorse or shame, Lily had told her. The jury needed to see a woman who had acted decisively to protect her children, a woman who would do it again.

"Mr. Samuels will call witnesses to tell you that Miguel Esperanza had turned his life around, and had moved on from his troubles with his ex-wife. We'll show you a man who defied a restraining order to threaten her...to make her sorry." She paused again so people could study on the threat as Maria saw it. "We shouldn't even be here today. Maria Esperanza sensed a threat from a threatening man who was taking her children from her home against a court order. How many stories have we read of men who did unspeakable things to their own children in order to make their ex-wives sorry? The defendant wasn't going to let that happen to her children. She acted to protect them, and that isn't a crime. It's an instinct."

* * *

Anna turned off her office light and skipped down the stairs
to the media room, where Andy was engrossed in a sales film for
the 760Li sedan, his grandfather's car. "Let's go, pal. I've made
us late." They were meeting the family at Empyre's to celebrate
Hal's birthday, but she had been dragged into an e-mail spat
between co-chairs of the Chamber's awards committee and lost
track of the time.

Their new family routine was working out just fine. Andy
loved spending afternoons at the dealership, and her father
didn't mind at all cutting out for a few minutes in the afternoon
to pick him up from school. Since neither she nor Lily had to
pick him up from the Big House after work, they all had an extra
half hour together at home. Her on-the-job kitchen training was
coming along nicely too. She had even mastered Andy's favorite
dish, macaroni and cheese, and she no longer took for granted
the opportunity to eat out in a nice restaurant.

"Did you get your homework done?"

Andy clicked his seat belt and stretched his neck to look out
the side window. He loved riding in the Z8 because he got to sit
in the front seat. "We don't have homework on Friday."

They caught every stoplight between the dealership and
Empyre's, which made them ten minutes late. A young valet,
dressed in dark shorts and a crisp white shirt with gold piping on
the shoulders, sprang to greet her as she pulled into the circle.
He was new to Empyre's, something she took as a good sign—
businesses were hiring again.

Andy dashed ahead as soon as he spotted the others at the big
round table in the back. Lily had saved his seat between her and
Jonah, as well as the one on the other side.

Anna leaned down and eyed Lily apologetically. "Excuse me,
madam. Is this seat taken?"

Lily gave her a sidelong look. "I've been saving that for

139

someone but she's very late. Go ahead and take it. We'll teach her a lesson."

The waiter took their drink orders, sparkling water, iced tea and sodas for the boys. For three years now the whole clan had passed on wine and cocktails whenever they gathered. They drank at home and out with others but never in Lily's presence. Though Lily insisted it didn't matter, Anna appreciated her family's gesture very much.

Her father immediately became engrossed in his grandsons while Martine entertained Alice in her high chair. Getting together with their parents gave the four of them a parenting vacation of sorts, since they could turn their attention to each other without worrying whether the children were being watched. It wouldn't be so easy to leave twins under her mom and dad's care, at least not for two or three years, but every set of hands and eyes lightened the load. She had learned that from her sister, because every time she showed up for a visit, Kim took a few minutes of time for herself.

Hal tapped his glass with his knife for everyone's attention. "We have something to celebrate today besides me getting older. All four dealerships posted profits in February. Sales were eight percent higher than last year—which isn't saying all that much since they were in the toilet—but now that we've adjusted our workforce we're happily back in the black."

Anna had been sneaking peeks at the numbers and had a feeling things were looking up. It was a relief to get his confirmation. "How are we trending?"

"Up three months in a row. And March is on pace to be our best month yet."

She stretched across the table to touch her glass to Hal's. "I would be willing to get older too for news like that."

No sooner had the waiter delivered their entrees than Alice pounded the table from her high chair, demanding something to eat. Kim set down her fork and began tearing off pieces of bread and bits of cheese. "Enjoy it now, you two," she said, directing

140

her remarks to Anna and Lily. "Life as you know it is about to change."

Anna dug into her piping hot souvlaki. "At least you don't have to worry that your Greek salad will get cold."

"And you think that's an accident? I haven't ordered hot food in five years. Babies have a sixth sense about these things. They get hungry the minute your plate comes, they wake up the second your bathtub is filled, and they wet themselves the instant you fall asleep. Without fail."

Hal nodded along. "She's right, you know. You probably think you've got this handled because there are two of you, but you're having two kids."

"Go home and go to bed now while you still can," Kim added.

After dinner they gathered in the parking circle. "Andy wants to ride with me because I drive the cool car," she whispered to Lily.

"Just wait till I get my Routan. He'll be begging me to take the long way home."

Anna handed her ticket to the valet, who looked at her with confusion.

"Do you have a red ticket?" the young man asked.

She felt her jacket pocket for a ticket she knew wasn't there, noticing with a sinking feeling that his sleeves didn't have gold piping like the other man's. "No, he gave me this blue one."

"Who did? I'm the only one working tonight."

* * *

"The State calls Serena Langdon."

Lily gave Maria a look of consolation at seeing her sister take the stand as a witness against her. Samuels had scoured social service records and found a reference to a threat Maria had made four years ago to kill Miguel if he ever laid a hand on her children.

141

The context was a custody issue, in which Serena argued that Sofia and Roberto needed to stay with her until the relationship between Miguel and Maria calmed down. They listened patiently as Samuels cherry-picked her testimony from the report.

Then it was Lily's turn. She didn't care that Maria had threatened to kill Miguel, and she didn't want the jury to care either.

"Mrs. Langdon, you're a state-certified foster parent, are you not?"

"Yes, I was certified when social services asked me to keep Roberto and Sofia."

"Can you tell us the circumstances of those occasions on which you took your sister's children into your home?"

"The first time was when Maria had to go to the hospital because Miguel broke her cheekbone."

Serena's recollections opened the door for Lily to present the court with all four police reports and a wide array of photos that depicted a battered Maria.

"Objection, Your Honor. Miguel Esperanza isn't on trial here. He's dead because the defendant killed him."

The objection was absurd, but Lily understood Samuels's intention. He needed to disrupt the focus on the damaging photos and testimony of abuse, even if only for a moment, to lessen their impact. Unfortunately for him, it gave her the opportunity to underscore Maria's state of mind. "The deceased's propensity toward violence is the reason his threat was perceived as genuine, and also the reason he is dead."

"Overruled."

She released the witness and gave Judge Anston a pleading look.

He slapped his gavel. "Twenty minute recess."

* * *

Anna drummed her fingers on her desk as she waited for Lily to pick up her cell phone. They had programmed unique ringtones for urgent calls, but this she dialed through the usual shortcut in case she was still in court, wanting only to commiserate about her stolen car.

"Hey, sweetie. I was just leaving court. One of the jurors started throwing up and we called it a day."

"I'm surprised you didn't follow suit."

"Tell me about it. I thought the bailiff was going to lose his lunch too, and that would've set off a chain reaction that would've shown up on the Richter scale."

Anna laughed at the mental image. "How did your case go today?"

"We're holding our own. I like it when the prosecution witnesses make our arguments for us."

"Speaking of making a case, I just got off the phone with the police department. The good news is that my theft system worked."

"They found your car?"

"No, they found my theft system. It was in a dumpster in Burbank. The detective said it looked like the work of a car ring they've been tracking for a couple of years...mostly high-end sports cars, like Ferraris and Lamborghinis." Anna let out a dismal sigh. "Most likely it's on a transport well on its way to South America by now."

"Aw, Anna." Lily sounded genuinely sympathetic. "I know I made a lot of jokes about you getting rid of it, but I know how much you loved that car. I'm really so sorry."

"It was just a car," she said drearily, not even convincing herself. It was a special car, just like the 850 that had been crushed in the parking garage during the earthquake six years ago. "I called Marco over at the VW dealership. They have a couple of Routans, but not with the package you want. They can't keep them on the lot."

"I guess I don't really need all those things. I just thought as long as—"

"Of course you need those things. Getting a new car is supposed to be special. You want something that catches your eye in the parking lot, something you can drive and know people are looking at you and admiring it. You learn how to play with all the new gadgets. You sink your butt into that leather and make it your own. You don't settle on a new car."

"Okay, I can certainly wait at least a couple more months until you get the one I want, but tell Marco to put my name on it. What about you though? What are you going to drive in the meantime?"

"I don't know…something." She heard Andy and her father on the steps outside her office. "I'll ask Andy to help me pick something out. See you at home."

Of all the cars on her lot, the new 650i convertible was by far her favorite. The downside was it was a coupe, and she couldn't drive it with the top down with two babies in the back. If the top was up, it would be nearly impossible to get in and out of the backseat to manage the car seats. Besides, it came only with an automatic transmission and she liked driving too much to buy a car that practically drove itself.

From her office window she looked down the row of gleaming 7s like her father's. Behind it were 6s, then the SUVs, the hottest vehicles on the lot. Not one of them offered what she wanted, a six-speed manual transmission.

Andy walked in behind her and dumped his book bag in the corner where he kept his toys and school supplies.

"Hey, pal. Let's go pick out a new car."

His face lit up. He often pretended to play car salesman and was delighted to have the chance to do it for real.

"Why should I get a BMW?"

"Because they're the best cars on the road," he answered, not hesitating even a second. He led the way down the stairs and outside to the lot. Then he put his hands on his hips and turned. "You look like someone who likes to drive."

She almost laughed aloud as he invoked her father's favorite line when a new customer came onto the lot. "As a matter of fact I do. What I really like is changing gears. What's the best car you have in a four-door with a six-speed manual transmission?"

Andy hung his finger on his bottom lip as he studied the rows of cars. Finally he pointed to the 7s and said, "Automatic." Then the 6s and SUVs. "Automatic."

She followed him toward the rear of the lot, chuckling to herself at his serious expression. One day he would make the most fantastic car salesman in all of California. When he reached the row of 5s, he turned in. Methodically, he stood on tiptoes and shielded his eyes to peer inside at the console of each.

"This one!" He proclaimed, pointing to a Tasman Green Metallic 550i with natural brown leather interior.

Anna grinned with pride. There weren't many five-year-olds who could have zeroed in on exactly the right vehicle the way he just had. "May I take it for a test drive?" She used her code to open the lockbox and the keys fell into her hand.

"I have to ride in the backseat."

"That's right, but just until you're six years old. Then you can ride up front with me."

She navigated the heavy traffic on Wilshire Boulevard before finally pulling north onto the 405. The car responded to her every impulse, even more so than the Z8, she admitted reluctantly. It was cushier too, much kinder to her thirty-seven-year-old bottom. And the smell...positively exquisite.

* * *

"We find the defendant guilty," the forewoman said, glaring angrily

at Maria Esperanza.

The case had turned on the testimony of Eduardo, who tearfully described his brother as a gentle and loving father, thwarted at every turn by his vindictive ex-wife. He feared for his children's safety, especially after learning Maria had acquired a gun, and wanted only to rescue them from their mother's volatile temper.

Rod Samuels sneered smugly, the price tag still hanging from—

"Hey, sweetie. I didn't want to wake you, but Andy's about to go to bed and I thought you might want to say goodnight."

Lily struggled to sit up as she got her bearings. She was still wearing the suit she had put on this morning for court, where Rod Samuels had wrapped up his case. Eduardo had done a fair job of painting his brother in a positive light, much better than she had expected.

"We had Chinese takeout for dinner, but I thought you might like something on the comfort side since it's so late." Anna indicated a glass on the dresser. "So I brought you a strawberry smoothie."

"Sounds perfect." Using both hands, she pushed herself off the bed. If she was this encumbered at twenty-nine weeks, how would she even be able to move in a couple more months?

She put on her cheeriest face and walked into Andy's room, awash in guilt that she hadn't seen him all night. He was already tucked in, but she pulled the covers back so she could stroke his chest. "Hey, sweetie. I'm sorry I slept through dinner and didn't get a chance to talk to you about your day. Did you have a good supper?"

"I had chicken and noodles, and Mom said there was enough left over for me to eat again tomorrow so I won't have to eat fish." Anna had finally struck a deal with Andy that he wouldn't have to eat fish if she didn't have to eat macaroni and cheese.

"Your mom takes good care of us, doesn't she?"

"And Grandpa."

It surely was only an innocent remark but it cut Lily to the bone to think she wasn't also on his list. "I'm almost finished with the case I've been working on. Then I'm going to take a long vacation from work, which means I'll be the one picking you up after school. We can come home and play together, and you can help me fix dinner for Mom like we used to do. Would you like that?"

"Will I still get to go to the dealership too?"

"Sure, sometimes." It was silly but she couldn't deny she was jealous of the new bond between Anna and Andy. "But here's the deal. Your mom and I both like to be with you so we'll have to learn to share. That means you can be with her some days and me some days."

When he fell off to sleep she ambled back to the bedroom and downed her liquid dinner, bone tired despite her two-hour nap.

Anna had changed into shorts and a long-sleeved T-shirt and settled into her reading chair with a magazine. "Did he get to sleep okay?"

"He did, but not before letting me know he didn't have to eat fish tomorrow night." She sloughed off her suit and let a soft cotton gown fall over her bare skin. Then she added fuzzy sleep socks to counter the persistent chill that came from her drop in circulation. "I know you find this look irresistible but control yourself if you can. I need my beauty sleep if I'm to have any hope of sustaining this sexiness."

"You ask a lot," Anna said, dropping her magazine. She guided Lily to the foot of the bed and stretched out behind her. With the heel of her hand, she began a firm massage of her lower back.

"You're doing a great job, Anna. Andy's really happy that he gets to spend so much time with you."

"We're getting by okay. Dad helps out a lot."

A sore point, but one Lily wouldn't belabor. "I feel like I'm not holding up my end anymore. I told Andy I was taking a vacation from work and his first reaction was to ask if he'd still get to go to the dealership. He must feel like we just hand him off when we have other things to do."

"It isn't that way at all. Dad and I both have been bending over backward to keep him entertained down there, but he'll love it once he's back home with you." She dropped a warm kiss on Lily's shoulder. "Everything's in an uproar right now. It's possible he's feeling a little neglected, but it's not something you can help. When you finish your case you'll be able to rest all day, and you'll have lots of energy to play with him when he comes home from school."

"But not for long. What's going to happen when the twins come? I won't have any time at all then."

"Yes, you will, because I'll take my turn with the babies so you and Andy can have your own time. And there will be lots of times when all five of us are here together." She snuggled closer and tucked her arm between Lily's breasts. "You aren't going to lose Andy."

Lily sighed, remembering a conversation she'd had with Maria Esperanza about being separated from her children. "Things got wild in court today. Samuels came to me after he rested his case and offered to lower the charges to manslaughter, but he wanted Maria to do at least a year in prison. She said no, that she couldn't stand being away from her kids that long, that they were depending on her now. When Miguel went to prison for a year she and her kids finally got a chance to relax without all the disruption and she started feeling like a good mother for the first time in her life. She's willing to risk a twenty-year prison sentence not to lose another day from them."

"That's a scary thought."

"Tell me about it. It made me so nervous I went back to the office today so Tony could look over my defense plan again. It's solid but you can't ever tell what a jury's going to do. It's all going to come down to whether or not they really believe the kids were in danger. I wish we could prove Miguel had a gun but it never turned up." Anna's fingertips tickled the hollow of her throat and she brought them to her lips. "The last thing I need to be thinking about is work. Tell me about your day."

"Nothing out of the ordinary...work, Chinese takeout, sexy

woman in my bed."

"Do you honestly expect me to believe that?"

"I can prove it. I still have two cartons of chicken lo mein in the fridge."

Lily didn't feel sexy at all this week, but that had to do with her growing discomfort, not with Anna. The desire was always there no matter how it played out. With her pregnancy they had been forced to find new ways to be intimate. One of her favorites was to hold Anna and whisper to her while she touched herself.

"You know I think you're the sexiest thing walking," Anna said. "You need to quit making up things to worry about. How long has it been since you went to an AA meeting...a month?"

Too long, Lily thought. She hadn't been tempted at all to drink but being around people in the program made her feel more in control of her life. "Virginia called me a few days ago. She's like a shepherd going after strays in her flock."

"Isn't that what a sponsor is supposed to do?"

"I guess. I told her I'd try to make some time next week, but honestly, I don't know when it would be." She was dangerously close to talking about work again. "I still haven't ridden in your new car."

"We can fix that this weekend. I'd like to take it up over the Grapevine, put it through its paces."

"Do you like it so far?"

"Love it, except my window fell off the track. That hardly ever happens in new cars, so I had them order a whole new assembly. Those things aren't that hard to pop off and snap back on, but who wants to do it all the time?"

It was interesting to hear of her problem in light of Eduardo's testimony that Miguel had the same problem with his car. "They really come off that easily?"

"Sure, if you have the right tools."

Lily sprang up and located her cell phone. In moments she was introducing herself to the desk sergeant at the LAPD. "I'd like to have Officer Joey McElroy meet me first thing tomorrow morning at the impound lot."

149

Chapter 10

Lily looked up each time someone walked by the door of the small conference room in the courthouse, and checked her watch again with growing annoyance. They were due in court in only thirty minutes for the opening of her defense. With her was Officer McElroy, who looked like he had lost his best friend.

"I don't know what to say," the officer mumbled, shaking his head. Clearly he didn't, since he had repeated that no less than a half dozen times since they left the impound lot. Four days ago he had testified for Samuels about the thorough search of Miguel's home and auto, which had turned up no gun. Now he was back, humbled by his error.

"We all make mistakes. What matters is that we correct them whenever we're given the opportunity."

Samuels finally entered and dropped his briefcase in a chair with a thud, grinning smugly. "Having second thoughts about my plea offer?"

Lily lifted her eyebrows and tipped her head in the direction of the police officer.

"What are you doing here?"

It occurred to her that her expression was probably smug too as she pushed the clear plastic evidence bag across the table. "As you can see, we found Miguel's gun. Turns out it was hidden in the doorframe of his car, where Officer McElroy had not previously searched."

If the contortions on his face were any indication, Samuels's stomach just flipped over. "It doesn't change the fact that your client shot an unarmed man."

"It's going to change how the jury sees it though. This gun matches the description my client gave to Officer McElroy when she first reported that Miguel had threatened her. The jury will believe her now, and they'll put it all together the same way she did. Miguel intended to kill their children. That's how he was going to make her sorry, and that's why he showed up at the house in violation of a court order to take them. If she hadn't shot him, your first felony case would've been a child killer, not a mother protecting her own."

All the bluster left his face and he slowly sank into a chair. "What kind of deal are you looking for?"

She snorted. Did he honestly think he had any cards left to play? "I'm not looking for a deal, Rod." She used his given name for the first time, hoping it would diffuse his competitive impulse. "We want dismissal. Nothing less."

He shook his head adamantly. "I can't do that. Your client killed someone. We can't just let people whip out their guns and go after someone who scares them. Ask Officer McElroy what happens when one of his fellow officers uses deadly force. We hold them accountable. We make them prove it was justified."

"In the public eye maybe, but not in court. Here the burden is on you to prove it wasn't." She turned to the officer, sensing she could take advantage of his remorse. "What do you say, Joey? If you'd heard Miguel's threats and known for sure he had a gun, what would you have done if he had tried to take his children?"

"I would have dropped him right where he stood."

The ominous words hung for several seconds before the fight finally left Samuels's face, replaced by a growing redness that was either anger or embarrassment. "It was a good case given the evidence we had."

Lily saw no point in arguing. If he actually believed that, someone in the DA's office had been blowing smoke up his ass, probably someone who resented his meteoric rise and wanted to see him get humiliated in court.

* * *

Anna flipped back through the first quarter financial report to make sure she was reading it right. "Please tell me this isn't an April Fool's joke."

"Nope, April Fool's Day isn't for a couple of weeks," Hal said, leaning in her doorway with his arms folded. "I thought you'd like that."

"Like it? We doubled our first-quarter sales over last year. I don't just like it. I want to marry it and live happily ever after."

Her father pushed through the doorway with a questioning smile. "Do I hear celebrating?"

Anna ran down the preliminary sales figures for March, holding up Hal's line graph that showed all four dealerships climbing in sales every month since November. "And that's not all. Holly said this morning she's taken deposits on all but three of the new vehicles coming in this week." At least some of the uptick was due to Holly's new advertising strategies. With her instinct for sales and knowledge of the vehicles, she was proving herself a much quicker study than Anna had anticipated. Once she got a handle on the finance end of things, she would be ready to take over as vice president of operations.

"It isn't all good news, I'm afraid," Hal said. "I got the new list of repos this morning. Your friend Dave Cahill's on it."

The usual practice at Premier Motors was to repossess leased vehicles after three missed payments and sell them as used. Dave had leased their high-end sedan, the 760Li, just before the recession hit and demolished his office supply business.

"Let it go," Anna said. "He'll be good for it once he's back on his feet."

Her father pushed his hands into his pockets and cast a gentle look of reproach.

"What? I own the place. I can do that," she said defensively.

"I know Dave is your friend, but you've cut your staff to the bone to save their jobs. You owe them more than you owe him." He had always preached that business was business.

"What about all the times you gave your golf buddies the family discount? Any one of them could have paid full price from what he had in his wallet. Dave Cahill has always cared more about giving a hand to someone who needed it, and I'm not going to turn my back on him now that he's the one who's down on his luck."

He visibly retreated, rocking back on his heels. "Good answer."

She wasn't finished. "Besides, I wouldn't say no to anyone at this dealership who came to me in a bind, and neither would you. Money is useless if you can't spend it to help people you care about."

He threw up his hands. "I take it all back…every word."

Her cell phone chimed with Lily's ringtone, and Hal tugged her father's sleeve. "I think we ought to get out of here before she fires you."

"Right behind you."

"Hey, baby."

"I did it," Lily announced. "Samuels caved when I showed him the gun and he dropped the charges."

"Good for you. Does that mean you don't have to go back to

work?"

"I'm walking out the door right now. Tony freaked out. He didn't realize when I said I was going to start my maternity leave when this case wrapped up, I meant the very minute we finished."

Anna was flooded with relief to know Lily would be resting through the home stretch. "Any second thoughts?"

"Not one."

"Good. If you're up for going out, I think we should celebrate. Andy and I can cut out of here early and we'll all go for pizza."

"I have a better idea. Tell George I'll pick Andy up today. We can be ready to walk out the door whenever you get home."

"That's perfect." Except that her dad was probably hiding by now.

*　*　*

Lily hadn't felt such relief since the day she walked out of Redwood Hills after twenty-eight days in alcohol rehab. The next few weeks were hers alone, the first time since her childhood summer vacations that she had only to relax and do the things she wanted. Most of all she was looking forward to her afternoons with Andy. These weeks would be special for the two of them, a time she could assure him that his place in her life was secure. As she pulled up to a stoplight she rested a hand on her bulging tummy and smiled. Thank goodness they had wrapped this case up when they did, or she wouldn't have had anything else to wear. At the rate her babies were growing, she would soon be spending all of her time in her bathrobe.

Her euphoria was lost when she pulled onto the Santa Monica Freeway. The inside lanes were stacked, and it took her forever to get out to where the traffic flowed. No sooner had she patted herself on the back when the cars in front of her came to a screeching halt. This was one part of her day she wouldn't miss at all, the eighty-minute crawl between her home and office. Not driving to and from work would add almost three hours to her day, time she could spend napping, reading or just sitting out by the pool thinking of baby names.

She had been studying on that question for months, hung up not just on how the names sounded but on who came to mind. Rod was definitely off her list, and Samuel too, for that matter. She would have liked naming her son after someone as wonderful as Hal, but he and Kim had used Harold as Jonah's middle name. Another man she really admired was her boss Tony, but he and Colleen had named their son Anthony, which was too much like Andres anyway.

The bottleneck gave way and she surged ahead again. By the clock on her dashboard, it was only two, which gave her just enough time to get to Andy's school before the final bell rang. He would be excited by the change in routine, even more so when he heard they were going out together for pizza tonight.

Sometime soon she had to schedule their childbirth classes at the UCLA Women's Center. That would be quite a feat, getting Anna to commit to two nights a week.

"And starting tomorrow I'm taking my kitchen back," she said aloud. Anna had been the perfect partner through all of this, but now she would have time and energy to do more at home. It was hard to believe that only a year ago they were heading off for their second try at getting pregnant. Now they were only eleven weeks away from—

Lily slammed on her brakes as the cars in front of her came to a dead stop. A sickening crunch hurled her forward and her head snapped back against the headrest. A split second later another crunch jolted her and her airbag exploded.

Tears erupted instantly as a sharp pain reverberated from somewhere deep inside her head. She was barely aware of a woman charging toward her window, screaming at the top of her lungs. A man began yelling too, and soon her door was snatched open and they looked at her in horror.

Her babies...

A fiery sensation ripped through her abdomen when she tried to move her leg, and she realized her skirt was wet.

"...and I promise I won't ever fire you," Anna said over her shoulder as she exited her father's office. They had made up rather easily after their little tiff, with him acknowledging that the recession made him stingier about his assets. She had reminded him how, during the gas crunch, he had allowed all of Premier's employees—from the garage mechanics to the office staff—to fill up their cars on the company account once a week. It was one of the things she had admired about him, and one of the reasons she too put people first.

As she neared her office she recognized Lily's ringtone again. "Hey, baby. I just told Dad that you were picking Andy up."

"...Michelle...told me to call you." The background noise was overpowering, but it definitely wasn't Lily's voice. "...helicopter."

"I can't hear you," Anna shouted. "Say it again."

After a few seconds she heard what sounded like a car door slamming.

"My name is Michelle. The woman asked me to call you—the pregnant woman. There's been an accident on the 10 at Fairfax."

Anna's pulse raced as she groped for her keys. "What's happening? Is Lily hurt?"

"They're putting her in the helicopter right now. The guy says they're going to UCLA Medical Center. That's all I know."

"Tell her I'm on my way. And tell her I love her."

Hal and her father had heard the commotion and were standing in her doorway.

"Somebody go get Andy and bring him to the Medical Center. Lily's been in an accident." She pushed past them and raced to her car.

* * *

An ice bag over her face prevented her from seeing much on her first ride in a helicopter. The pain in her head was now only a dull ache, but the one in her belly was coming in agonizing waves. Over her protest, someone had started an IV drip, but they promised not to give her anything that might hurt the babies.

The ride ended with a bump and within seconds she found herself at the center of organized frenzy. Through bright sunlight she glimpsed the chopper's blades whipping overhead as blue-clad people clustered around her gurney shouting numbers and terms she didn't understand. She was whisked across the building's roof and into an elevator, where it went deathly quiet the moment the door closed. An African-American woman, her hair tightly braided in rows and decorated with brown and ivory beads, was shining a penlight into her eyes.

"Take care of my babies, please."

"It's your lucky day, sugar, 'cause ol' Darla here don't lose babies, and she don't lose mamas neither. Tell me what hurts most right now."

Lily shook her head. Didn't they understand that her pain didn't matter?

"Come on, sweetie. Don't you play tough with me. I'm asking 'cause I need to know."

She focused and realized her abdominal pains were coming mostly from one side and she indicated the area just as a cramp seized her.

The doors opened and her gurney lurched forward. "Her doctor's waiting in ER," a male voice behind her said. She was wheeled into an examination bay where a swarm of nurses seemed to talk without words as one went to work cutting her suit from her and another started taping leads to her bare chest and belly. A third snapped a hospital gown to her shoulders.

She had only a vague recollection of the chaos on the freeway,

157

where she had given them Beth's name and told the paramedic she was having twins. What she remembered clearly was the woman running back to say Anna loved her.

More cuffs, clips and leads were attached, and a nurse mounted her IV bag to a pump. In only seconds, the machines hummed, beeped and clicked to life. Someone laid a fresh cold compress across the bridge of her nose, but she pulled it aside at the sound of Beth's familiar voice. She needed to see what they saw, as well as the looks on their faces.

"Lily, we weren't supposed to meet like this. I see they gave you my best obstetric nurse."

Darla nudged her shoulder. "See, I told you."

Beth went right to work, checking her eyes, ears and extremities. Then she touched the tender points across her lap where the seat belt had grabbed her, causing her to grimace. "Looks like you were buckled in just right. That's in our favor."

As Beth finished her cursory pelvic exam, a thin, bald man in a striped shirt and tie entered holding a clipboard. "Anything for me?"

"Nothing pressing," Beth answered, pulling a sheet across Lily's exposed abdomen. "Probable broken nose…some bruising. We may have woken up a pair of sleeping babies though, so I'd like to get her moved upstairs for a sonogram."

He shrugged. "Call if you need me. I'm here till midnight."

Beth continued the assessment, pressing a stethoscope to various points around her abdomen. "Someone page Dr. Saint-Laurent to obstetrics."

Lily studied her face for signs of concern. The attention she was getting from everyone seemed steady and methodical, not at all frantic. "What's happening?"

Beth blew out a breath that rippled the hair on her forehead. "Well, I've got two strong heartbeats, which I like very, very much, and no bleeding. But you've lost some amniotic fluid so we have to see if that's a permanent problem or something that will fix itself. I'll get a better look upstairs." She snapped off her gloves and left, setting off another burst of activity among the nurses and orderlies.

Frustration gripped her—along with another contraction—as she tried to make sense of the cryptic clues Beth had given her. "Darla, what did she mean about it being a permanent problem?"

"She said you woke up the babies. Now she got to see if they going back to sleep or coming out to say hello."

"Say hello? You mean they might be born now?"

"That's right, sugar. But don't you worry. We got you covered."

The next few minutes were a blur of faces, doorways and lights as they navigated the hospital's maze to the obstetrics floor, and into a room filled with the familiar equipment she had seen in Beth's office. She wished Anna would hurry. If there were decisions to make—

"On three," Darla said, grunting as they lifted and transferred her to the bed. Then they went about their flurry of tasks again, reconnecting her equipment and activating the machines.

She pulled the blanket they had draped over her torso up around her neck and lay perfectly still, concentrating on her various points of pain. Her knee had hit something on the dashboard, the ignition switch perhaps. The worst of it—besides the all-too-frequent searing contractions—was her nose, which radiated an ache throughout her whole head.

"In here," the nurse said, and suddenly there was Anna rushing to her side.

"Sweetheart, you're hurt."

"I'm all right, but they're worried the babies might come." In a rapid jumble of words, she related everything she knew, which wasn't much. "Beth has that look again...you know, the one where we know she's worried but she won't say anything."

Anna's hands were all over her face and arms, checking... caressing. "They just have to make sure they cover all their bases. I'm sure it's all going to be okay."

"What you doing, mama?" Darla barked, setting the compress

back into position across her nose and cheeks. "You leave that there or your nose be looking like my sister's butt, and believe me, you don't want that. No, ma'am."

"This is Darla," she said drolly to Anna. "Don't give her any shit."

Beth returned with a woman of about fifty wearing a crisp white lab coat and a pageboy haircut that suggested an all-business persona. "Glad you got here, Anna. I want you both to meet Dr. Saint-Laurent. She's a neonatal specialist and I've asked her to sit in on the sonogram."

The new doctor greeted them brusquely with a pronounced French accent and positioned herself to peer over Beth's shoulder as the graph came to life.

"There's some good news," Beth proclaimed.

Braving the wrath of Darla, Lily whipped off her compress again and twisted so she could see the image.

Beth used a pointer on the screen to indicate what pleased her. "See how your babies are positioned? It looks like most of the pressure from the seat-belt was against the buttocks of this one…and the feet of this one."

"Placenta remains adhered," Dr. Saint-Laurent said with a steady nod, "but the amniotic sac was clearly breached. Did you give the antenatal steroids?"

"About thirty minutes ago, as soon as they got her off the helicopter." Beth looked up at Anna and Lily. "Steroids speed up the lung development in case we have to deliver…which we'd do by C-section."

Lily clutched her abdomen as her panic rose. "Deliver? But I'm not even seven months along."

"That's why Dr. Saint-Laurent's here. My job is to take care of you, Lily, but hers is to take care of your babies."

Anna gripped her hand and mouthed a silent reassurance before addressing the doctors. "Do you see anything that makes you worry about them?"

Dr. Saint-Laurent nudged Beth to the side and took her stool.

160

With a few clicks of the mouse she drew lines on the screen and busied herself with computations. "Both fetuses appear viable, in particular, the female. She is—"

"Female?" Anna asked. "We're having a girl?"

"Indeed, and a boy as well. You did not know?" She looked at Beth and winced. "Apologies."

Lily barely gave herself a moment to think about her babies' genders. "Is there something wrong with the boy?"

"I can't say with absolute certainty, but he looks perfectly fine considering the trauma of having his pool drained while he was swimming in it," the neonatal doctor said perfunctorily. "He is significantly smaller than his sister, probably less than two and a half pounds. However, survival rates are quite high at gestations above twenty-eight weeks, though admittedly they are clinically exacerbated in the instance of multiple births."

Beth put a hand on the other doctor's shoulder and gave her a stern look. "Doctor, this is what people are talking about when they say you sometimes scare patients half to death."

"Oh, apologies again. Perhaps I should just tell you that I don't see anything here beyond our usual scope of treatment for preterm births, if it becomes necessary to deliver these babies early. We're quite good at what we do, if I do say so myself, and we have the best neonatal facilities your tax-free endowments can buy." She turned to Beth. "That said, if we continue without distress I'd recommend waiting a few hours for the sac to regenerate. Could be this was just a pressure pop around the cervix that's already sealed itself, and once the little ones stop squirming they'll go back to sleep. Then we monitor fluid volume for forty-eight hours before we send the patient home for permanent bed rest. We can discuss delivery options a few weeks down the road."

"Agreed," Beth said. "The contractions have decreased in frequency from what the paramedics reported so maybe they're settling back down already. And if it turns out our leak continues, at least we'll have given some time for the steroids to work. In the meantime we'll start a course of antibiotics. We don't need an infection to complicate things any worse." She turned to Darla. "Let's go ahead and do the prep just in case we get surprised. Small sips of clear liquids only until further notice."

With the doctors and nurses gone from the room, Anna perched on the side of the bed. "They don't seem as worried as I thought they'd be. Sounds like we've got all the bases covered."

"How can you tell? I never know how to read Beth, and this Dr. Saint-Laurent talks about survival rates like she's taking bets at the horse track or something. Did you get the idea she's had a few problems with her bedside manner?"

"I don't care if she comes off like Attila the Hun as long as she knows what she's doing. I can't imagine Beth would have called her in here if she didn't." Anna gently set the compress back in place. "Tell me what happened."

Lily recounted the accident as best as she remembered. "The guy in the helicopter said my nose was broken."

"It's pretty swollen, but it still wrinkles when you're worried… like right now."

"I'm scared, Anna. They're so little."

"But we've got all the angles covered, sweetheart. You heard what the doctor said. She sees this kind of thing all the time, and I bet Beth has too. They act like they've got it all under control."

"But what if one of them is hurt from the wreck? I should have listened to you. If I hadn't been so stubborn about working I wouldn't have been on that highway in the first place. I should have been at home taking care of myself."

"Shhh…this wasn't your fault. They're going to be okay." She brought her face close and smiled. "Did you hear what she said? We're having a boy and a girl."

Anna's optimism was unshakable, so much that Lily finally gave herself permission to relax a little.

Darla returned and scattered several items on the bedside table and drew the curtain so it blocked the open door. Casually holding up a box labeled Urinary Catheter, she addressed Anna,

"Girlfriend, this might be a good time for you to take a long walk."

* * *

Anna paused and gripped the wooden handrail that ran the length of the hall, hoping to steady both her legs and her stomach. She was physically sick from having worried all afternoon, something she had masked upon seeing Lily in a state of near-panic.

Eagerly heeding Darla's advice, she had broken away to find Kim, who had texted her to say she was with their father and Andy in the maternity waiting room. Anna had only a brief window to connect and let them know what was happening. It would be even more important to keep up her spirits in front of Andy, who was probably already scared by what little he had been told. He was too smart not to realize everyone was worried. Her decision to have him brought to the hospital in the first place was impulsive in case things had...she didn't even want to entertain the thought. With Lily set to stay at least a couple of days, the best course would be to send Andy home with his grandparents.

Kim's was the only face she recognized in the waiting room. Without makeup and clad in sweatpants and a hoodie, it was obvious she had rushed to the hospital just like everyone else.

"Hey, where's Andy?" Anna asked.

"Dad took him down to get something to eat. They should be back any minute. How's Lily?"

"She's a little banged up, but not too bad. She's resting now. They think everything's okay but they're going to keep her for a couple of days just to be sure."

"What's up? Are they worried about the babies?"

"I wouldn't say worried...call it cautiously optimistic." As she laid it out for Kim, she started feeling better about where things stood. "She's been having contractions all afternoon, but Beth said that was just the babies repositioning on account of the amniotic sac. Apparently it ruptured in the accident, and a lot of her fluid leaked out."

"Her water broke? That means she's going to deliver."

"Maybe not. She doesn't seem to be leaking now, so Beth says if everything's still intact the babies could make more fluid and fill it back up in a few hours. She called in a neonatal specialist, a woman by the name of Saint-Laurent, and she said the babies looked good." She decided to keep secret the news about their gender, since it didn't feel right to be boasting about anything when she wasn't yet sure they were safe. "One's a little smaller but their heart rates are good, and the sonogram showed them sitting up higher than the seatbelt so they missed the impact."

"So the only question is whether or not the sac fills again?"

"That's it. The contractions aren't coming as often, so Beth says that's a good sign too. They're prepping her for a C-section just in case and gave her a shot of steroids to help speed up the lung development. Just precautions though." She pulled a hospital-issued pager from her pocket. "They gave me this and told me to get lost while they were putting the catheter in."

"How are you holding up? And don't even think about lying to me."

It was useless to lie to Kim anyway. She had an uncanny ability to see right through her, even to uncover feelings she didn't know were there. "I've been scared to death ever since that woman called me, but I feel better now. I couldn't let Lily see me worrying because she feeds off it and gets even more anxious than she already is. I got really scared when I saw the babies on the sonogram—they're tiny. The littlest is not even two and a half pounds. My foot weighs more than that." What if their son didn't make it?

"Oh, Anna."

As Kim's arms went around her shoulders, she realized she had started to cry. "I couldn't stand it if something happened to one of them…or to Lily."

"Listen to me," Kim said, her voice more serious than Anna had ever heard it. "You sat out here in this very room for sixteen hours waiting for Jonah. I was freaking out just like you are because it was taking so long, but Beth was like"—she threw up both her hands and twisted her face into an exaggerated look of nonchalance—"we got this. She was in total control the whole time, and if she thinks Lily or one of the babies is in trouble, she'll be on it like Rambo."

Anna wiped her eyes with her sleeve and sniffed loudly, knowing she couldn't go back in the room with Lily until she pulled herself together. "That's what I told Lily, that they saw this kind of thing all the time."

"And you know what? They probably do. My friend Mona delivered at twenty-five weeks and her baby turned out just fine. They do miracles every day."

Andy came through the door, sliding his feet forward and holding his arms out like an airplane. He was probably bursting with pent-up energy.

"Mom!" He raced across the room into her open arms.

"Hey, pal. Mama said for me to give you a great big hug." Tears stung her eyes again as she poured fierce emotions into her embrace. "She had a wreck in the car but she's going to be okay."

Her father joined her and put a comforting hand on her shoulder. "How is everything else?"

"I'll let Kim fill you in. Can you keep Andy for a day or two? I want to stay here at the hospital with Lily."

"Sure."

"You all right with that, pal? Grandpa will take you to our house so you can pack a few clothes and toys, and then you'll go stay at the Big House."

"But I have school."

"That's okay. Grandpa or Grandma will take you and pick you up. And I'll call you tomorrow so you can talk to Mama on the phone."

He frowned and jutted out his lower lip. "I don't want to. I want to stay at the hospital with you."

Her heart broke at his whimpering plea. "I wish you could, but they won't let little kids visit. That's why you had to stay out here with Grandpa and Aunt Kim."

Kim tugged him to where she was sitting and wrapped her arms around his waist from behind. "I know…why don't you come stay with Jonah? You can teach him his alphabet."

"What about Chester?"

"You can bring Chester too. He can teach Peanut to pee outside."

Chapter 11

Even at four thirty in the morning the hospital buzzed with activity. Lily had dozed off and on, taking advantage of the fact that her abdominal pains were much milder and coming less frequently. The attending OB-GYN physician had come in overnight and conducted another sonogram, which confirmed a significant increase in amniotic fluid. That was the best news they could have gotten.

Soon after he left, the overnight nurse, a young Asian woman named Wendy, had wheeled in a recliner for Anna, who had nodded off for a few minutes but now was wide awake and gazing transfixed at the array of monitors.

Lily studied her profile from the dim light that streamed from the hallway. It was undeniable she was worried about their situation, but Anna didn't worry like most people. She took charge, even if it meant putting problems in someone else's hands, as it did in this case. When she was satisfied she was on the right path she usually went forward with confidence. That's where they stood now, waiting for Beth to walk in and decree that their babies were out of danger.

A faint smile crossed Anna's face, causing Lily to wonder what had just passed through her thoughts. "Are you thinking about baby names?"

Anna chuckled. "No, I was thinking about something Kim said about Chester and Peanut. I hope one of our children grows up with her sense of humor."

"Something tells me Alice will be just like her mother. The faces that child makes…I bet her first full sentence is a smart-aleck remark."

"I wonder if our kids will be as opposite as Jonah and Alice."

"I don't know. With Andy in the mix—" Another contraction shot through her midsection and she moaned. It was nothing compared to the ones she'd had right after the accident, but she would be glad when they stopped altogether. "I have a feeling one of these kids will grow up to be a lumberjack."

"Is there something I can do?"

"Just be here." She was tired, and could only guess that Anna was much worse, since she had been sitting up in the chair all night. "We should probably try to get some sleep. I imagine there will be people in and out of here all day."

"And then you'll get to go home for bed rest, while I go back to work."

"You should take a couple of days off too." It was comforting to hear Anna talk about the days ahead. Her confidence helped hold back fears that something horrible was yet to happen. The worst part was over, the trauma of the accident. Now they had only to wait…

"How you doing, sugar?" Darla's exuberant voice brought the room to life.

Lily opened her eyes to daylight creeping through the blinds. Anna had apparently fallen asleep also because she suddenly sat up and twisted her neck from side to side.

168

"Wendy done told on you. Said you stayed up and played all night like you was having a slumber party in here."

The aroma of breakfast was wafting in from the hallway and Lily's mouth began to water. "What time is it?"

"Seven fifteen. Time to get you all jellied up again so we can look at those babies." She tugged the ultrasound machine to the bedside and laid out fresh supplies. "Dr. Beth will be here in about two minutes."

"Sooner than that," the doctor announced from the doorway. With her hands on her hips and a broad smile she looked pleased. "I got the report last night on your sonogram. Amniotic sac was intact and filled again with fluid. Looks like we dodged a bullet."

Lily and Anna exchanged looks of relief.

"We'll do another one right now, but I believe these little ones have gone back to sleep." She ran the wand across Lily's abdomen and lit up the display. "Yes, indeed. Dr. Saint-Laurent was probably right about this being just a pressure breach. No rupture at all…and the vitals look good."

"So what does that mean?" Anna asked. "You think we're out of the woods?"

Beth answered with a pensive nod. "I'd like to keep tabs on her for another day just to be sure, but I don't expect anything to happen. After that she goes home for bed rest. That'll bring its own brand of craziness, but it beats worrying about your babies."

"It sure does," Lily said. She had been looking forward to some free time to prepare for the babies' arrival and reclaim her kitchen for a few weeks, but what mattered was the babies' health, and if that meant staying in bed, she would. She was through taking chances. "Do you think I'll go to term?"

"Ennnh…" Beth squinted and cocked her head. "I kind of doubt it. Twins usually come early anyway, and I think under the circumstances we might want to assert a little more control. I hope you didn't have your heart set on natural childbirth."

"I just want them to be healthy." She would have sat on a nest for the next nine weeks if that had been determined as the best

169

thing for her babies. "Does this mean I get to eat?"

"I'll order up something." She looked back over her shoulder at Darla. "You can disconnect that IV but leave her clip in until I wrap this up with Dr. Saint-Laurent."

Anna stepped out to call Kim, who was the conduit for everyone else in the family.

"Let me give you a little inside info on the breakfast around here," Darla said, lowering her voice. "The eggs are real eggs, but that bacon ain't bacon, just like their hamburgers ain't hamburgers. It's all turkey."

She didn't have the heart to tell Darla that she preferred the leaner offerings. "Usually—" She was interrupted by a contraction, quite a bit stronger than the last one, but it was over as quickly as it came. "I don't mind it so much, but usually when I want turkey, I order turkey."

"Ain't it the truth? But here you order pig, you get turkey. You order cow, you get turkey. I don't even want to think what you get when you order turkey."

Lily tugged the catheter tube from underneath her as she shifted onto her hip. "Please tell me you're going to take this out too. I've felt like I've had to pee ever since you put it in."

"Hmm...I don't know if..." Darla was distracted by the monitors that read out her vitals, as well as the heartbeats of her babies. "Dr. Beth didn't say anything about that." She left the room as Anna was returning.

"Did you check in with Kim?"

"Sure did, and Andy went right to sleep last night with Chester at the foot of his bed. Even Jonah had a quiet night, relatively speaking. The only problem was that—I wasn't even going to tell you this because I didn't want you to worry—he wet the bed again."

The news, though not surprising, made her sad. "Poor little guy. He was just getting used to the idea of sharing us with two babies. This is really going to make him feel left out. At least you can be home with him tonight."

"Maybe, but I can't leave you if things are still up in the air. We'll just have to make it up to him later. And I'll call over there as soon as school's out."

Darla returned with the doctor in tow. They both studied the monitor for a few seconds before Beth withdrew her stethoscope and pressed it to several spots on Lily's abdomen. "Page Dr. Saint-Laurent to obstetrics. Tell her to scrub in."

"Scrub in?" With the monitor still attached, Lily could hear the ping of her own pulse rising with alarm. "What's going on?"

"The little one's heart rate is falling. We need to get them out now. Darla, get me a team set up stat."

"No," Lily protested. "He was fine just a minute ago."

"Whatever it is, it happened just now, Lily. I can't explain it, but at this point he needs Dr. Saint-Laurent. You have to trust us here. We're going to do everything we can."

Anna had moved close enough to hold her, and when Beth walked out she pressed her lips to Lily's temple. "Listen to her, sweetheart. This is exactly what we were talking about before. They handle things like this all the time."

"But something's wrong with him."

"I know, but that's what I'm saying. There's always something wrong when babies come this early, but they're set up for this kind of thing here. He's going to be all right."

Warm fingers gently brushed the tears from her swollen face. "If I"—she choked back a sob—"if I don't get to see him, I want you to give him a name."

"That's not our deal. Besides, you'll see him. I'm counting on it."

* * *

Anna touched the floor to make her cushioned chair rock, expecting to hear it squeak. Instead there was nothing...not a sound emanating from the small tiled room. Nearly forty minutes had passed since they took Lily into surgery. Though she had hoped to be present for the delivery Beth advised otherwise, since Lily had gone under general anesthesia in case of complications.

On her way to the room, she had peeked into another neonatal unit to see a woman looking down through the glass incubator at her small child. The mother cooed and made faces, probably needing the connection even more than her baby did. She wondered how the woman's desperate hours of delivery had passed, and how the baby's father had endured the agonizing wait.

Unable to stand it anymore, she went to the doorway and leaned against the jamb, half in and half out of the room, training her eye on the hallway. How hard could it be to make an incision, pull out two babies and sew it all up? She refused to think anything was wrong, and consoled herself with images of all the things they probably had to do before bringing the babies to their room. After all, they had just come out of surgery too.

A smiling man walked into the room where she had seen the mother talking to her child. Anna said hello and returned to her seat. Seeing the parents so happy made her feel better.

"There's your mom, little girl," a woman's gentle voice suddenly sang.

Anna jumped to her feet as the incubator rolled across the floor to its bay, its tiny red occupant clad in a diaper and white knit cap. "Oh, my God." Though the baby's face was partially obscured by tape that held tubes in place, she knew immediately this was her biological daughter. "How is she?"

"Beautiful, just like her mom." The nurse smiled to reveal a mouthful of orthodontic braces and held out her hand. "I'm Kathy, the pediatric nurse. I'll be in here with you till seven tonight when Deidre comes on."

Though her voice was melodic and calm, Anna's anxiety soared. "What about..."

"Your son? He'll be along in a little while. And their mom

came through it all like a trouper."

She blew out a breath of relief and finally allowed a smile as she turned her attention back to the incubator.

"As you can see, this little angel's got a bunch of stuff going on," Kathy said. "See those tubes going into her nose? One is her feeding tube—gavage tube, we call it—and obviously, it goes to her stomach. The other is just an oxygen cannula, but Dr. Saint-Laurent said her lungs were pretty strong for her weight."

"How much?"

"Two pounds, twelve ounces, just a hair under the average for twenty-nine weeks, but that isn't unusual with twins." Kathy made all the connections and the room came to life with a mechanical hum. "Her immune system isn't fully developed, so we have to be very careful about bacteria, especially for the first couple of weeks." She directed Anna to scrub her hands with antibacterial soap before demonstrating how to use the inverted pockets on the side of the incubator.

Anna tentatively pushed her hand through the opening and tickled her daughter's clenched fist until it opened and closed around the tip of her finger. Nothing had ever felt so miraculous.

"That's it, Mom. You're officially bonding."

She watched mesmerized as the baby's spindly toes spread and curled, and her chin—Anna's chin—twitched in what appeared to be an effort to adapt to the strange new tubes.

Darla had sneaked up to stand beside her. "She's a cutie-pie. Your son will be out in a minute. He gave us a little trouble, but then boys tend to do that."

Anna sucked in a breath as her stomach tightened with fear. "What kind of trouble?"

She shrugged. "Nothing we ain't seen before. Lily said she had a name picked out for him and wanted you to go ahead and name this little girl."

"Here, you can write it down," Kathy said as she pulled a card from the slot at the bottom of the incubator.

Anna looked again at her daughter. Strong, Dr. Saint-Laurent had said. "Eleanor. Eleanor Cristianna Kaklis after both our mothers."

She cooed and smiled as she held Eleanor's tiny hand, trying not to panic over why it was taking so long to bring her son out.

"She's as close to perfect as you can get at twenty-nine weeks." The new voice belonged to Beth, who was still in her scrubs and sweating around the collar.

"How's Lily?" The next question she hated to ask. "And our baby boy?"

"Lily's fine. The surgery went just as it was supposed to, and she's in recovery now. Someone will come and get you when it's okay to go back and see her." She ran her hand lightly across the top of the incubator as if caressing the glass. "Dr. Saint-Laurent is still with your son. As we feared, his lungs are very immature. He had some problems with an air pocket and she had to drain it, so I want to warn you that you'll see a little tube coming out of here." She indicated an area in the middle of her chest. "And he has a breathing mask. We call it a CPAP. It pushes air into his lungs until he's strong enough to inhale on his own. Almost all of them can do that by thirty-four weeks or so, even the ones that have problems."

"Is he going to make it?" Her voice rattled with fear.

"He's in good hands, Anna, and he's active. Those two things matter more than anything else." She dropped her doctor persona to draw her into a hug. "I'll be checking in on Lily for the next few days, but I'm handing you off to Dr. Saint-Laurent. She's the miracle maker now."

"Thank you, Beth…thanks for everything."

"You're welcome. Nothing will make me happier than to watch all of you leave here together."

It was another thirty minutes before Dr. Saint-Laurent appeared. Her surgical gown, which had tiny smears of blood on the chest, was pulled off by a passing nurse and stuffed into a waste container. Underneath she wore gray knit pants and a Montreal Canadiens T-shirt. "Apologies. I was called out in the middle of breakfast."

"How's my son?"

"He's a pistol," she answered, clapping her hands for emphasis. "If he gives you as much trouble as he gave me, you're going to need a lot of therapy."

A nurse entered pushing a second incubator and Anna rushed to look inside. Even though Beth had prepared her, she was shaken by the sight of all the tubes leading to and from his doll-like body. All of him would fit in her open palms. "How big is he?"

"Two pounds, two ounces. Quite a little one but we've had much smaller. By now they're riding their bikes and playing baseball."

Darla bounded back in. "I have two messages for you. Here's the first." She handed Kathy a name card, which she slid into the end of his incubator.

Anna looked at her tentatively before peering around to read the name. *George Stewart Kaklis.* "Oh, my." Her eyes flooded with tears.

"And the other for you is to stop crying and go see your wife." Darla tipped her head toward the two incubators. "Kathy's got your babies. She won't let nothing happen to them."

Dr. Saint-Laurent wrapped an arm around her waist and steered her out the door and down the hall. "This is going to be a long and difficult journey for you and Lily, probably six weeks here in the hospital and then special care for a few more weeks at home. But your children will grow bigger and stronger every day, even as they seem to struggle. No one expects the two of you to carry this burden alone. When people offer to help you, let them. When they tell you to rest, tune out the whole world and go to sleep. It is the only way all of you will get through it."

It was compassionate advice for someone not known for her bedside manner, Anna thought. "We also have a five-year-old."

"He is on the journey too. He can help, but he also needs his time, just like you and Lily will need yours. It's a mother's instinct to sacrifice herself for her children, but meaningful martyrdom went out with the Middle Ages. Search for the joy in all of it because that will sustain you. And then one day you'll realize your fear is gone."

Anna entered the recovery bay to find Lily sitting up, her bruised eyes pronounced against her pale face. Her expression was a mixture of exhaustion and angst. Anna planted a kiss on her forehead and smiled, determined to show nothing but joy. "I've noticed that every time the biggest day of my life happens, you're right there…the cause of it all."

A flicker of relief passed Lily's eyes, and she looked for a moment as if she would cry. "I had nothing to do with the earthquake."

"No, but that wasn't the biggest thing that happened to me that day. Far from it." She pushed a lock of hair off Lily's brow and caressed her cheek, which now seemed to have more color than only moments ago. "They're both precious, sweetheart… and the doctor promises me that everything's in place to help them along. Now it's up to you to get better, and to rest up while you can. Life's about to get crazy."

"I didn't have a chance to see our little girl."

"She's perfect. But I think the nurse might have misunderstood what you meant to name our son."

Lily chuckled lightly and pressed her lips together in a tight smile. "I figured that would guarantee us free babysitting for life."

"I don't think there's any doubt about that."

"And what about our daughter? Is she Ruby?"

"No, sorry. I went with something else."

* * *

Lily could barely contain her excitement as Kathy helped position her in the recliner. From the beginning Eleanor had shown an interest in physical contact, and Dr. Saint-Laurent had determined she was stable enough to move to the next phase. That was Kangaroo Care, so called because Eleanor would be laid against her bare chest to experience her warmth and nurturing. To get ready for the delicate exchange, Lily untied the top sash of her gown, a soft cotton wraparound, opening it from her hip to her neck.

Kathy then eased the sleeping infant into the valley between her breasts. "Support her bottom with this hand and hold her head with the other."

She was immediately captivated by the splendid feel of Eleanor's skin next to hers. Her tiny fingers curled into a ball, which she tucked beneath her chin. "This is heavenly."

"Apparently she thinks so too. I can't believe how fast she settled down. They usually wiggle at first and some of them even cry."

"I'm the one who feels like crying." Beth warned her the days of raging hormones would return, but not to fear, that she would be quicker to cry with joy than anger.

"No need for tears. You can hold her for as long as you want... hours even." Kathy fingered the gavage tube that stretched from the incubator to provide continuous nourishment. The oxygen cannula also remained in place, and the heart monitors continued to beep. But the tubes and wires, and even the oversized diaper, did little to detract from the glorious skin-on-skin contact.

Lily eyed the feeding source, a bottle of her own milk expressed only hours earlier using an electric pump. The urge to feel Eleanor's mouth on her nipple was almost overpowering, but Kathy had said it would probably be two more weeks before they could attempt breast-feeding, and with that came the caution that some preemies had problems getting the hang of it, while others simply found it too exhausting. Each baby was different, she said, as if Lily needed any proof.

From where she sat cuddled with Eleanor, she was able also to keep a steady eye on George, who remained connected to his

CPAP, though the drainage tube had been removed from his chest after only one day. Beyond their health issues, the physical differences between George and Eleanor were astonishing, especially considering they had the same anonymous father. Unlike his sister, who presently sported a head of thick dark hair, George had only light brown fuzz on his crown. His digits were small in relation to his hands and feet, while hers were long and lively. The one thing they had in common—and which set them apart from everyone else in the Kaklis family—was their brown eyes, clearly a gift from their Latino father. According to Beth, blue eyes or green eyes were subject to change for the first couple of years of life, but these brown eyes were here to stay.

"If we could bottle that look, we could sell it as world peace."

Her eyes had been closed and Dr. Saint-Laurent's voice startled her. "They were already growing up in my mind's eye."

"It will happen before your real eyes soon enough." She scrubbed her hands before slipping on gloves and a sterile gown. Then she opened George's incubator and inspected him thoroughly. "He is stronger already but he still has far to go. It will be a while yet—perhaps two weeks or more—before he is able to sit with you that way."

The ache to hold George against her had begun almost the instant Eleanor settled on her chest. It wasn't just her need, but his too. In such a fragile state, what child would not yearn for the touch of his mother?

"How are you feeling?"

Lily sighed wistfully. "To be honest, I'm feeling pretty good…which is bad, I guess. Under normal circumstances I'd be chomping at the bit to get out of here. But getting out means leaving my babies behind and I don't know how I'm going to be able to do that."

The doctor pulled up a chair and propped her feet on the trashcan, revealing wrinkled blue socks decorated with pink kittens. It was funny to think only a couple of days earlier she had given off such a stiff clinical image when, in fact, she was as down to earth as anyone Lily had ever known. Her attention to the care of their babies was enough to win them over, but she had gone beyond that to offer her friendship, even insisting they call her by her given name, Sylvie. They would be spending a lot of time together over the next few weeks, she said.

"I already gave your wife the lecture about taking advantage of every opportunity she had to rest."

"She told me all about it," Lily said. "I just think it's a lot easier to rest when I'm with them or when I know they're just here in the next room. Don't get me wrong. I like everyone who works here, and I trust them. But if I went home now I'd feel like I was leaving them at the very moment they needed me most, to say nothing of the fact that I doubt I could sleep away from them anyway."

"Rubbish. It isn't as if they'll take their first step or call someone else Mama while you aren't here." She nodded her head in the direction of George's incubator. "Even that one over there...he knows who his mothers are already. Not that he actually knows *what* a mother is, mind you. But he knows that the ones who come and hold his fingers for hours are his people. And I believe he knows this even when you're gone."

Lily dipped her chin as Eleanor mildly squirmed on her chest. "I'm not as worried about their missing me as I am about missing them. I hadn't planned on being away from them at all until September when I went back to work, and now it's going to be tomorrow. I know it'll kill me because it already kills me to be away from Andy."

"I bet you'll see one very happy boy tomorrow when you're discharged."

"At least I have that to look forward to."

"That and a whole night's sleep."

In her own bed with Anna's arms around her, and with Andy just down the hall. She had to admit she was looking forward to that feeling.

Sylvie tugged up her fallen socks and stood. "For your sake

and everyone else's I hope you'll come visit for only a few hours a day. Let Anna have her time here too, maybe in the evenings while you're having special time with Andy. She can give them Kangaroo Care too just like you, and while I always recommend my mothers breast-feed, you and Anna will have your hands full with two of them for at least a couple of years. It's very likely they'll take the bottle first anyway, so I see no reason you shouldn't let them do that sometimes. They'll still be drinking the nourishment you provide, and the two of you can share the load."

"What about all the research that says it's best to breast-feed?" It was easy to imagine all the ways Anna would help with the babies, but she had never really considered bottle-feeding her babies.

"Most of that argument is nutritional. As long as you're providing breast milk, the emotional and physical advantages of mother-child bonding can be realized by Anna as well, which in my view, more than evens the tally. Besides, I'd never advise you not to breast-feed, just to let Anna help where she can. She seems excited to do it, and certainly capable."

"If there's one thing she is, it's capable." She gently rocked and watched with amusement as Eleanor's fist tightened and relaxed in rhythm to the sway. Once Anna held her daughter this way, she would never want to stop.

When Anna showed up at six o'clock with Andy, Lily dressed and took him downstairs to the cafeteria for dinner. Anna took a turn holding Eleanor and, as Lily had predicted, was so captivated she didn't want to leave.

"You have to get this young man to bed," Lily said, and hugged Andy. "I'll be there to help tuck you in tomorrow."

The neonatal ward always quieted in the evening, with nurses popping in for occasional checks and attending physicians making their circuit through the ward in the middle of the night. Lily loved these peaceful hours when she could commune with her babies. Deidre, the night nurse, helped move the recliner next to George's incubator so she could be close to him too as she held Eleanor. It was easy to imagine nights at home like this, rocking one of her babies while the other slept. She could probably get used to sleeping in the chair too...

"Get the attending, and page Sylvie at home," a woman's voice snapped.

Lily's eyes shot open to find Deidre examining George's connections, and two other nurses coming to her aid. The clock on the wall said a quarter to ten.

"Susan, help Lily put Eleanor back in her bed so we can move that chair out of the way."

"What's happening?"

"Tachycardia...rapid heart rate. He's in respiratory distress."

It was all Lily could do to wait for Susan's help with Eleanor. By the time she was up the attending physician had arrived and was calling for new IVs to deliver chemicals and drugs she hadn't heard of before. The other nurse reported that Sylvie was on her way.

Deidre patted her arm. "Dr. Tomlinson knows what he's doing, Lily. Maybe you should step out and give Anna a call. She might want to be here with you while they make decisions."

Lily was in full-scale panic mode, so much that she dropped the phone twice before finally dialing home. "George is in trouble. I need you here."

Sylvie arrived at twenty after ten and took the lead. After a thorough assessment, she pulled Lily aside. "It's called respiratory distress syndrome...not at all uncommon for preemies, but I had hoped we'd gotten past the rocky part."

Anna rushed in, dressed in jeans, a T-shirt and denim jacket, her hair tied back in a ponytail. Andy was draped over her shoulder, still pajama-clad and clearly half asleep. Deidre took him and laid him in the recliner, which had been moved to the corner, and covered him with a blanket.

"What's happening?" Anna gasped.

Sylvie delivered her update again. "We need to do an

181

endotracheal intubation."

"Why something so drastic? I thought he was already getting air from that mask."

"The CPAP pushes air into his lungs, but his body still has to do all the work inside, and right now his lungs are at risk of collapse. The intubation ensures the appropriate gas exchanges whether he's able to breathe on his own or not." She took a set of papers from Deidre and drew a pen from her lab coat. "We need a consent form. We do this all the time, but the procedure isn't without risk. His airways are tiny and there's always the danger we'll nick something on the way in. But I'll be honest with you. If we don't do this tonight, his condition will deteriorate rapidly."

Anna didn't bother to read the forms, going straight to the back page to affix her signature.

Lily tried to get closer to George but realized her knees were weak, and she grasped Anna's arm for support. "Oh, God...we could lose him right now."

"No, no." Anna drew her into an embrace, cradling her head as she murmured assurances. "He's in good hands. Sylvie does this all the time. She said that. He'll be okay."

Though it pained her to watch, she followed Anna's lead and looked on as Sylvie assembled her tools and ordered the CPAP mask removed. She made quick work of inserting the thin tube and attaching it to a hand pump, which she gently squeezed several times while Deidre assembled the tubing for the mechanical ventilator. As soon as it was ready, Sylvie made the switch, laying the tubing alongside George's tiny body and taping it into place over his mouth. The whole procedure took less than two minutes.

"That went about as well as it could go," she proclaimed, looking up briefly to give Anna and Lily an encouraging smile. "We need to watch him for a little while or so and make sure that's all he needs."

Anna squeezed her. "See? I told you he'd be okay."

Lily's relief was palpable, though she was still shaking with fear. "What happens if he still isn't breathing right?"

"He'll be breathing just fine...or rather the ventilator should be breathing for him just fine. We can give him a few things to adjust the gases if we have to, but I'm hoping he'll take over from here."

"Is he out of danger?" Anna asked.

"I've done all I can do right now. Let's give him a couple of hours."

It was possibly the longest two hours of Lily's life, but when Anna finally hoisted Andy onto her shoulder at two a.m., George was stable. Sylvie assured them he would rest well for the night and they should do the same. And to prove it, she put on her own jacket and headed for the door.

"Go to bed," Anna said, pausing in the doorway to give Lily a quick kiss to her temple. "Our days will be even longer starting tomorrow."

"Thanks for coming so fast. I would have lost it if you hadn't been here."

"Just a few more weeks, Lily...then we'll bring all of our babies home."

* * *

"...because the membership won't support that this year," Anna said, holding her hand over the receiver to stifle a groan. Her longtime compatriots at the Chamber were drawing up a platform strategy for their candidate, one she knew would go down in flames in next month's officer elections. "We need to shift our priorities back to the small businesses or we could lose half our membership."

As she finished her call, Andy walked into her office and dropped his book bag in the corner.

"Hey, pal."

183

Trina, the payroll clerk who had moved out of the back office to take Carmen's place in reception, beeped in. "Anna, Marco called and said to tell you four, whatever that means. And Nancy is in the conference room with Walter."

"Great, another migraine on the horizon," she mumbled. If Nancy, her human resources chief, had driven all the way up from Palm Springs to meet with Anna and the dealership's attorney, it couldn't be good news. She glanced up to see Andy taking her ledgers off the bookshelf to use as buildings in the make-believe town where he would drive his toy cars. "Not those, please. They aren't toys."

Across the hall in the conference room, Nancy and Walter were already speaking in agitated tones. "From a legal perspective, it's a pretty tough case to make. But I wouldn't go so far as to say he doesn't have a leg to stand on," Walter said.

"Who doesn't?" she asked, foregoing the offered chair to pace the room. It had already been a long day, with calls to Lily every hour to check on George.

Nancy sighed and pushed a letter across the table. "Ricky Hill filed a grievance over JoAnne Cowens getting the service manager position at the VW lot in Palm Springs. He's been working for the company four years longer than she has, and he's claiming reverse discrimination because he's a white man."

"Yes, a white man who spent his entire career working on BMWs. All of JoAnne's experience is in the VW garage, and if I'm not mistaken she worked somewhere else before taking that job. On paper she's the better candidate." Anna hated to micromanage personnel issues and it irritated her that this one had been brought to her attention. "Maybe I'm missing something, but I really don't understand what this meeting is about."

"Normally it wouldn't be an issue," Nancy explained, "but Ricky is saying it's part of a hiring pattern. Ever since you acquired the new dealerships, all the top jobs and promotions have favored women and people of color. Four of the managers in Palm Springs have submitted letters for Ricky in support of this fact, but they all wanted me to tell you they weren't taking sides, just stating the facts."

"It's called a business strategy," Anna said, rolling her eyes in exasperation. "We hire and promote a variety of people because we want to attract all potential buyers, not just young white guys, who held almost all of the managerial jobs when we acquired the other dealerships. Walter, are we covered here?"

"After the Supreme Court ruled for the firefighters in that Connecticut case, there will be less inclination to accept diversity for diversity's sake when it comes to hiring and promotion practices. But I like that you're casting it as a business strategy. That changes the argument substantially. I think a reasonable—"

"Cut to the chase. Is this going to be a problem?"

"I think it could be annoying and perhaps time-consuming, but I don't think it's a winnable case for Mr. Hill if he takes it to the next level."

"And I'm not sure he's inclined to," Nancy added. "He's basically a nice guy. He's always worked well alongside everyone in the garage, and people like him a lot. I think he's just frustrated that there probably won't be any opportunities to move up for a long time. He honestly feels that since both the BMW and VW dealerships in Palm Springs have always been part of the same company, his tenure and job performance earn him the promotion over JoAnne."

"So talk to him, Nancy. Let him know we appreciate his loyalty, and encourage him to apply for any future opportunities that might arise." Perhaps he would make trouble, but it was situations like these that called for the courage of her convictions. "I think our choice of JoAnne was the right one, and I'd make it again tomorrow. I'll defend it in court if I have to."

Walter closed his leather portfolio and put away his Mont Blanc pen. "I agree. Mr. Hill deserves a respectful response, but not one that gives support to his grievance."

Nancy scribbled a note to herself and gathered up her papers.

"Thanks, Anna. That was my gut instinct, but I thought under the circumstances—with the potential for legal action and all—you should make the call."

Anna left them to find their own way out and returned to her office where, much to her annoyance, her ledgers remained scattered across the floor as Andy played with his cars around them. "What did I tell you about those books?" she demanded sharply. "When I tell you to do something, I expect you to listen. You know those ledgers are important to me. I don't come and get your favorite toys and leave them out where people can step on them. Do I?"

Looking ashamed, Andy began sliding the books back into the slots on the shelf.

"You're putting them in backward. They go...never mind. Just leave it alone. I'll do it myself."

As she approached the bookshelf, he burst into tears and darted past her out the door.

"Damn it," she muttered. Her whole day had been one disaster after another. Yes, she was annoyed he hadn't listened to her, but dressing him down the way she had was uncalled for. Last night had been just as hard on him as it had been on her.

Hal appeared in her doorway only moments later. "Is everything all right? I heard..."

An array of emotions bombarded her—frustration, fear and no small amount of shame, and she realized she was crying too. "We're just tired. George had a setback last night and we had to go back to the hospital. They put an air tube down his throat and we didn't get home until after two."

"Oh, Anna." His strong arms went around her shoulders, a comforting reminder that her family would be her rock if she needed them. "Is he all right?"

"He's stable again. It's something called respiratory distress syndrome. It's pretty common for preterm infants, but once their lungs reach a certain threshold they're usually out of the woods."

"You should have called us. We could have picked up Andy,

186

or I could have stayed over with him. It's bad enough that you had to be out so late, but him..."

She shook her head. "No, we wanted him there. That's his little brother fighting for his life, and we all needed to be there to support each other. Besides, Andy's already feeling like he's on the outside of the circle since we're spending so much time at the hospital. And to make matters worse, now I've gone and hurt his feelings."

"I don't even know why you're here. Take him and go on to the hospital."

"That's where we're headed after work. Lily's being discharged today. We'll probably have to drag her out of there, especially after last night."

"Seriously, beat it. Your dad and I can hold down the fort, and if we absolutely need you, we'll call."

Given the kind of day she'd had, leaving work now probably wasn't a bad idea. First she had to make up with her son.

"I saw Andy run into the conference room."

She could barely make out his dark figure huddled among the chairs beneath the long table. "Hey, pal. I'm sorry I yelled at you. I'm tired and I'm worried about Georgie, but I shouldn't have taken it out on you." She pulled out a chair and crawled to sit cross-legged beside him. "Will you forgive me?"

His only reply was to sniff loudly and wipe his nose on his sleeve.

"I bet you're tired too. Are you worried about your brother?"

He nodded. "It makes Mama sad."

"It sure does, just like when you have asthma. We want all of our children to be healthy—you, Eleanor and Georgie." She tugged him into her lap and kissed the back of his head. "The doctor is taking real good care of him though. When he grows bigger and stronger, he won't be sick anymore."

"Mama says I might not have asthma anymore when I get big. And if I get better, and then he gets better too we'll both be big and strong."

She loved his optimism, and decided then and there to share it, since it felt so much more uplifting than fear. "I bet you're right. Mama comes home today, you know. She'll be sad to leave your brother and sister at the hospital but it'll make her happy to be with you again. I think we should take her a present. Would you like that?"

"What would we get?"

"Marco just called and said he has four new Routans. What if we went over there now and picked one out? We could drive it to the hospital and surprise Mama."

His face lit up at the prospect of choosing another family car. "Can we get a silver one that's black on the inside?"

"We'll have to see what they have." He squirmed to climb out of her lap but she held him fast. "Wait, we still have a couple of things to clear up. I think the way you've helped Mama and me these last few days has been very brave. I'm proud of you and I love you very much."

"I love you too."

"Do you forgive me for yelling at you? I'll try not to do it again."

He poked her shoulder emphatically as he answered, "I... forgive...you."

"Good, I feel better now." She truly did, lighter than she had felt in days.

Chapter 12

Lily folded the last towel and added it to the stack on top of the dryer. The basket probably wasn't that heavy but Anna had read her the riot act about carrying even small bits of laundry or groceries. Beth's four-week restriction period had passed and she felt plenty strong, but that made no difference to Anna. At least her itchy stitches were gone, though the scratchy pubic hair was just as bad.

Since coming home from the hospital almost five weeks ago she and Anna had settled into a routine that maximized the time they spent with Andy while also providing lots of hands-on nurturing for Eleanor and George at the hospital. After dropping Andy at school, she would spend the entire day in the neonatal unit, usually holding Eleanor, who after a week of training had finally been persuaded to take a breast. Lily was thrilled to finally experience this maternal connection, though Eleanor seemed indifferent when it came to the choice of a breast or bottle. At least it meant Anna could help handle feedings.

Whenever Eleanor fell asleep on her chest, she would snake an arm through the hole in the side of George's incubator, urging him to clutch her finger as she tickled his hand. He grew more responsive every day and had been off the ventilator for over a week. Sylvie said his lungs would soon be strong enough to ward off the risk of infection outside his sterile cocoon. She couldn't wait to hold him.

It was all she could do to tear herself away from the babies when school let out, but her reward was one-on-one time with Andy until Anna got home for dinner. She appreciated that his needs were different from those of Eleanor and George, and that she wasn't confined to a small physical space or required to give him her undivided attention. He was happy with their time too, bursting with stories the minute he climbed into their new silver minivan.

Most nights after dinner she returned to the hospital for a couple of hours before coming home to fall exhausted into bed. Anna usually juggled a hospital visit during the day, along with a couple of brief evening visits with Andy during the week. It was less than ideal but it was workable, though the road time was wearing all of them out.

That would change somewhat tonight because they were going to the hospital after dinner to bring Eleanor home, five weeks to the day from when she was born.

"Mrs. Dooley let us draw pictures after music," Andy proclaimed, unfurling his art so she could study it while she stirred his dinner on the stove. "It's Georgie and Eleanor. See?"

Indeed she could. It wasn't at all surprising to see what had impressed him about their differences. Both figures wore triangular diapers but one had lines leading from various points on his body to a box with buttons and dials. "This one's Georgie, isn't it?"

"Yeah, 'cause he has a hose in his mouth…and these wires."

"Did you show this picture to the boys and girls in your

class?"

"Just to Jeremy. He said Georgie was electric because he's plugged in."

"Except this one isn't there anymore," she said, pointing to the tube that ran to his mouth. "He can breathe all by himself now."

"I can draw another one."

"Maybe you'll draw a picture of Eleanor after she comes home." He was more interested in George, but who wouldn't be more fascinated by an electric brother? "Are you ready for your supper? I fixed you a hot dog and some macaroni and cheese."

"Where's Mom?"

"She's on her way home but she asked me to fix her a peanut butter sandwich so we can go as soon as she gets here."

"But she's supposed to—"

"She said she had macaroni and cheese for lunch." Anna had become quite creative with her excuses.

When Anna arrived she insisted on eating her sandwich in the car on the way to the hospital. It was more than just her eagerness to bring Eleanor home, she said. She had left work early so they could get home before Andy's bedtime. He was likely to be wired from the excitement and she wanted him wound down so they all could get rest tonight.

Andy led the way into the neonatal unit where Kathy greeted him exuberantly. "Andy, your sister is so excited about coming home with you. She's been talking about you all day."

"She has not," he said with a grin, knowing he was being teased. "She can't talk yet."

"No, but she smiles whenever I say your name. Come here and see for yourself."

She leaned over Eleanor's bed and sang Andy's name, prompting her eyes and mouth to open wide. "See?"

It was a relief to see Andy so delighted with his sister. Ever since they had made a concerted effort to give him special attention, he had calmed considerably and the bedwetting had stopped. Once the babies were home it would be impossible to concentrate solely on his needs, but Lily was confident they could find the right balance between having him help with his siblings and giving him his own time to play.

Kathy handed her a towel for her shoulder. "She ate a little bit about an hour ago but I bet she's still hungry if you want to feed her while they're visiting George."

Anna helped Andy wash his hands so they could play with George. He had grown more alert in the last few days, gripping a finger without hesitation and even meeting their eyes when they tried to entertain him. Sylvie assured them his progress would accelerate now that he was breathing better, and he would follow his sister home within a matter of weeks.

Lily opened her shirt and lifted Eleanor from her bed. *Home.* The word resonated in her head as she took in the decorations of the room that had been her second home for over a month. Cards, balloons and stuffed animals lined the shelves, one of the few reminders there were other people in the world besides just the five of them and the hospital staff, practically the only people she had seen since the accident.

She held her breast until Eleanor latched on, and then settled back into the sublime sensation. Andy came close to watch and even held out his finger so Eleanor could clutch it while she ate.

A flash went off as Anna took a picture with her cell phone. "That's too perfect not to save. I should send that out to our friends."

Lily rolled her eyes. "Just what I need, my boob on someone's screensaver. But you know, there is someone I would like you to send it to. Karen Haney. She'd really like that." Karen had sent pink and blue stuffed rabbits for the babies and an enormous Easter basket for Andy, saving the day, since she and Anna had totally forgotten the holiday.

Anna caught her eye and pointed first to her watch then to Andy.

She gestured to Eleanor, who had stopped nursing but had

dozed off still clinging to her breast.

"She could stay that way for an hour or more," Anna urged gently.

"I know." But Lily couldn't bring herself to move. This moment—all five of them together in such a tranquil setting—was too precious to disrupt, and she felt her tears gathering at the realization it had to end.

"What is it?"

"I don't want to leave George. He'll be here all by himself."

"Sweetheart," Anna said, kneeling beside her. "We're not leaving him behind. We're giving him what he needs, and we have to be strong enough to do that. If we just hold on for a little while longer, we'll all be home." As she spoke, she scooped Eleanor onto her shoulder and patted her back. "Go give George a little love so we can get these two tucked in. I promise I'll be back here in the morning to sit with him, and you can come back tomorrow night as soon as I get home."

The promise of seeing him again soon wasn't much of a comfort, but Anna's plea that she be strong gave her the courage to do what they had to do. As Anna got Eleanor situated in her carrier, Lily leaned over George's bed and snaked her hand through the opening on the side. When her finger stroked his head, he opened his eyes to watch her. "Be strong, little guy. We love you, and it won't be a real home until you get there."

* * *

Anna sucked in a breath so she could fasten her skirt. She hadn't worn this gray suit for several months, not since eating on the run had become the standard. Too many sandwiches and muffins. She usually wore slacks and a jacket to work, but today she had a meeting downtown for the Chamber of Commerce, one she would enjoy immensely, since it was her first since handing over the gavel of the presidency last month.

In the kitchen, Andy and Lily were finishing breakfast as Eleanor took her morning nap in her carrier, which sat on the kitchen table.

"Hurry up, pal. We're going to be late."

"Don't forget to take George's lunch," Lily said, holding up two bottles of expressed milk. The bruises under her eyes from her broken nose had faded to almost nothing, but she still appeared tired. They all did.

"Maybe I'll even stick around while he eats. My meeting isn't until nine thirty, and it won't matter if I'm a few minutes late because I'm not in charge anymore."

"Hallelujah!" They all felt relief to be out from under the pressure of the Chamber.

Anna brushed her nose against Eleanor's. "You're getting to be such a big girl."

"Four pounds, seven ounces. Can you believe it? Almost a pound more than her brother."

"Kathy says he'll take off too once he starts to nurse."

"Who knows when that'll be? I wish Sylvie would get back from vacation."

"At least he's out of the woods. She never would have left if she'd been worried about him."

Anna dropped Andy at school and drove to the hospital, where she found George alert and instantly attuned to her presence through the glass top of his incubator. "Hi there, sweet boy. Did you sleep well?"

"He slept splendidly," Sylvie declared, appearing by her side.

"Welcome back. How was your trip?"

"*Je suis fatigué*," she answered with a moan before smacking her forehead. "Apologies. I visited with my family in Québec, and it takes me a day or two to shift the gears in my brain back to English."

"Have you had a chance to see George yet? How do you think he's doing?"

Her answer was a low chuckle, and she rubbed her hands together. "I think it's time he told you himself." She gestured toward the recliner where they had given Eleanor Kangaroo Care.

"You're kidding. Are we ready?" Anna wasted no time changing into one of the hospital's cotton tops and getting situated in the chair. Her heart raced with excitement as Sylvie drew him from his bed and placed him face down upon her chest.

He squirmed at first to find himself in such a foreign position, but when his tiny fist closed around her finger it was as if he knew he was okay.

Anna gestured toward her purse. "Quick, find my phone and take a picture."

Sylvie took several photos, finally zooming in as George fell asleep against her bare breast.

"Now do me a favor and send that one to Lily."

Seconds later the phone rang to Lily's excited screams. "I can't believe I'm missing this. I'm so jealous."

"Don't be jealous. I'll tear myself away from here eventually and trade places with you. In the meantime, how about giving Trina a call and telling her to cancel everything on my schedule? I don't see how I could go into work today."

* * *

Eleanor sat wide-awake in her carrier watching Lily sort through the pile of clothes on her bed.

"Which one do you like? Blue...or red?" She held two tops for Eleanor's approval. "Take your time...no pressure. Here they are again. Blue...or red?" It was fun to watch her delayed response as she shifted her eyes from one top to the other. "You like the red, don't you?"

Lily had amassed a closet full of clothes, but hardly anything

195

she owned worked well for breast-feeding. It was easy enough to lift a pullover shirt, but she couldn't see Eleanor as well, and she missed the luxurious feeling of having their bare skin in contact. She preferred shirts she could open all the way in the front, like the red and blue ones.

"'Bye, Mama," Andy called from downstairs.

She walked onto the landing and looked down to where he waited with Jonah and Hal. "What are you fellows doing today?"

Hal broke into a grin. "We're headed to the boat show."

"Sounds like trouble to me. Does Kim know you're out looking for boats again?"

"We thought it would make a nice surprise."

Lily chuckled. "Good luck with that. Andy, don't come home with anything that won't fit in the bathtub, and you know the rules. Listen to Uncle Hal, not to Jonah."

Anna trudged up the stairs carrying a basket of cloth diapers. "What time do you want to go see George?"

"Let's go together after lunch." They had spent last weekend at the hospital celebrating Mother's Day, but Sylvie said they had only one more week of running back and forth to the hospital. George was finally gaining weight and would probably be discharged next Saturday.

The doorbell rang as Anna deposited the basket on the landing. "Wonder what they forgot." She took off downstairs to answer the door.

"What about you, little girl? You ready for lunch?" She scooped Eleanor out of her carrier and jostled her across the landing into their nursery. Their cribs were set up in the master suite, but this room had two rocking recliners like the ones in the neonatal unit, a changing table and bassinet, and a large bureau to hold baby clothes...if they ever got any. Kim had brought over a few things that had belonged to Jonah and Alice, but the premature arrivals had put all their shopping plans on the back burner. Pretty soon she would have to bite the bullet and leave Anna at home with Eleanor so she could go pick up a few things.

It wouldn't do to take her baby out without clothes.

They were still tweaking the new routine. Anna liked doing the first feeding, usually around midnight. Then she managed a solid six hours of uninterrupted sleep. Without that she was a zombie. Lily went to sleep around ten but got up at four, napping again along with Eleanor after everyone else left for school and work. It was tiring but not unworkable. However, all bets were off once George came home.

No sooner had Eleanor started to nurse than the doorbell rang again. She couldn't imagine why the boys were having so much trouble getting out the door. Probably one of them coming back to use the bathroom.

She looked at the empty rocker beside her and smiled, envisioning the day soon when Anna would be sitting there holding one of their babies. Having their whole flock under one roof, no matter how often the babies cried in the night, would bring both of them deeper and more restful sleep. Not having George at home stirred memories of those early days after Andy had come to stay with them, when she was uncertain of his long-term fate. The fear of losing him had been unbearable.

Eleanor's sucking had slowed and her eyes were heavy with sleep, but they shot open when the doorbell rang yet a third time.

"What in the world are those boys doing, Eleanor? They just won't let you sleep."

Anna peered through her doorway, smiling and shaking her head. "You aren't going to believe this."

"Let me put her down," she whispered. "I think she's ready to go to sleep."

"Let me have her." She put her back in the carrier and buckled her into place.

Lily refastened her front-hook bra and buttoned her shirt. "I take it we're going downstairs."

"Oh, yes. We have company."

Company didn't quite describe the crowd that had gathered in their living room. Martine and Kim sat with Alice on the loveseat. Beside them on the sofa were her friends from work, Colleen, Lauren and Pauline. Virginia and Holly had pulled chairs from the kitchen.

Sandy and Suzanne appeared in the doorway that led to the dining room. "All the food is out. Everyone come help themselves."

Lily's jaw dropped to see the mountain of gifts on the coffee table. "What is all this? I have the sneakiest friends."

"You can thank Sandy," Kim said. "She arranged all of this back in February, but of course you were supposed to wait until June to have your babies."

Colleen and Virginia shot up from their seats to peek at Eleanor, who never stirred. "Except this way is better because we get to see the baby."

"If you had timed it for next weekend you could have seen George too," Anna said.

"He's coming home?" Martine asked.

"A week from today," Lily answered, still stunned at the room full of women. She greeted everyone with a hug, finally reaching Sandy, who was grinning triumphantly. "You are absolutely the best friend a person could possibly have."

"Surely you didn't think I was going to let you off without a baby shower. What kind of friend would I be?"

For more than an hour they snacked and chatted, shifting seats periodically so everyone had a chance to watch Eleanor sleep. Even Suzanne, who professed no affinity for children whatsoever, found herself mesmerized when Eleanor awoke and gripped her finger. "It's a good thing I didn't know about this ten years ago."

Sandy hugged her from behind as she peered over her shoulder. "Does this mean I can get a cat?"

"If kittens are half this much fun, you can get two."

They all laughed as Sandy mouthed a silent thank you upward, her years-long crusade for a pet finally answered.

Lily followed Lauren into the dining room and fixed herself

a plate of appetizing snacks—brie and crackers, cocktail olives and for dessert, strawberries dipped in dark chocolate. "I haven't eaten anything this rich since our spa day in Palm Springs. I plan to enjoy every decadent bite."

"You've earned it. Did your doctor put you on any restrictions?"

She chuckled. "No alcohol...like that was even an option. Don't tell Virginia this—I wouldn't want her to feel obsolete—but alcohol couldn't possibly be the drug motherhood is. I feel euphoric all the time."

Lauren nodded along. "I know. Babies are like little endorphin machines. You can look at them, smell them or even think about them and get this happy rosy glow. It wears off on their second birthday though."

Lily laughed. "What do they produce then?"

"Let's just say you'll want to keep your AA sponsor's number handy." She edged a brownie onto Lily's plate. "You won't be coming back to work, you know."

"I...I haven't even had time to think about it."

"It wasn't a question, Lily. This is your life now and you're in love with it. I can see it in your face and in Anna's too. You both look like you've won the lottery, and there's no way you're going to walk out of here and leave your precious children for a job you don't absolutely need. Believe me, if Will and I didn't have such a big house payment, wild horses couldn't have dragged me back to work after Peter was born."

Lily's resistance to being a stay-at-home mother had never been rooted in financial need or independence, or even Kim's lament of not having adult interaction, but in a desire not to let her identity be subsumed by motherhood. The irony was that she now embraced it as the most important thing about her, and she couldn't stand the thought of leaving her babies for a selfish pursuit. "I might take a few years off...maybe until they start school. I can keep my law license up."

"Sure, you could come back to Braxton Street one of these

days, but who knows? This is life-changing. You might find yourself on a different path in a few years, and you can come back to the work world on your own terms when you're ready."

She already had support from Anna to stay home with their children. Now she was getting it from another mom, one who walked in her shoes at work. It was what she wanted most in the world, and she needed only permission from herself. "I won't ever regret it, will I?"

Lauren shook her head. "Not for a second."

Chapter 13

Anna congratulated the young couple on their choice of the 330i and signed off on their finance package. She hated working Saturdays, but with Holly off to visit her family in San Diego for Memorial Weekend she had no choice. At least work was fun again. Their sales hadn't fully recovered from the dive last year, but with a smaller crew they were processing sales all day long. Everyone at the dealership was buoyed by the steady work.

Only twenty more minutes to closing. Then it was home to add the final piece to their family puzzle. Tonight they would go as family to pick up George and bring him home. At four pounds, four ounces, he had finally started to thrive. No more setbacks, Sylvie assured them. And not only that—he was sleeping up to five hours at a time without crying for food.

As she walked back into the showroom, Trina grabbed her elbow and pulled her aside. "There's a detective waiting upstairs in your office."

"What? Did he say what he wanted?"

"She, and just that she had to speak to you."

Anna bounded up the stairs and into her office, where a stocky redhead in slacks and a sport jacket was bent over her desk peering at the family photos. "Can I help you?"

The woman spun around and flashed a smile that showed deep dimples on both cheeks. She was tall—even taller than Anna—with the muscular physique of an athlete. "Ms. Kaklis, I was just admiring your beautiful family. You must be very proud."

"Thank you, I am."

The woman held out her hand. "Detective Shawna Butler, LAPD. Pleased to meet you."

"Same here. What can I do for you?"

"Not a thing. I'm here with good news. We found your car."

"My Z8? They told me it was probably trucked across the border the day after it was stolen."

"That's what we thought, since we were assuming it was the work of one of the car rings we'd been watching for a while. But then we stumbled on another gang, and last night our guys raided a warehouse down by the port. Your car was one of a couple dozen we found ready to load onto a Shanghai-bound freighter. The officers nearly came to blows over which one would get to drive it out of there. I settled it and drove it myself. Very sweet."

Anna was stunned. "Wow, I feel like you've found my first wife after I remarried."

Detective Butler laughed. "No, one wife is enough for anyone. Especially a wife like mine." She nodded in the direction of the photos. "And from the looks of things, that goes for you too. We've got two little ones, hers from when she was married. Gave me a whole new respect for my mother."

It was amazing how quickly her feelings of kinship with the detective materialized at the revelation of their similarities. "It's all trial and error if you ask me."

She handed Anna a business card. "If you learn any mommy tricks, don't hesitate to pass them on. I could use all the help I can get."

Anna lifted a card from the holder on her desk. "I will if you will."

"It's a deal." Detective Butler explained the procedures for reclaiming the car and promised to follow up with any developments in the case.

Anna's ambivalence about the Z8 surprised her. Not only had she gotten used to driving the 550, she enjoyed the fact that Andy had picked it out, and she could say without any shred of embarrassment that she now drove a family car. The Z8 would bring a pretty penny through a broker and would no doubt make someone very happy to have found such a rare prize. She would see it into the proper hands, like finding a new home for a pet.

The low lights came on in the showroom to announce closing and she hurried out to her car and eagerly left her workday behind. Her father was pulling out of the driveway at her home as she was pulling in, and he waved and went on his way. It was unusual for him just to drop by, and Lily had probably shuffled him off so they could go get George.

"Hey, baby. I just saw—" She stopped abruptly in the doorway, confused about why the aroma of dinner was wafting from the kitchen. "I just saw Dad pulling out. Did you tell him we were—"

"Surprise!" Andy yelled. He was standing at the end of the kitchen table, which held not one but two infant carriers.

"What's this?"

"We couldn't wait," Lily said, sporting a proud grin. "I knew you'd be tired tonight so I called your dad and asked him to drive us to the hospital."

Her mouth agape, Anna brushed past to see George fast asleep in his carrier. "He's here already."

"We're all here. No more running out the door to deliver milk in the morning, no more fighting rush hour traffic to see him at night."

"And best of all," Anna said, nuzzling first George then Eleanor, "no more telling him goodbye."

"You know what Andy said?" Lily wrapped one arm around Anna's waist and the other over Andy's shoulder. "We have everyone here…"

"So we can start now," he said.

Anna nodded pensively. "I like that, pal." In fact, it summed up her feelings almost perfectly. Each day since the twins were born had begun and ended with the stress of uncertainty and the feeling their lives were on hold. No more. They were free now to get on with living, to have friends over or to go out, and to celebrate their new family without holding back out of fear that something bad might yet happen. Life was ready. They could start now.

* * *

Anna loved the sight in the rearview mirror of the minivan. Lily had the whole backseat to herself and looked as if she relished the momentary solitude. In the middle seats were George, who seemed to fall asleep each time the car started, and Eleanor, who was wide awake and alert to take in all her surroundings. Andy rode beside her in the front passenger seat for the first time on this, his sixth birthday. And despite all her previous vows to never drive this "box on wheels," here she was doing just that.

When they reached the Big House, George and Martine ran out as if they had been watching at the window for their arrival. Her father made an elaborate fuss over Andy's birthday, but he didn't seem to mind when Andy ran past him so he could tell Jonah all about riding shotgun. He was already focused on snatching his namesake from his car seat.

Martine came around the van to retrieve Eleanor, leaving Anna and Lily with the task of hauling in both of the infant carriers, the diaper bag with the baby supplies, and a large shopping bag filled with Andy's birthday presents.

Anna made a circuit of the van closing all the doors. "Have you noticed that no one even says hello to us anymore? It's like we're invisible."

"It's payback for how we treated Kim and Hal when Jonah was born. I think it comes with the territory."

"Wonder if anyone would miss us if we just got back in the car and drove off. We could go back home and get in the hot tub... have our own little party." She arched her eyebrows suggestively.

"Best offer I've had all day. Georgie would starve before we got back, though."

"Need a hand?" Hal asked, arriving at the front door as they juggled their load.

Anna thrust the gift bag into his hands and told him to put it with the others. Then they wound through the house to the sunny patio and settled into side-by-side chaise lounges beneath an umbrella.

Andy had already stripped down to his swim trunks and jumped into the pool with Jonah. Kim stood in waist-deep water swirling a delighted Alice back and forth in a small inflatable raft. Hal burst from the kitchen to do a cannonball into the deep end where the boys played.

"I almost feel disembodied from my own life," Anna said, nodding toward her father, who was sitting beneath the covered patio with a sleeping George.

"And look at that," Lily said, gesturing to Martine, who was parading Eleanor through her garden to inspect the colorful flowers. "I'm not even sure they know we're here."

"Dad was telling me last week that they had talked about selling the house once he retired for good. They were thinking of downsizing into one of those luxury condos on Wilshire and buying something up in Tahoe too. I said that would be nice, that we could come up a couple of times a year and hang out. Next day he said never mind. I think he and Mom would go nuts if we didn't come over here at least twice a month."

"If you ask me, that's only going to get more intense as the children get older. I guess we could always gather at our house, but it wouldn't be the same."

"Remember the first time you came here?"

Lily chortled. "When your homophobic father insulted me? How could I forget?"

"You won him over though. He loves you like a daughter now."

"I know." And Anna knew she loved him like a father, whether she admitted it or not. "You know what I also remember? That weekend we brought Mom over here to meet the family."

Anna nodded. "She walked through the garden with my mother just like her granddaughter is doing right now."

They looked at each other with sudden tears at the poignant reflection.

"That was just four days before she died," Lily said sadly. "You really honored her by giving our daughter that name...and you honored me too."

"I never seriously considered anything else. But George? That one blew me away."

"What can I say? I was still under general anesthesia."

Birthday cake and presents followed the pool party, and by the time they called it a day, even Jonah was exhausted. Before they left, Anna took one last look around the patio. Every summer at the Big House seemed to bring momentous change... Lily, Jonah, then Alice and Andy. And now George and Eleanor. As a family they had known phenomenal joy and devastating loss. She couldn't bring herself to think about loss again, not after the scary episodes they had gone through with George. She preferred to dream about the happier times, looking ahead to the day she would sit with her father in the shade while Lily paraded her grandchildren through the garden.

The table lamp cast a soft glow in the alcove by the front window of the master suite creating the perfect ambience for winding down at the end of the day...and winding down Eleanor and George. Anna had rearranged the master bedroom to accommodate not only the two cribs but also the reclining rockers from the other bedroom. She had argued it was easier to cram everything in one room, especially since Eleanor had a tendency to wake up as they were walking back across the hall to her crib.

Lily liked how this new arrangement gave them a couple of hours to relax together every night. In the old days they would lounge on the couch in the family room and watch TV after putting Andy to bed. Now they sat and talked about their day, trading off one baby for another as Lily nursed them both. George in particular enjoyed being rocked, while Eleanor seemed to prefer being jostled gently as she was carried around the room. TV with sound was a thing of the past, but that didn't cut into Anna watching Dodgers games.

As Anna rocked George, Lily tried to persuade Eleanor to take her breast. "It's funny how she prefers the bottle sometimes. I think she has trouble seeing everything when she's pressed against me. She doesn't mind it so much when she's ready to go to sleep though."

"I'll feed her if you want, and you can nurse this one."

Eleanor suddenly seized the nipple and began to nurse. "There she goes. Let's see how long this lasts."

"That's the most beautiful thing I've ever seen," Anna said as she set George into his crib.

"I felt the same way whenever Kim would nurse her babies. Except hers always loved it. Eleanor's fussy about it sometimes."

"Not this little guy, though." She tickled his tummy and he waved his arms. "He doesn't care where his food comes from."

Lily snickered. "As long as you keep it coming."

"Didn't you love that look on Kim's face when you told her both of them slept from midnight till five?"

"I don't think she believed us. I'm just glad you're getting enough sleep again. You were dragging around here like you'd run a marathon."

"It's easier now that school's out because I can sleep in till seven. That extra hour in the morning was a godsend."

Eleanor fussed and turned her face away from Lily's breast. "I think she's done already."

Anna scooped her daughter onto her shoulder and began to pat her back.

"She has the sweetest disposition," Lily said.

"I know. She doesn't mind who's holding her as long as their feet are moving."

Eleanor's wide brown eyes took in every detail, and she seemed especially fixated on things that were red. Anna had come up with the bright idea of strategically placing interesting objects—stuffed toys, pictures and trinkets—at shoulder level throughout the room. Eleanor never tired of the circuit.

Lily picked up George from his crib and with hardly any coaxing at all brought him to her breast. "Sylvie couldn't believe Georgie was six and a half pounds already. I told her he ate nonstop. At this rate he'll pass Eleanor in another week or two."

Eleanor let out a burp then dribbled onto the towel on Anna's shoulder. "It's amazing how he's taken off all of a sudden. You can't look at him now and tell he had any problems whatsoever."

"Sylvie always said once his lungs developed he would be out of the danger zone. I guess I expected him to be kind of...not really puny, just sort of picky or take it or leave it about eating. Instead he eats like a teenager."

"Seven weeks...I don't know how we kept from going crazy, especially that night his heart rate shot up and Sylvie put him on the ventilator. That scared the crap out of me."

"You?" Lily could still picture Anna's stalwart expression as

Sylvie walked them through the risks. "If that was scared, I must have been petrified. And I would have been a whole lot worse if you hadn't been so calm and confident about everything. You're the only thing that kept me sane."

Holding Eleanor firmly against her shoulder, Anna bent down to kiss the top of Lily's head. "Trust me, all was not as it seemed. I was scared out of my mind, just like you were."

"No way. You don't get rattled. You just buck up."

"Not always. Sometimes I melt down, like the day we came to pick you up in the new minivan. That was the night after Georgie had to go on the ventilator. I nearly took Andy's head off in my office because he dared to touch one of my ledgers. That's why you got a new car, by the way—not because I agreed with you, but because I had to make up with Andy."

"Anna Kaklis, you are full of it."

"You're just now figuring that out?"

"Are you telling me you were just as worried as I was this whole time?"

"Maybe more. But seeing you upset made it even worse for me, so once I saw how much calmer you were if I acted less worried, I figured it was better for both of us."

Lily didn't know how she felt about that. On the one hand, she actually had endured the ordeal better because of Anna's confidence. She had been able to convince herself she was overreacting. On the other hand, she felt foolish now to realize she had been duped. "It was dishonest for you not to share how you really felt. We should have gone through it together."

Anna gently laid a sleeping Eleanor in her crib, sat in her recliner and kicked off her shoes. "We went through it together, but neither of us needed to feel worse than we already did. I tried to stay positive because you needed that. And what I needed most was for you to be okay."

"But that means you worried all by yourself. You were scared too but you didn't come to me for support. How is that supposed to make me feel?" George seemed to pick up on her dismal tone and started to fuss. She shifted him to the other breast and drew a deep breath to still her unpleasant mood.

"You should feel like we're partners. To me, that means we work together in a way that's good for both of us. In this case I put what I thought you needed first. Don't you do that for me sometimes?"

"Of course, but…" It still meant Anna had bottled up her feelings inside. "Who was there for you?"

"Andy, mostly. It was good that I spent more time with him because he ended up giving me extra attention too, whether he realized it or not. The more I reinforced how great it would be for him once his brother and sister got here, the more I was able to stay focused on that. I didn't let myself think too much about everything in between."

"And what else did you keep from me? Were you upset that I didn't quit work sooner?"

Anna made a sheepish face. "Upset isn't the right word. I was disappointed, but I got over it in Palm Springs that day you called me on it for not supporting you. You were right and I was wrong."

"Yeah, except you were the one who was right. If I'd been home, that accident wouldn't have happened."

"It might not have happened on the Santa Monica Freeway, but it could have happened anywhere else, even if I had been behind the wheel. What really matters is we're home now and we're all safe. No need to second-guess anything."

From the very beginning, it had been as easy as that, Lily realized. Anna wasn't one to dwell on problems between them or punish her for their differences with something as immature as the silent treatment. That was Lily's habit, and she vowed at that moment to put it behind her. "How did I ever get so lucky?"

"I ask myself the same thing. A part of me wants to rush ahead and dream what we'll be like a year from now, or five years from now. I like to imagine that first day Andy comes to work at the dealership. I'll be fifty years old by then, and all I can think is how happy we'll be. But then I try to put it out of my head because I don't want to miss a second of right now."

George began to squirm and Lily handed him off to Anna and climbed into bed. "It's funny...this time last year I was dreaming about a night like tonight, going to bed with our baby in the crib beside us. All of those fantasies pale next to reality."

"My whole life is like that," Anna said sweetly.

Lily closed her eyes and tried to quiet her thoughts, not an easy task with Anna tossing about such profound pronouncements. Her fantasies of Anna Kaklis had begun the day they reconnected after the earthquake, when her divorce had become final. There was Lily, dreaming the love of her life would be someone so beautiful, so kind and so charming. Anna was everything a fantasy was made of.

Then she discovered a reality that was far beyond those meager dreams. Never had she dared imagine Anna would come to cherish her in the same way, and that she—and now these three precious children—would be Anna's fantasy fulfilled.

Anna's recliner creaked and moments later the lamp clicked off. Her long nude body then slipped between the sheets and nestled next to her, a physical display of her happiness with their life.

Lily wriggled closer and opened her eyes, seeing Anna's tranquil face in the glow of the tiny nightlight in the alcove. "Hey, Amazon...wake up and make love with me."

Epilogue

"You're late," Lily said, looking up from the stove. She was barefoot, with baggy shorts that barely showed underneath one of Anna's button-down shirts. Her blond hair hung into her eyes, evidence it had been too long since she had made time to get to the salon. She had her hands full at home with Eleanor and George, who at three years old, were too young for the preschool in Westwood.

"That's because I stopped to pick up ice cream."

Lily shook her head and sighed with resignation. One of her ongoing complaints was that she had never quite recovered her figure from when the twins were born. "Why do you torture me like this?"

"I've learned that torture—properly applied—makes you quite happy." She dropped to a squat to catch Eleanor in a hug as she raced into the kitchen from the dining room, which was wall-to-wall toys. With gangly arms and legs and prominent cheekbones, her daughter looked more like her every day.

"Eleanor swam across the shallow end all by herself today."

"That's my girl!" Anna ignored Lily's faux cranky mood and embraced her from behind, groaning as she saw what was in the pot. "Please tell me that isn't what I think it is."

"Andy needs a pick-me-up. He had a tough day."

"What happened?"

"The kids were teasing him at school."

"Not the lesbian thing again. You'd think people would get over that already." One of the kids in Andy's second-grade class had teased him year before last.

"No, it was—"

"Stop it, Georgie! Give me that back," Andy yelled from the family room.

"Uh-oh." Anna went in to see about the ruckus.

"He took my car," Andy pouted.

George, who was small and blond like Lily but with the dark complexion of his Latino father, appeared to be starting a competing garage on the other side of the cramped family room.

"Which one do you want back?" Her implication was that Andy might consider sharing a few from his massive collection.

"The Vette."

"Hmm." Anna picked up another car from George's purloined stash and swapped him for the Vette in his hand, and handed it to Andy. "I might have chosen the Porsche, pal."

"They're all mine."

"I know, and that's what makes you such a great brother. Georgie is lucky because you share your toys."

"He's not my brother."

"Excuse me?" She invoked her stern voice, the one that meant she had heard clearly but wanted an explanation.

"He's not my brother because I'm adopted."

"Of course he's your brother. Just because we—"

"Dinner's ready!"

"Come on, pal. We'll talk about this while we eat. Mama

213

cooked something special just for you." She nudged him up from the floor and turned back to George. "Let's go, son. Mama's calling."

"Mrs. Rueggle sent a note home," Lily whispered as the children took their places at the table. "They were talking about different kinds of families and he told his classmates he was adopted. Some of the other kids started saying they had *real* families."

Anna bristled. "Kids can be cruel."

"She set them straight, but she said he had his feelings hurt and might need a little reassurance at home. Judging from his mood since he came home I'd say she was right."

They had remodeled their breakfast nook to seat the whole family, still favoring the cozy kitchen over the formal dining room. Now the padded bench that lined the bay window seated Andy on the inside, Eleanor on one end and Anna on the other. George preferred sitting in a regular chair, as did Lily.

Anna rubbed her hands together. "Yum! I see we're having mac and cheese again."

Andy knew she didn't like his favorite dish, so when he didn't respond at all to her remark, it was a sure sign he was genuinely depressed about the events of the day.

Lily leaned over to cut Eleanor's chicken strips. "Andy, I told Mom we were having macaroni tonight because you had a tough day and I thought it would cheer you up."

"I don't like macaroni," Eleanor said, making a horrid face.

"I do," George announced seconds before he shoveled an enormous spoonful into his mouth.

"Not such a big bite, Georgie," Anna said, pulling his plate closer so she could cut his meat. "So what happened today, Andy? Does this have anything to do with what you said about Georgie not being your brother?"

Andy remained glum, only picking at his food. "He isn't. I'm adopted and he was born."

"You were born too, honey," Lily said. "But you grew in my

sister's tummy."

"But Georgie and Eleanor grew in your tummy, so they aren't my real brother and sister."

"Wait a minute," Anna said. "It doesn't matter whose tummy you came from. Families are connected by love."

"That's right," Lily chimed in. "And we all love each other, so that makes us a family."

Andy looked directly at Anna and asked her pointedly, "How come you always call me pal and you call Georgie son?"

Stung by the indictment, she consciously held her casual expression to mask her hurt. "Those are just nicknames. I've always called you my pal. I thought you liked it."

"I do," he admitted, his voice small and seemingly contrite.

"You and Georgie are both my sons, and you are both my pals. Eleanor's my pal too."

"I want more macaroni," George said, prompting Anna to scrape hers quickly onto his plate before Lily could get up for more.

"But Russell said real families all had the same blood."

"Russell's wrong," Lily said indignantly.

"He said he got his blood from both his mom and his dad. Who did I get mine from?"

Anna set her fork down. "Okay, it's like this. We're all connected by blood." She pushed aside her plate. "Everybody put down your spoon or fork."

Andy complied and rested his hands in his lap. Anna practically wrestled George's spoon from his hand and set it out of reach. "You can have it back in a minute. Okay, we'll start with Mama. She and her sister had the same blood, right?"

Andy nodded.

"And since you grew in her sister's tummy, that means you have the same blood as Mama."

That realization brightened his face. "We share the same blood?"

"That's right, so I want you and Mama to hold hands."

215

Lily reached across the table and took Andy's hand.

"All right, now it gets a little complicated." How did one explain in vitro fertilization to a nine-year-old? "Georgie grew in Mama's tummy and he came from her blood. So Georgie, I want you to hold Mama's other hand, okay?"

George did, and now he, Lily and Andy were connected.

"You and Georgie and Mama share the same blood, right?"

Andy nodded, obviously spellbound.

"Eleanor grew in Mama's tummy too, but she came from my blood." Anna stretched across the table to reach for her daughter. "Take my hand, sweetie."

Now Anna and Eleanor were connected, but the most difficult aspect of the link remained—the sperm donor.

"Before a baby can grow in someone's tummy, it has to have blood from a woman, like Mama or me"—she watched Andy's eyes to see if he was following along—"and blood from a man. We don't know who that man was. The doctor did that part while we weren't looking. But she took blood from the same man to give to Georgie and Eleanor. That means Georgie and Eleanor are connected to each other by blood too. Georgie, take your sister's other hand."

George hoisted himself onto his knees to stretch across the table.

"So look what we have, Andy." What they had looked like an octopus in the middle of the kitchen table. "You're connected to Mama. She's connected to Georgie."

Andy started to mouth the words along with her.

"Georgie's connected to Eleanor. And she's connected to you!" By the look on his face, he was thrilled by the proof they all were related by blood.

"That was a pretty amazing story," Lily said, giving her a satisfied nod.

Anna was indeed pleased with herself, but the point Lily had made earlier was still more important than her little demonstration. "But Russell's still wrong, Andy. Even if we weren't connected by blood, we're a family because we all love each other."

George lunged for his spoon.

"And you know Georgie's your brother because he likes mac and cheese as much as you do, right?"

"Right." Andy dug into his dinner enthusiastically.

When she got up to help clear the table for ice cream, Lily tugged her aside for a quick kiss. "Have I ever told you I think you're brilliant?"

"Not nearly enough."

"Maybe when the kids go to bed we can lock the door and I'll tell you some more."

"Promises, promises," Anna said. "Once we turn the lights out, you never want to talk about my brain."

Publications from
Bella Books, Inc.
Women. Books. Even Better Together.

P.O. Box 10543
Tallahassee, FL 32302
Phone: 800-729-4992
www.bellabooks.com

THE GRASS WIDOW by Nanci Little. Aidan Blackstone is nineteen, unmarried and pregnant, and has no reason to think that the year 1876 won't be her last. Joss Bodett has lost her family but desperately clings to their land. A richly told story of frontier survival that picks up with the generation of women where Patience and Sarah left off.
978-1-59493-189-5 $12.95

SMOKEY O by Celia Cohen. Insult "Mac" MacDonnell and insult the entire Delaware Blue Diamond team. Smokey O'Neill has just insulted Mac, and then finds she's been traded to Delaware. The games are not limited to the baseball field!
978-1-59493-198-7 $12.95

WICKED GAMES by Ellen Hart. Never have mysteries and secrets been closer to home in this eighth installment of this award-winning lesbian mystery series. Jane Lawless's neighbors bring puzzles and peril—and that's just the beginning.
978-1-59493-185-7 $14.95

NOT EVERY RIVER by Robbi McCoy. It's the hottest city in the U.S., and it's not just the weather that's heating up. For Kim and Randi are forced to question everything they thought they knew about themselves before they can risk their fiery hearts on the biggest gamble of all.
978-1-59493-182-6 $14.95

HOUSE OF CARDS by Nat Burns. Cards are played, but the game is gossip. Kaylen Strauder has never wanted it to be about her. But the time is fast-approaching when she must decide which she needs more: her community or Eda Byrne.
978-1-59493-203-8 $14.95

RETURN TO ISIS by Jean Stewart. The award-winning Isis sci-fi series features Jean Stewart's vision of a committed colony of women dedicated to preserving their way of life, even after the apocalypse. Mysteries have been forgotten, but survival depends on remembering. Book one in series.
978-1-59493-193-2 $12.95

1ST IMPRESSIONS by Kate Calloway. Rookie PI Cassidy James has her first case. Her investigation into the murder of Erica Trinidad's uncle isn't welcomed by the local sheriff, especially since the delicious, seductive Erica is their prime suspect. 1st in series. Author's augmented and expanded edition.
978-1-59493-192-5 $12.95

BEACON OF LOVE by Ann Roberts. Twenty-five years after their families put an end to a relationship that hadn't even begun, Stephanie returns to Oregon to find many things have changed...except her feelings for Paula.
978-1-59493-180-2 $14.95

ABOVE TEMPTATION by Karin Kallmaker. It's supposed to be like any other case, except this time they're chasing one of their own. As fraud investigators Tamara Sterling and Kip Barrett try to catch a thief, they realize they can have anything they want—except each other.
978-1-59493-179-6 $14.95

AN EMERGENCE OF GREEN by Katherine V. Forrest. Carolyn had no idea her new neighbor jumped the fence to enjoy her swimming pool. The discovery leads to choices she never anticipated in an intense, sensual story of discovery and risk, consequences and triumph. Originally released in 1986.
978-1-59493-217-5 $14.95

CRAZY FOR LOVING by Jaye Maiman. Officially hanging out her shingle as a private investigator, Robin Miller is getting her life on track. Just as Robin discovers it's hard to follow a dead man, she walks in. KT Bellflower, sultry and devastating...Lammy winner and second in series.
978-1-59493-195-6 $14.95

LOVE WAITS by Gerri Hill. The All-American girl and the love she left behind – it's been twenty years since Ashleigh and Gina parted, and now they're back to the place where nothing was simple and love didn't wait.
978-1-59493-186-4 $14.95

HANNAH FREE: THE BOOK by Claudia Allen. Based on the film festival hit movie starring Sharon Gless. Hannah's story is funny, scathing and witty as she navigates life with aplomb—but always comes home to Rachel. 32 pages of color photographs plus bonus behind-the-scenes movie information.
978-1-59493-172-7 $19.95

END OF THE ROPE by Jackie Calhoun. Meg Klein has two enduring loves— horses and Nicky Hennessey. Nicky is there for her when she most needs help, but then an attractive vet throws Meg's carefully balanced world out of kilter.
978-1-59493-176-5 $14.95

THE LONG TRAIL by Penny Hayes. When schoolteacher Blanche Bartholomew and dance hall girl Teresa Stark meet their feelings are powerful—and completely forbidden—in Starcross, Texas. In search of a safe future, they flee, daring to take a covered wagon across the forbidding prairie.
978-1-59493-196-3 $12.95

UP UP AND AWAY by Catherine Ennis. Sarah and Margaret have a video. The mob wants it. Flying for their lives, two women discover more than secrets.
978-1-59493-215-1 $12.95

CITY OF STRANGERS by Diana Rivers. A captive in a gilded cage, young Solene plots her escape, but the rulers of Hernorium have other plans for Solene—and her people. Breathless lesbian fantasy story also perfect for teen readers.
978-1-59493-183-3 $14.95

ROBBER'S WINE by Ellen Hart. Belle Dumont is the first dead of summer. Jane Lawless, Belle's old friend, suspects coldhearted murder. Lammy-winning seventh novel in critically acclaimed mystery series.
978-1-59493-184-0 $14.95

APPARITION ALLEY by Katherine V. Forrest. Kate Delafield has solved hundreds of cases, but the one that baffles her most is her own shooting. Book six in series.
978-1-883523-65-7 $14.95

STERLING ROAD BLUES by Ruth Perkinson. It was a simple declaration of love. But the entire state of Virginia wants to weigh in, leaving teachers Carrie Tomlinson and Audra Malone caught in the crossfire—and with love troubles of their own.
978-1-59493-187-1 $14.95

LILY OF THE TOWER by Elizabeth Hart. Agnes Headey, taking refuge from a storm at the Netherfield estate, stumbles into dark family secrets and something more… Meticulously researched historical romance.
978-1-59493-177-2 $14.95

LETTING GO by Ann O'Leary. Kelly has decided that luscious, successful Laura should be hers. For now. Laura might even be agreeable. But where does that leave Kate?
978-1-59493-194-9 $12.95

MURDER TAKES TO THE HILLS by Jessica Thomas. Renovations, shady business deals, a stalker—and it's not even tourist season yet for PI Alex Peres and her best four-legged pal Fargo. Sixth in this Provincetown-based series.
978-1-59493-178-9 $14.95